Indigo Lounge

HIGHER

An Erotic Novel

Zara Cox

Copyright © 2014 Zara Cox
All rights reserved. No part of this book may be reproduced or transmitted in any form or by any means without the written permission of the author.

Edited by Laura Kingsley
Cover by Angela Oltmann

ISBN-10: 1499293127
ISBN-13: 978-1499293128

BOOKS BY THIS AUTHOR:

Wreckless

High
Higher
Spiral

One

"YOU...YOU *KILLED* her?"

Of the three emotional grenades Zach Savage had just thrown at her feet, this was the one that had wreaked the most devastation. Not that she wasn't shattered by the other two...

Farrah was my wife...

We were married for a day...

Bethany Green shook her head, unable to fathom how to begin to process those pieces of information the man to whom she'd confessed her love had just flattened her with. Her mind was locked on this last statement.

Around her crickets chirped in the dark Moroccan night, uncaring that two people stood frozen in the middle of what should've been a sultry paradise, but was instead ground zero of epic proportions.

Zach had paled alarmingly following his stark confession, his vibrant golden beauty turned into a taut, cold statue. He looked shell-shocked as if his own revelation had stunned the hell out of him.

She was equally stunned. Stunned that she wasn't fleeing his presence as fast her legs could carry her. He'd just confessed to... to...

"Say something!" The words were propelled from the depths of her ravaged soul, the consuming need for an answer greater than the fear that she could be in danger from Zachary Savage.

He jerked out of his stasis. Grey eyes pierced through the darkness at her and he suddenly lunged for her.

"No!" Bethany scuttled out of reach, narrowly missing the

shallow pool to her left. Renewed fear slammed into her as she adjusted her position to avoid yet another looming threat.

Zach checked himself and froze, looking from the water to her face.

"Bethany, come here."

She looked from his tormented expression to the mound of stones behind her. The beautiful shrine he'd built to his dead wife.

Oh God. Oh God. "Oh God."

"Bethany!" His voice was sharpening, his focus strengthening as determination and that iron control began to reassert itself.

"Tell me what you meant."

His eyes darkened until she could only see black holes, fraught with chaotic despair. A breeze wove through the garden. They both shivered.

"I can't. It's…Bethany, I can't tell you anything more than I already have. I've already said too much…"

The ice that had engulfed her soul hardened several degrees more. "You can't? You brought me to the place where you've built a *shrine* to your dead wife and you can't tell me how she died? How *you killed her*? Please, God, tell me you meant that metaphorically?"

The words jerked out of her and dropped into the yawning space between them.

Zach made a sound, like a wounded animal, before he twisted away from her and dragged his hand through his hair. "God, this whole thing is a fucking mess. I shouldn't…you shouldn't have…"

"I shouldn't have what? Watched you sleep? Been awake to hear you talking to another woman in your dreams?"

He whirled back round. "That wasn't what I meant," he bit out.

"Then tell me what the hell you meant!"

"I shouldn't have let you this deep under my skin. I shouldn't have let myself crave you this desperately. And you shouldn't have told me…"

She took another shaky step back, her heart hammering hard enough to snap her rips in half. "I shouldn't have told you what? That I loved you? That's what you mean, isn't it?" Her lips barely moved. Her fingers felt numb. The stone she'd half-forgotten she held, the one that formed part of Zach's monument to his wife, fell from her nerveless fingers.

Eyes, bleak but no less intense, stared back at her. Then his gaze dropped to the stone at her feet.

Wordlessly, he picked it up, walked to the mound and placed it back where it belonged. The gentleness with which he did so shattered her heart smash a few more million pieces.

He faced her. Opened his mouth. No words came out. He sucked in a heavy breath and his shoulders hunched.

She could barely work her vocal cords to speak. "Message received." She shook her head in derision. "And you're right. We've known each other what, a handful of days? How could I possibly be in love with you? How could I possibly believe that I can't imagine my life without you?" The words burned her throat so badly she was surprised she could swallow around the pain ricocheting through her heart.

He made another rough sound. "Baby—"

"Are you really a killer, Zach?" He flinched and a tiny part of her felt hope for that action; a foolish part of her that wanted something to hold on to in a world suddenly gone nuts.

I should be running!

But she couldn't force her feet to move. All she could see when she looked at him was the man who'd made love to her like she was part of his soul; who'd taken the patience to help her overcome her fear of water.

Then she looked at the stones, and a shiver coursed down her spine. The evidence of death was too hard to refute.

She took a step back. "Don't worry, Zach, you can hang on to your secrets. Stay here with your precious shrine and your sacred memories." She started to walk down the centre marble walkway that divided the pools and realised she'd have to walk past him.

His eyes narrowed on her as he saw her hesitance and her heartbeat tripled. She couldn't risk him touching her for fear she would break into a million useless pieces.

She stared down into the shallow pool and fought the rising panic. On top of everything else, she couldn't deal with the terror that stemmed from her fear of water. Not right now.

Holding her breath, she stepped into the water and felt it close over her ankle. Panic flared higher. Her legs started to turn to jelly and her arms flailed.

Zach stepped toward her. She looked at him. At the man who'd been so gentle with her, who'd called her brave and worshipped her body over and over this past week.

The man who'd just confessed to killing his wife.

She darted sideways before he could touch her.

Feeling solid tiles beneath her feet, she ventured another step. Then another.

And then she was running.

"Bethany!"

She didn't stop until she was in the bedroom. Grabbing her weekender, she shoved as much of her belongings as she could find into the bag.

"What the hell do you think you're doing?"

She froze as Zach entered the room and stalked to where she'd just slammed the bag shut.

She licked her lips and sucked in a breath. Here in the well-lit bedroom, she couldn't miss the fact that he was only wearing boxers. His sleek body gleamed under the golden lights, and even in the midst of despair, something inside flared to life.

That, on top of having her life turned upside down it was just too much to bear.

Hot, choking tears scoured her throat and pricked her eyes. Hands shaking, she tugged the button of her jeans and shoved her feet into her heeled wedges.

"You can physically stop me from leaving if you want to. But I know you won't. I know that because the only reason I'd stay is if you tell me what you meant. And we both know that's not going to happen. Don't we, Zach?"

His eyes hardened. "Emotional blackmail doesn't work with me."

"And secrets don't work with me! You know what I went through with Chris."

He growled. "Do not compare me to that asshole."

Her fingers tightened around the handle of her bag. "Then prove you're different from him!"

Anger flamed through his eyes and his fists clenched. But he remained silent.

Pain raked her insides raw. "That's what I thought. Goodbye, Zach."

She yanked her bag off the bed and stalked past him.

At the last moment, he grabbed her arms, lifted her clean off her feet and pressed her against the bedroom wall. His large body imprinted hers from head to toe, his large body bracketing hers, reminding her how powerful he was, how overwhelmingly male, even as his large hands gently cradled her face.

A fierce, indomitable light burned in his eyes as he stared deep into hers.

"You're seriously deluded if you think that, baby. We're not over. Not by a long shot."

Two

New York, One Week Later

"HE KILLED HER. He actually said that?"

"Yes. He did."

"But...I don't understand." Keely looked at a loss, the way she had since Bethany had finally broken down and blurted out the scalding, condemning words screeching through her brain.

Bethany's fingers convulsed around the cushion in her hand. Consciously relaxing her fingers, she hugged the velvet square to her chest, blinked hard, and concentrated on just breathing. Her eyeballs were gritty and aching with the tears she'd shed over the last seven days. Her ass was numb from being permanently glued to the living room sofa, and her heart thudded every now and then - normally when her phone rang - with some mocking semblance of beating.

All because of Zachary Savage.

Keely made another incoherent sound of disbelief and shook her head. She started to speak but Bethany interrupted.

"Well, he said, quote: 'Farah was my wife. We were married for one day. Then I killed her.'"

Keely flinched, then reached for the bottle of red she'd brought with her. "Jesus." She poured and took a huge gulp. "I can't believe you kept this to yourself for a fucking week before you told me."

"I didn't...I couldn't..." she heaved in a huge breath. "The way he was with me, Keel. No one's ever taken care of me like that. I couldn't cope with the fact that he could do anything like that...

that he could...Oh God!"

Keely patted her knee. "I'm sorry, baby girl," she said softly.

"Please don't do that. It'll make me cry and I sure as hell have no fucking tears left." Even as she spoke, her eyes brimmed. "Shit. I hate myself for doing this. I feel so pathetic. So fucking weak. After what he said, I still want him. I can't stop thinking about him." She realized her whole body was trembling and she breathed in deep. The damn pain just grew larger. "God, how did I end up here?"

"You took a chance."

"And it backfired horribly."

For once her friend didn't have a quick come back. She just nodded and drank some more. But Bethany could see the questions in her eyes, the puzzlement in the slight shake of her head every now and then.

Yeah, join the fucking club.

Angrily, she brushed away the tears and reached for her glass of wine. With a defiant toss of her head, she drained the full glass and set it down to find Keely watching her, one perfectly plucked eyebrow cocked.

"Umm...atta girl?"

"Yeah. Go me."

"Bethany, maybe he didn't mean it literally? Maybe—"

"You weren't there. You didn't see the guilt on his face. The anguish. He looked as though his heart had been ripped out. He didn't just blurt it out, he *confessed* it. Trust me, he meant it. And you know what that said about me? That I'd been sleeping with a man I had no clue about."

"But you don't really think he did that, do you? *Killed someone?*"

Bethany jumped up, her insides roiling with pain and heartache. "I don't know! I've asked myself that same question a thousand times. And yes, I asked him. He told me he couldn't talk about it!"

"Why the fuck not?"

Her heart did that thing it'd perfected over the last seven days every time she thought of Zach. It bungee-jumped from her chest into her stomach, set itself on fire and streaked about like a firework. "Because he was so damned ripped up about it? Because he loved her more than life itself and things went horribly wrong between them? I was merely the woman he was fucking six ways to Sunday at every opportunity who just happened to find out his dark secret at a weak moment."

She clawed her hand through her hair and barely felt the pain of her tingling scalp at the rough movement. "Bottom line is, I found out, it scared the hell out of him, and he clammed up. And I got the hell out of there."

"How did you leave Marrakech?"

"He had his driver take me to the airport and his pilot flew me home."

"Okay, that kinda floors me a bit. But you trusted your instinct with him, B, or you would never have ditched the Indigo Lounge trip to go with him."

The reminder that had been both her pain and her hope through this hellish week, threatened to overwhelm her again. "I know. Which is why I can't think straight! My gut tells me he's incapable of…whatever he did, that there's more to the confession. But my head…I can't unhear the words." She shuddered.

Her phone buzzed loudly. They both jumped and stared at the number on the screen.

"Looks like *he's* not ready to give up either," Keely murmured. "Should I turn it off?"

Bethany swallowed, shrugged, and tried to keep breathing. More than anything she wanted to pick up that phone and hear his deep, dark, pulse-destroying voice again. Seven days had felt like a million lifetimes. She wanted to hear him call her *Bethany* in that husky, growly way of his that promised insanely decadent things. She wanted to see his gorgeous face, run her thumb over his lower lip the way he loved her to do. Hell, she wanted to climb into him and never come down.

Too damn bad.

She backed away from the ringing phone, her heart now making a slightly more valiant effort to do its job. "He'll go away," she replied shakily.

"I hear wishful thinking but I also hear yearning and denial. Which is it, baby girl?" Keely eyed her, then eyed the phone as if she wanted to incinerate it with just her thoughts.

"You didn't come here expecting coherency from me. Jesus, am I not allowed some leeway to be confused out of my goddamned mind?"

Contrition gentled Keely's face. "Of course. I'm sorry."

They both stopped as the phone cut off mid-ring. A second later, a text message beeped.

Bethany's knees gave way and she subsided back onto the sofa. Keely eyed her again and snatched the phone off the table.

She read the message, then sucked in a deep breath.

"What?" Bethany blurted, unable to stop her belly from flipping over.

Silently, Keely handed the phone over.

We need to talk. But until you're ready I need to know that you're okay. I'll respect your decision for me to stay away but only up to a point, Bethany. Avoiding my calls will not make me go away. I think we both know that.

Jesus. Zachary Savage couldn't help his arrogance even as he *respected* her decision. There was a mild threat to the text that promised punishment for her silence.

Punishment. As in, retreating to nurse her completely shattered heart and reeling senses would only be tolerated *up to a point*.

Sliding her finger across the interactive surface, she tapped her keypad.

I'm not okay, Zach. I think we both know *that*. And I don't see the point of talking when you won't answer the questions that are creating the problems between us. Hell, is there even an *us*? Or was there always going to be me, blowing my stupid feelings out of *proportions and you taking advantage of that?*

She pressed SEND and dropped the phone beside her.

"More wine?" Keely asked.

"Why not?" She held out her glass and took another big, fortifying gulp. Getting hammered was a stupid idea, especially after the first time she'd replied to Zach's incessant attempts to contact her all week. The likelihood of her weakness and pain bleeding through was very high, but her own silence was eating away inside like acid.

"Feel better?" Keely asked.

"Not even a little bit. But keep it coming."

"What—" she stopped at the sound of another text message. "He's fucking persistent. Gotta give him that."

Bethany made a sound between a snort and a sob. "You don't know the half of it." She picked up her phone and read the message.

Her shaky sigh had Keely's eyes narrowing. "What did he say?"

"He's calling in thirty seconds. He wants me to pick up. God."

"And are you going to?"

Bethany typed *No*, pressed send and held up the phone to Keely.

Her best friend slowly nodded her approval. "You know that's bought you like one minute, of course. But hey, I'm happy to kick his ass for you?"

Bethany attempted a smile. "Thanks, sweetie. I appreciate it."

The phone rang. They both ignored it. "Okay, let's talk about your birthday," Keely said brightly. "We could hit *Shades*, that new club downtown. I organised a premium tequila taster there last month for some bigwigs from Mexico. The owner was so impressed he put me on the permanent guest list. Or we can do karaoke? You missed a hell of a Fourth of July Karaoke Special at…Oh fuck, what did I say?" The touch of gentleness was fading from her eyes to be replaced by exasperation as tears welled up in Bethany's eyes.

"It's not you. Zach told me not to make any plans for my

birthday…Christ, I'm sorry. This is just a little unbearable."

"Don't fucking apologize. If he wanted to make your birthday special, then he shouldn't have confessed to being a *possible* murdering psycho." Bethany's flinch made Keely groan. "Fuck. I'm sorry but I kinda wanna tear his head off right now. In fact," she snatched the phone off the table and jumped up.

"Keely! What are you doing?"

"Sorry, B, this needs to be done." She hit dial and put it on speaker. Bethany insides turned over as she listened to the loud ringing.

"Bethany."

Dear Lord. His voice hasn't changed. Of course it hadn't. It still dripped sex, danger and dark secrets. And despite every heart-wrenching emotion she'd been through, it still curled so very effortlessly around her heart and held on with a vice-like grip.

"No such luck, Savage. You're stuck with the wicked stepmother." There was a dark delight in Keely's voice that a tiny part of Bethany was proud of.

"Put her on," Bethany heard him say. "Now, please."

"No can do, hot shot. Now, listen up. Remember what I said about coming after you with a blunt instrument if you hurt my girl?"

Deathly silence.

"Well guess what? You've just been upgraded to a hot poker stick up the ass if you don't stop calling."

"Let me speak to Bethany."

"You're still not getting the message, Savage. Stop. Calling. Or fucking else."

More silence. Maintained long enough for Keely to purse her lips and raise an eyebrow at the phone.

Then, "How is she?" Even from the distance, the gravity of his voice made Bethany's breath catch. God, he was so good at that. So good at making her believe he cared.

Except how could he genuinely care about her when he refused to give her the one thing she'd told him time and again would make things right between them? A little access. Was that too much to ask for?

"Tell me how she is. Please."

Right before her eyes, she saw Keely waver and begin to crumble. Bethany wanted to tell her that she'd graduated to the big leagues because Zach Savage didn't beg. But she was too busy holding her breath so she could catch every single thing he said.

"She's fucking *peachy*. What do you expect?" Keely attempted to snap but it came out half-hearted. When her eyes met Bethany's she rolled hers, and shrugged in an I'm-not-quite-sure-how-to-handle-this way. Another first from her friend.

Bethany's eyes widened.

As if realizing just how easily she'd succumbed to Zach Savage's wizardry, Keely shook her head. "Was that all? Because we have lives to be getting on with and wild birthday parties to be planning."

"Whose party?" he snapped, the solemnity gone from his voice. Keely's eyes narrowed.

"None of your business."

"*Miss Benson—*"

"Oh, is that tone supposed to frighten me? Try again, Savage. Or no, actually, don't try again. Give it up. Or I will make good on my promise."

She stabbed the end button and sucked in a breath. Striding over to the sofa, she collapsed beside Bethany and looked over at her with a slightly stunned understanding.

"I'm getting why you've been avoiding him. He can get kinda intense when he doesn't get his way, huh?"

A shiver went down Bethany's spine as she recalled just how intense Zach could be. He'd pursued her with a single-minded focus from the moment he'd seen her. Giving in had been an exhilarating experience and a crash course in diving in off the deep end. "Yeah. A little."

Keely blew out a breath. "So, what now?"

Bethany took her friend's hand and squeezed it tight. "I really want to high-five you right now for having my back. But I'm terrified you've just made things worse."

Three

8:03: BETHANY, TALK to me. Pick up the phone.
Bethany shoved her feet into the black pumps and attempted to ignore her phone and the messages that were starting to pile up.

She wasn't due back to work yet - Keely had taken one look at her when she picked her up from The Indigo Lounge VIP area last week and emailed Sheena to tell her Bethany wouldn't be in for another couple of weeks.

Leaving Marrakech the morning after Zach's atomic revelation, she'd never thought she'd be in the frame of mind to ever function properly again. But reality had a way of forcing itself on you, even when you were an emotional wreck who wanted nothing more than to stay in bed forever with the curtains drawn.

And reality had come in the form of a Friday morning email from The SMC Group, asking if she was available for an interview at ten. She'd wanted to ignore the email, to pull the covers over her head and drown in the misery she was wading neck-deep in.

Then the anger had started to build. She'd done nothing wrong, except fall in love with a man who'd been ultimately unattainable. It made her a whole lot stupid, yes, but it didn't mean she had to crawl away and die. Even if every single cell in her body craved to do just that.

And, seriously, there was a bright side to all of this. She'd had, hands down, the best sex of her life. Something memoir-worthy should she be so inclined to memorialize her very brief experience at some distant date in the future…

Jesus. She stopped and sucked in a breath. She was losing it. Perfectly understandable but if she was to have even a hope of making any form of impression at her interview, she needed to get her head out of Marrakech and back into New York mode *asap!*

She picked up her phone just as another message came through.

8.37: I can't stop thinking about you. I'm in agony, baby. Please, pick up the phone.

She turned her phone to silent before the inevitable ringing started and tried to get her thoughts into professional work mode. She had time on the ride to SMC's Midtown office to brush up on what she'd said in her resume. She just needed to stop her brain from deciphering every single nuance of Zachary's message. The man had a way with words. And he was particularly ruthless when it came to getting his way.

Well, she was done rolling over for Zach Savage. And if the thought immediately caused another shattering of the fragile pieces of her heart, that was just something else she would have to suck up today.

The interview passed in a blur of polished questions and equally polished answers with a mildly out of body feel to the hour she spent in the CEO's office.

Before she left, Bethany was certain she wouldn't take the job even if it was offered to her. Her potential new boss was a carbon copy of Sheena, and taking anything they had to offer would be making a bad situation worse.

She'd made enough of a mess of that in her private life. Feeling another vibration in her purse, she tried to tell herself she wasn't really interested in what else Zach had to say but found her hand reaching for the phone anyway.

10:14: Fuck. Stop this. I miss you. Z.

But as she read the latest one, her heart started to pound.

10:49: You made promises too, Bethany. You promised I wouldn't lose you no matter what. You promised you wouldn't hold yourself back from me. You're reneging on both promises.

She stopped in the middle of the sidewalk. Someone bumped into her and followed through with the classic New York response of *watch it, bitch*.

Her fingers shook as she pressed the button.

He answered immediately. "Bethany?"

Just like that the world fell away. She was back in his arms, in that exhilarating place that felt like nothing else in her universe. The way Zachary Savage said her name made her want to break down and weep with equal amounts of joy and sorrow.

He exhaled noisily down the line. "Please say something, baby."

The world snapped back into sharp focus. Horns blared and people rushed past at breakneck speed. Sights, sounds, smells. But all the wrong ones. She yearned to be back in Paris or in Marrakech. Before everything had gone to shit.

"You want me to say something? How dare you pull me up on my promises when you never kept even one of yours?" Her voice, husky from all the emotions she was trying to keep inside, sounded like she'd smoked a pack of cigarettes for breakfast.

"Bethany—"

"You expect me to keep trotting after you like some horny puppy after you dropped a bombshell at my feet and walked away? Let's try this for a second. What if I'd been the one to throw that grenade at your feet? Would you want to carry on blithely, as if what I'd said didn't matter?"

"No. But I wouldn't have walked away either. I let you go because—"

"You *let* me go? FYI, I am my own person. I may have let you have too much of your own way back in Paris and Marrakech but don't mistake willing for spineless."

"I never thought you were spineless."

That appeased her a little but anger still burned in her gut that he would use her promises against her. "Your last text was a low blow. I'm disappointed that you would sink that low."

"I wanted to get your attention."

She noted that he hadn't apologized. That Zach was still very much in play. "Well, you succeeded. For a minute. Goodbye—"

"No! Dammit, don't hang up."

Her grip tightened on the phone. Someone else bumped into her and a hiss of anger was swiftly followed by a rude suggestion of what she could do to herself.

"Where are you?" Zach demanded.

"I'm standing in the middle of the sidewalk somewhere in Midtown," she replied before she could think better of it.

She heard the distinct sound of a chair being shoved back. "I can be there in fifteen minutes. Tell me exactly where—"

"Wait a minute. You're in New York?" Shock rocked through her. Somehow, she'd imagined he was calling from his base in San Francisco. Learning that he was in the same city made her hot and cold at the same time.

The idea that he was *fifteen minutes* away made her heart flip over.

"I'm trying not to be disturbed by the fact that you think I'd be anywhere else but where you are."

Words, she reminded herself. They were just words. And Zach Savage was very good with his words, even when they hid his true meaning.

When she was bumped a third time, Bethany forced herself to move. She found herself want to ask him how long he'd been in New York and clamped her mouth shut.

"I took the next commercial flight out right after my plane left to bring you home," he volunteered softly. "You needed time so I didn't want to force my presence on you on my plane. Tell me where you are."

She reached an intersection and stopped. "No."

"Please, baby."

"You were right about me needing time."

He breathed out and Bethany could imagine his eyes narrowing into laser-sharp focus. "It's been a week, Bethany. It's felt like three fucking lifetimes but it's been a *goddamn* week."

The lights changed and she went with the flow of human traffic. She had no idea where she was headed but moving was a little better, and not like a robot only attuned to Zach's voice. "I know exactly how long it's been. Are you ready to explain what you meant in Marrakech?"

His silence lasted a few seconds but felt like a year. "I told you, it's not that easy."

The permanent vice-like grip around her chest tightened another notch. "Then I guess I'll be taking more time."

He sighed. "Dammit, Bethany, stop these games."

"Fuck you, Zach. You don't get to say that to me. If there's even a tiny shred of game-playing, it's not on my part. If you trust nothing else, trust me on that. You've taken pleasure in fucking with my head since we met. You won't be given the opportunity to mind-fuck me anymore."

"I know you want answers—"

"Answers you've made clear you're not prepared to give me. Knowing I'm not worthy of your trust hurts and I refuse to hurt anymore. So unless you're about to propose anything remotely close to what I need, I fail to see what the point of this phone call is."

"The fucking point is *I need you*. I miss you. I can't sleep without you. I can barely fucking function," he growled.

She stumbled, hating herself for the betraying flow of warmth that started in her belly and arrowed straight between her legs. Spying a coffee shop ahead, she quickly darted inside and found a pre-lunch time empty seat.

"I know you're not functioning well either, baby," his voice softened, almost crooning in her ear.

"Right. And you know this, how?"

"Because I *know* you. Inside and out. Tell me where you are. I need to see you. We can talk."

"By talk you really mean fuck, don't you? Because you know there's only one thing I want to talk about. And since we both know you don't want to talk about that, there can only be one thing on your mind."

He sighed. "I need more time, Bethany. There are other factors involved beyond me revealing what happened six years ago. But I'm working on it."

Her heart slowed with a painful thud. "You know something, Zach. Ever since we met you've used some variation of that line to keep the important parts of your life from me. Why did you even bother to tell me about your...about Farrah? Oh wait, you didn't. I only found out because you were *dreaming* about *her* while you were in bed with *me*."

"Christ, Bethany—"

She gave a laugh that scraped her throat and drew the wary attention of the guy on the next table. "And now I sound like a fucking neurotic bitch for wanting to control who you dream about. That's what you've reduced me to. You need more time? Sure. Go ahead and take all the time you need."

She ended the call. Her phone rang immediately. She flipped it to silent and sucked in a shaky breath.

The guy glanced at her again. Slowly she watched his expression turn from wary to appreciative. She stared back, forcing herself to look properly. He wasn't bad looking. He was well built with a pleasantly charming face and thick brown hair that flopped over one eye. Earphones rested over his buff shoulders, and he was dressed in a casual trendy way that flattered his body.

Her gaze clashed with his again. His interest was definitely sparked.

Once upon a time she would've been extremely flattered.

Now she felt nothing. Not even mild feminine satisfaction of catching another man's attention.

Because the only attention she wanted was Zach's. First and always. Except Zach only had one interest. Her body.

She looked away from the guy and didn't even feel bad when she sensed his disappointment. Her heart hurt too much. Her body hurt even worse.

Zach Savage Withdrawal was a condition she'd become agonizingly familiar with over the past seven days. The ache hadn't been gradual. The pain of walking away from Zach had been immediate. And excruciating.

She'd shut down completely once she'd boarded his plane to come home. She'd slept the whole journey, as if her body was preparing her for the rough ride ahead.

When she'd woken a half-hour before they landed at Newark, she'd relived the events of the night before and been stunned Zach had let her leave.

She may have been angry when he'd reminded her just now, but the truth was that if he'd asked her to stay she would've seriously considered it. In that moment after his stark declaration he'd been vulnerable enough for her to have pulled the information out of him had she so chosen.

Of course, shock had played a huge part in rendering her mindless for those precious minutes. The triple whammy of Zach being married for just one day before he…he…

God. She couldn't think about that last statement. No matter how much it'd knocked about in her head, demanding an answer, she couldn't wrap her mind around Zach's stark confession.

I've never wielded an axe in my life…

He'd said that to her in Paris. He'd looked like he meant it. And seriously, if Zachary Savage, billionaire extraordinaire had taken an axe to anyone, surely it would've made breaking news?

A bark of hysterical laughter startled from her throat.

Cute guy veered back to wary guy. The waitress walking past barely glanced her way. She was probably used to nut jobs stopping by to reminisce about their axe murderer ex-lovers just before the lunch crowd descended. Another laugh threatened to burst out but she swallowed it down.

You've finally fucking lost it, Bethany.

Standing, she picked up her bag and sucked in another breath. She was walking out when her phone pinged again.

Heart jumping into her throat, she read the message.

11:46: There's a time limit on how long I'm prepared to live without you. The clock's counting down fast and I'm slowly losing my mind. One way or the other, this will have to end soon. Z.

Four

THE FLOWER ARRIVED the next morning. A single vintage-yellow rose with a note - *Thinking of you. Z*

Bleary eyed from another sleepless night, Bethany stood on her doorstep for several seconds clutching the flower and note, blinking to stop the tears from forming.

She'd dreamt of him. Of Marrakech. Of dancing in his huge, magical ballroom. Of hot hands, hotter lips, wicked tongue and his thick, delicious cock.

In the dark of night, her body had screamed for him. She'd been so turned on, so needy and horny, she'd come in her sleep.

Opening her eyes to her dark New York apartment and her cold bed had been beyond rough. She wanted to hate Zach Savage. But right now she wanted to see his face so badly, she could barely breathe.

The silence between his texts had grown progressively longer as the day went yesterday. The last one had been at midnight. She'd snort-laughed at his imploration to *sleep well, baby.*

She'd texted back with a *fuck off.* Then she'd laid awake for hours expecting a response, hating herself for clutching her phone to her chest and jumping at each imaginary beep.

Now she slowly closed her door and stared at the flower. It wasn't a replica of the one he'd given to her in Marrakech, thank God. She was barely holding it together as it was. She didn't need another reminder of Marrakech. When she found herself trailing a finger over the sprawling *Z*, she shook her head and dropped the note on her coffee table.

Life. She needed to get one.

She changed into her jogging pants and tank top and pulled on her trainers. Tying her hair into a ponytail, she plugged in her iPod and tucked her keys into her hip pouch.

Vladimir, the Ukrainian daytime doorman smiled at her as she stretched in the foyer. "You have a good run, Miss Green."

"Thanks, Vlad. It's been a while. Hope I haven't forgotten how."

Two weeks ago, she'd been engaged in another, more mind blowing form of exercise. Her face flamed and she walked quickly to the swinging doors.

"You never forget how. Not that easily," Vlad said.

She waved her thanks as he held the door open for her. She blinked as she walked out into the dappling sunlight.

The stretch town car wasn't out of place in her relatively affluent East Village neighbourhood. All the same she found her footsteps slowing as she walked past it. It was driverless, with black-tinted windows that made it impossible to see inside. Aside from the high polish and silently opulent model, there was nothing distinctive about the car.

And yet...

She caught her reflection in the glass and realised she'd walked so close to it, she was in danger of looking like a total creep.

Turning, she hurried away and broke into a jog. After several minutes, the sound of her feet pounding the sidewalk slowly soothed her.

By the time she'd run a mile, Bethany was daring to believe she could rescue a few worthy crumbs from the pile of ashes her life had become. By the time she'd run two miles, she was daring to believe she could put Paris and Marrakech out of her mind some time before winter arrived in New York.

By the time she turned around and started back, her pounding heart was making the argument with her brain that one day she would forget that Zach Savage existed.

Bethany never found out which organ won the argument. She rounded the corner of her apartment block and jogged the last few meters, grateful that her body hadn't let her down. And stumbled to a halt.

The town car was still parked in the same place but this time its occupant was very visible.

Mouth agape, heart racing, she watched Zach's head turn to where she stood. Slowly he straightened from where he'd been leaning against the car.

From across the space between them, he stared at her with those mesmerizing eyes. Then his gaze slowly raked her from head to toe, lingering for several seconds at her breasts and hips. With depressingly eager enthusiasm, her body reacted to his stare, her pulse slamming higher, her nipples tightening into painful nubs as fire flared through her belly to heat her clit. She felt dirty in a delicious way, as only Zach could make her feel.

Hell, in that moment, feeling those eyes on her, even the sweat drenching her skin turned her on.

A wave of dizziness washed over her as she devoured him in turn, her senses jumping wildly at the sensual feast Zachary Savage offered.

"Hello, Bethany."

Despite the high volume of Pink blaring *The King Is Dead* in her ear, she couldn't mistake the low, dark voice. Or the distinct edge to it.

Or the fact that in the morning sunlight, his tall, arresting body was a sight her hopelessly deprived senses were lapping up with a greed that was truly frightening.

He wore an indigo shirt - God, the man could work that colour like no other - and dark blue jeans that rode low on his lean hips. Powerful thighs she remembered far too well bunched as he took a step toward her. His shirt was folded back to reveal his brawny forearms and his beautiful skin was thrown into stunning relief. He hadn't lost the tan he'd acquired under the hot desert sun.

"What are you doing here?" She didn't bother to ask him how he knew where she lived. The arrival of the flower this morning had reminded her that Zach knew most of the pertinent details of her life, thanks to the forms she'd filled out for the Indigo Lounge flight and also because, unlike him, she'd held nothing back during their short time together.

That admission of total access made her exhale noisily. She didn't want to dwell on just how openly she'd shared her life with him and how much less she'd received in return. Now wasn't the time. Right now, she needed to get her roiling emotions under control.

"Are you really surprised to see me? You knew this was inevitable." Dark grey eyes rested on her, watched her with an intensity she'd thought she'd imagined but was rudely reminded was very real. "Did you get my delivery?"

Pink raged on the *truth about love*. She pulled out the earphones and left them dangling uselessly from her side. "I got the flower. And I got the note. That changes nothing."

A hard smile curved his lips. "I didn't expect it to. I just wanted you to know how I was feeling."

"Why? So I can feel sorry for you? You're thinking about me. Big deal. I thought about you too. I thought about how I never want to see you again. I made that very clear in Morocco."

His jaw tightened and he folded strong, muscled arms across his chest. She tried very hard not to stare at the silky dark hairs that coated those arms. To remember how much she'd loved to run her hand up and down the bunched strength of it. How they felt banded around her waist as he pounded into her.

"Baby, you don't mean that," he said quietly. "I refuse to accept that you mean that."

"I know you make your own rules. Ones that don't apply to us lesser mortals. But please do me the courtesy of at least pretending to think that I know my own mind, Zach."

He regarded her for several seconds before he tapped on the front window. It wound down smoothly to reveal Philip, Zach's driver, bodyguard and Bethany imagined, all round Mr Fix-It. Philip looked her way and nodded his greeting. Then he picked up a Styrofoam tray containing two large coffees and a bag with a familiar bakery logo on it.

"What's that?"

"Breakfast. I missed you leaving for your run when I popped round the block to get it earlier. I got you a fresher cup a few minutes ago. Invite me up, Bethany."

Her gaze snapped back to him. "Hell no!" Her voice emerged screechier than she'd intended. Simply because the effect of seeing Zach again had hammered home the fact that she was still on precariously shaky ground where her feelings for him were concerned. Inviting him up to her apartment was inviting trouble and temptation to feast on her already ravaged heart.

"Fine. Have dinner with me tonight."

"I have other plans."

His jaw clenched and he walked slowly to where she'd stumbled into immobility five minutes ago. When they were inches apart, he stopped. "Plans. Who with?" he grated, his tone icy and commanding.

"None of your business," she replied, struggling not to inhale his hauntingly familiar scent like a bloodhound on a juicy trail. Her gaze reached the pulse throbbing in his neck and warmth shamelessly flooded her mouth.

"Tell me who you're going out with, Bethany."

She raised her head and glared at him. "Go away, Zach."

"Christ," he muttered. "How did I not know you were this stubborn?"

"Because as much as you like to think otherwise, you don't know everything about me."

His face hardened. "I know you're not stupid enough to go out with another guy when you still belong to me." Her gasp got lost in the morning air because he was still speaking. "No matter how much you think you hate me right now, you're still mine and I'm not letting you go. I never will. I'm telling you that right now so we're both clear on the matter and there's no room for misinterpretation. Nod if you understand what I'm saying to you."

Her head moved before she gave it permission to and Bethany exhaled roughly, ready to kick her own ass for that weak slip.

"I guess that will have to be enough for now," he rasped. He continued to stare down at her for a full minute, his eyes raking over her face and her body with a hunger that threatened to flatten her where she stood.

Finally, he held out the bakery bag to her. The scent of sugared pastry rose to tease her nostrils. She was fast reaching her breaking point. Seeing him again felt like being plugged into an electric socket with the voltage racing higher by the second. She risked a full-body electrocution if she didn't retreat fast.

"If I take this will you go away?" she ventured bravely.

His eyes narrowed further. "I'm hanging on by a fucking thread here, baby, so don't push me. Take the food," he instructed.

She took the bag and the coffee cup he held out to her. With both hands full, she couldn't stop him when he reached out and traced his thumb over her lower lip. It tingled and trembled before she bit desperately on it and jerked her head away.

His eyes darkened and he made a rough sound under his breath.

"Drink some water first before you drink the coffee. And next time you run, take some water with you. It's July in New York for fuck's sake. I don't want you stroking out on some street corner because you're careless with your health."

She really needed to get out of here. "Are you done?"

His fingers twitched again as if he wanted to touch her.

"Not nearly. I'll call you in twenty minutes. Make sure you pick up."

Every nerve in her body screamed in anticipation even as she raised her chin. "Or what?"

"Or I'll just turn around and come back here. You have no idea how much it hurts to be this close to you and not take you in my arms and show you how much I've missed you. But I'm playing by your rules for now. So throw me a fucking bone, Bethany. Pick up the phone when I call. Or I will come back.

And if you think that puny excuse of a doorman I can see glaring at me from in there is going to stop me, think again."

With one last, intense look, he took two steps back and pulled the back door open. She didn't want to watch him leave. She swore she wouldn't do it as she turned and walked quickly toward the swinging doors.

And yet, as Vlad moved forward and held the door open for her, she found herself looking over her shoulder.

His eyes were riveted on her. When they dropped to her ass, she saw his grip clench hard on the door. His gaze reconnected with hers and the stark, fiery hunger on his face slammed into her so hard she moaned.

She rushed indoors and stumbled toward the elevator, nodding jerkily at Vlad's concerned query if she was all right. She was still shuddering long after she was back in her apartment, her body screaming with all the emotions rampaging through her.

He called exactly twenty minutes later. Freshly showered and sipping the last of the delicious freshly ground coffee, she told herself she was answering so he would leave her alone and not return to shatter her peace of mind.

"I've answered your call. Can I go now?"

"No, you can't. You sent me away when I wanted to lick every fucking drop of sweat off your gorgeous body. Now I have a hard on that won't subside and an appointment in five minutes. You'll pay for that, Peaches."

Her breath caught at his dark promise. Desperately, she tried to think of anything else besides Zach's cock and what form her punishment would take.

This man had turned her life upside down with a revelation that should make her run a thousand miles away...he continued to devastate her with his silence while blatantly disregarding the fact that she considered them over.

And yet her heart and body craved him with a hunger that defied reason. Despair warred with anger inside her and still she hung on, her pulse hammering and waited to hear that deep, gravel-rough voice again.

"Did you eat yet?" he asked.

"Yes." She'd devoured the cream-filled pastry within minutes of entering her apartment. Stress eating had never felt so good and the deep shame she'd felt afterward was well worth it.

"Good." Satisfaction reeked in his voice.

"What kind of appointment do you have on a Saturday?" she asked before she could stop herself.

"I'm apartment hunting. I'm seeing four today. I could use your help if you want to come meet me?"

Several thoughts tumbled through her mind but the one that lit like a neon sign in her brain was - *Zach was staying in New York*. Yeah, big deal. It changed nothing. Their problems still loomed as large and would remain insurmountable until Zach got the message - that open communication was non-negotiable. "I told you I have other plans."

"Tell me about these plans."

"Why?"

"Because I need something to take my mind off the fact that my dick is about to explode and you're not next to me," he rasped. "That I'm missing you madly and you won't give me the time of day."

Heat cannoned into her belly then detonated outward. "I'm meeting Keely for lunch. Then she's taking me shopping for tonight."

"Tonight?"

"We're going out for my birthday."

Silence echoed ominously down the phone. "Your birthday's not till tomorrow."

"I'm seeing my parents tomorrow so we're celebrating tonight."

"You were supposed to celebrate with me."

"Yeah, we both know how that worked out."

He sighed. "It doesn't have to be this way. What time are you seeing your parents?"

"They're taking me to lunch."

"So we can still spend tomorrow evening together."

Her heart lurched. "No. We can't, Zach. Not if we're going to ignore the herd of elephants in the room."

"We will fix this, Bethany."

"I can't see how, not without discussing what needs to be discussed."

His breath hissed out. "So you're saying everything that came before means nothing to you?"

Pain ripped through her insides. "Of course not. But I can't ignore what came afterward. I have so many questions, Zach, not just that one question you won't answer."

"Ask me one of them," he grated out.

The tense invitation shocked her into silence for a handful of seconds. Then, heart thundering, she gripped the phone tighter. "Okay. Why did you take me to Marrakech? Of all the places in the world you could've taken me, why there? We both know that place means more to you than just a house. So why did you take me there, Zach?"

He exhaled harshly. "My answer won't please you."

She licked dry lips. "Try it anyway."

"I needed to put some ghosts to rest."

Cryptic as ever. "Zach—"

"Remember what I said when we were there, that you were a risk I knew I was taking?"

"Yes."

"Do you know what usually happens when I feel that way?"

"No."

"I walk away. I only take calculated risks in business. My personal life before I met you was based on one thing. Sex, on my terms. That went out the window the moment I saw you. But I still took the risk."

"What are you saying?"

"I'm still taking the risks now. Some of the answers you need we can work through. We don't need to be apart to do that."

Her heart lurched. "*Some?* What if I said I want to know

everything? I want to know about Farrah? What if I said that's the only way I'll contemplate us moving forward?"

Tense silence. "I'd ask you to rethink that."

"Why?"

"Because you told me you loved me. And that you'd give me time. Or did you lie?"

Scalding tears welled in her eyes. Angrily she brushed them away. "You bastard," she croaked, her whole body going numb.

His breath hissed out. "Fuck. Bethany—"

"No. Enough, Zach. Enough." She hung up.

Five

ZACH ABSENTLY TUNED in to the realtor yammer on about south facing versus west facing lighting, Poggenpohl kitchens and parquet floors and tried to stem the panic flaring through him.

He pressed the call button again and listened as the call went straight to voicemail.

The message he wanted to leave couldn't be said out loud in the presence of the realtor and Philip who hovered a few steps behind him.

"As you can see, the floor to ceiling views are rather special," the realtor continued. Blonde, in her late twenties, she'd been doing her best to catch his eye since they met downstairs ten minutes ago. Impatience crawled over him as he struggled to keep the frown from his face.

"The space is *ideal* for entertaining, and has the perfect blend of home and office. And the square footage is one of the largest on our books at the moment. The specially selected concierge…"

Zach bit back a sharp retort, blocked her out, and forced himself to look around properly. As his needs went, the duplex was more than adequate, with a large office complete with the meeting room he'd specifically demanded. Setting up here for the foreseeable future shouldn't be a problem. And out of the four properties he planned to view today, this was the closest to Bethany's place in the East Village. Which made it a no brainer, really.

"I'll take it," he said abruptly. "On condition that I can move in immediately." He fingered the call button again, desperately hoping that Bethany would pick up this time.

The realtor's face lit up with pleasure. "Oh...that's great, Mr Savage. Yes of course to moving in immediately. I'll draw up the papers. Umm," she started to move toward him and Zach noted her hips had taken on a sexier sway, "we also offer a remodeling service if you need it, with highly sought after designers—"

He turned away. "No, thanks. Philip will take care of the papers." He nodded to Philip and walked out of the living room.

He dialed Bethany's number again and cursed under his breath when he heard the distinctive click.

You've reached Bethany. Leave me a message.

He walked into the study, shut the door and crossed over to the large window overlooking Central Park. Heart thudding dully in his chest, he leaned forward until his forehead touched the cool glass.

"I fucked up. Again. I'm sorry, baby. I just...this distance... being without you...I can't handle it." He stopped and tried to breathe. But just like everything else since that moment in his garden in Marrakech, his breathing was off. Every damn thing was off. "I'm sorry..." he stopped again, his mind spinning with all the things he wanted to say but couldn't.

He'd been floundering every day since admitting what he did six years ago, like he was on a rollercoaster that was taking him farther and farther away from Bethany with each passing second. And he couldn't get off.

He'd gone through moments of detesting her for making him feel these alien, confounding emotions. But the underlying factor had always remained the same.

He needed Bethany like he'd never needed anyone else in his life. That last night in Marrakech had ripped away any illusions that what was going on between them was run-of-the-mill. Even before his near meltdown in the toy room and the way he'd taken Bethany, he'd known his craving ran deeper than mind-blowing sex. It was that knowledge that had sent him into a disturbed sleep, making him dream - on that night of all nights - of Farrah and the events of six years ago.

The moment he'd woken from the dream he'd known something was seriously wrong. In his short time with Bethany, he'd grown accustomed to her emotions in a way that stunned and confused the hell out of him.

Hell, he could blame that confusion for his stark confession. Or he could admit he'd been terrified that not giving her something would've made her walk away.

His lips twisted. Well, he'd gambled and she'd walked away anyway. After she'd looked at him with confused terror in her eyes. After she'd paled to the point where he'd been petrified that she would actually shatter from the grenade he'd thrown at her feet.

When she'd asked to leave, he'd fought his every instinct to make her stay. And really, how could he have asked her to stay knowing he'd brought her to the place that was special to Farrah?

What sort of asshole would that have made him? What sort of asshole had he been to take her there in the first place?

Sighing, he stared down at his phone and contemplated calling one more time. In the distance he heard the realtor leave and Philip shut the door behind her.

A few seconds later, Philip knocked and entered the study. "It's done," he said quietly.

Zach nodded at the loyal right hand man who'd been with him longer than any friend or acquaintance. "Let's get the usual people in to get things sorted in here."

Philip nodded. "The extra works included?" he asked.

A dark throb started inside him and he sucked in a breath at the acute hunger threatening to tear him apart. "Yes. Use the room next to the master bedroom. I want it done ASAP."

"Understood." Philip left as quietly as he'd entered.

Striding to the desk, Zach switched on his laptop and quickly located the file he sought. Scrolling through, he found the phone number and dialled.

The phone was answered after one ring. "Keely Benson,"

barked the no-nonsense voice.

"Miss Benson," he greeted, slightly gratified that someone was answering his calls. "It's Zachary Savage."

"Hey, Zach. Call me Keely. If my red-hot poker is soon to become intimately acquainted with your delectable ass, I think we should at least be on a first name basis, don't you?" she snapped icily.

Zach's lips twitched. She was a pit bull when it came to protecting her friend. He definitely respected that. But even that wouldn't be allowed to stand in his way. Although he was prepared to remain cordial. For now, Keely Benson may be his only immediate access to Bethany.

"Very well. I'm doing my best to make sure my ass remains poker free."

"That's good to know. How can I help you?"

"I need five minutes of your time, if it isn't too much to ask?"

"Go ahead. I'm all ears," Despite the easy rejoinder, he heard the wariness in her voice.

Zach gritted his teeth and forced himself to remain calm. His first question was met with frostily negative response. His second request brought a marginally easier reply. By the time he made his third request, he dared to think that Keely Benson's voice had grown considerably less chilly.

"You do recognize that there's a mildly stalkerish quality to what you plan to do, don't you?"

"It's her birthday. I had in mind quite different plans for her birthday. This contingency is all I have."

"Fine. But I'll be keeping an eye on you. If you so much as twitch in the wrong direction, your ass is mine. Are we clear, Savage?"

He knew the use of his surname was deliberate. He chose to let it slide. "I'd expect nothing else. And Keely?"

"Yep?"

"You may not believe this right now given the circumstances, but know that I'd rip out a vital organ before I harm a single hair on her head."

Keely remained silent for several seconds before she sighed. "Yeah, the circumstances are not swinging wildly in your favor. But I'm holding you to that promise. I'm also hoping you'll make things right between you two. She's been through enough." The line went dead.

He swallowed hard and jerked away from his desk. Raking a hand through his hair, he paced to the window and back again. But no amount of pacing could put distance between him and the knowledge that Keely had just lumped him in with the other assholes who'd hurt Bethany in the past. The very idea made him sick to his stomach.

But he *had* hurt her. And was continuing to do so with his silence.

I'm also hoping you'll make things right between you two.

Fuck.

Striding to his desk, he snapped up the phone again. He didn't care that it was early and a Saturday to boot on the West Coast. At moments like these he appreciated having a few billion dollars attached to his name.

His lawyer answered almost immediately. And much to Zach's satisfaction the man was instantly alert despite the early hour.

"Where are we on the Farrah issue?" Zach bit out.

Stanley Reed cleared his throat. "I reached out like you asked. The family attorney thinks her father may agree, but her mother and brother could be a problem. Especially the brother."

Zach's jaw clenched hard. "He was my brother-in-law for less than twenty-four hours and she—" he stopped before he gave anything away. His lawyers had been given enough information to draw up the agreement but not even they knew the whole truth. Secrets. So many secrets threatening to tear him apart. Threatening to rip his most precious possession from his arms. He sighed.

"We haven't seen each other in six years. No feathers have been ruffled. How hard can it be to get them to change their minds?"

"The brother is an attorney now. He knows the law and is determined to stick to every word in your agreement."

"Can't you make a deal with him?"

"I'm looking into it but..." Stanley hesitated.

"But what?" Zach's patience shredded even thinner.

"It looks like he's about to make partner at his law firm. He's understandably anxious of any unsavory details getting out that could jeopardize that. Perhaps in a few months once he's made partner—"

"No. Dammit, I don't have a few months. I need a way around this *now*, Stanley. Find it for me. And find it soon."

"As always, I'll do my best."

Zach slammed the phone down and cursed long and hard. He knew he was playing hardball but he was fast running out of options. He could feel Bethany slipping through his fingers and he was damned if he was going to stand by and let it happen.

But a signed agreement wasn't that easy a hurdle to get over, not to mention the chaos it would bring. But he would find a way around that too.

If it came down between that and losing Bethany, it was a fucking no-brainer.

He glanced at his watch and noticed only ten minutes had passed since his last attempt to reach Bethany.

Christ. Had time ever dragged this slowly in his entire life?

His phone rang and he pounced on it, only to recognize the familiar number of his assistant back in San Francisco.

He answered. "Jeff. What's up?"

"I just wanted you to know there's been a slight change in the delivery date for the latest IL plane."

"Sooner or later?" he queried.

Jeff laughed. "After your threat to rip them a new one if they delayed again, what do you think?"

Zach forced a laugh. "So it's sooner. When?"

"It touches down in Newark on Monday. I've emailed the final layout pictures to you. They're incredible. I think they've outdone themselves this time." Jeff's excitement was palpable while Zach had none.

"Great. I'll go and check it out on Monday. Thanks for letting me know." He ended the call and leaned his hip against the desk.

Staring out the side window towards the East River, he started to smile at the idea forming in his brain.

Perhaps Keely Benson wasn't his only avenue to Bethany after all.

*

Bethany slipped the twenty to the cab driver and turned to watch Keely slide gingerly out of the cab. Watching her friend maneuver her dangerously short hemline made her laugh for the first time in what felt like years.

"Is there any particular reason you feel the need to show the world the color of your thong?" she teased.

"Shut up." Keely flipped her hair and primped her scarlet lips. "I have great legs. What's the point of hiding them?"

"There's showing them off, and there's *showing* them off. Don't blame me if you get jumped before your first *cosmo*."

"If anyone's gonna get jumped, girlfriend, it's you. Your curves are fucking dangerous tonight." She blatantly eyed Bethany's black tube dress and the one inch gold belt that cinched in her tiny waist.

The gold bangles at her wrists and long necklace jangled as she fidgeted under her friend's scrutiny. There was something strange about the way Keely was acting. Something about the way Keely had kept glancing at her since she'd arrived at Bethany's apartment earlier that made Bethany nervous. It was a cross between speculation and anxiety.

Bethany had been an emotional wreck over the last seven days but Keely hadn't appeared fazed by her breakdown. And Bethany honestly thought she'd been less of a wreck in the last day or so. Sure, she was still shaky from her conversation with Zach this morning. She hadn't recovered from *that*. Or from listening to the dozen messages he'd left for her since then. But she hadn't cried since midday and she'd carefully applied enough makeup to hide the bags under her eyes.

So, what gave?

She opened her mouth to ask her friend just that but Keely was exchanging greetings with a skinny, trendily dressed host wearing an earpiece and clutching a leather clipboard. They exchanged air kisses and admired each other's labels before Keely dragged Bethany forward.

"Travis, this is Bethany. It's her pre-birthday drinks tonight, so you need to make her feel special."

Travis held out his hand to Bethany, gave a limp handshake and raised a carefully trimmed eyebrow at Keely. "Every girl who walks through *Shades'* doors is a unique little snowflake, darling. But I've put you in the Gold VIP room upstairs anyway. Enjoy," he drawled lazily. "I'd have given you the Platinum room but some guy with bigger balls than mine has commandeered it." He executed a perfect pout before giving a tiny *shaking-it-off* shimmy.

More air kisses were exchanged. Then Keely was sashaying her way into the interior of the nightclub, her pert little ass twitching in the red micro skirt she'd worn with her black backless top.

Shades was all about the lighting. One section - the first floor bar, was lit in bold shades of green and purple, with more subdued colors of gold and silver cutting across the dance floor.

A wide cordoned-off staircase bathed in amethyst light led to the upper floors. On the wraparound balcony overlooking the downstairs bar, guests sipped cocktails and grooved to the sound of hip-hop blaring from the speakers. A walkway connected to an upper level dance floor. Two girls, clearly well on their way to being hammered, danced provocatively in the middle of the dance floor.

Bethany felt a tug on her arm, and followed Keely to the sitting area marked Gold VIP.

"What would you like to drink?" Keely indicated the touchscreen listing the various cocktails. Bethany read through the list and laughter bubbled up her throat.

"Are these names for real?"

Keely laughed. "Yep. Wanna try the *Studded Reverse Cow Girl*? I'm having one."

"How about just a plain *Dirty Cowgirl*?"

"Chicken." Keely clicked their order through and flung her tiny clutch on the seat just as Justin Timberlake started crooning about taking back the night.

Keely was a fabulous dancer with very little inhibition. And in her tiny skirt and endless legs, she was soon attracting avid male attention. When she urged Bethany to join in, she groaned under her breath. Refusal wasn't an option, however. Keely had been determined all week to do something special for her birthday and Bethany hadn't had the heart to refuse her best friend's efforts to cheer her up.

Their cocktails arrived, followed steadily by more drinks until Bethany's inhibitions, heartache and misery began to dull around the edges. They never went away but the alcohol flowing through her bloodstream helped her believe she could finally take a breath without her heart contracting with pain.

Perhaps things weren't as bad as they felt. Perhaps she could welcome her twenty-fifth birthday with laughter and pleasure, not tears and heartache.

With a whoop, she threw herself into the music.

She was popping her hips to the addictive beat of *Blurred Lines* when her gaze connected with a tall, dirty blond haired guy in dark trousers and a wine shirt. He was leaning against the balcony railing, one leg crossed over the other, with a smile on his face. There was an appreciative gleam in his eyes that made her want to smile back.

She glanced away. Beside her, Keely laughed as the long haired, spectacled guy she was dancing with murmured something in her ear. The guy looked as if he was about to spontaneously combust with adoration.

Bethany looked back at the guy in front of her. She watched as he slowly straightened and mouthed, "Dance?"

She was about to nod when the tingle shot down her spine. There was nothing subtle about it. It slammed through her, nearly knocking her off her feet.

Heart racing, she whirled, feeling momentarily dizzy. Keely grabbed her arm, concern stamped on her face. "Hey, are you okay?" she yelled to be heard above the music.

Bethany shook her head and turned her head sharply her gaze darting around the ambient space. Aside from a few VIP guests who'd drifted in to join them about an hour ago, nothing seemed out of place.

And yet…

Remembering when she'd first experienced that sensation - on the first day of her Indigo Lounge trip, staring up at Zach's office in Newark - she shivered.

Heart hammering faster, she glanced around again but all she could see were bodies moving to the music and her own reflection on the mirrored walls. Her face appeared flushed and her eyes sad and haunted. She looked away quickly, unable to face the truth that stared back at her.

"Hey."

The guy who'd asked her to dance stood in front of her, his smile wider, his gaze expectant. From the loud speakers, Rihanna demanded to know where some guy had been all her life.

Bethany started to smile just as another tingle surged up her spine.

She heard a gasp beside her before Keely's "Shit!" exploded in her ear.

Zachary Savage materialized out of the darkness, pure fury vibrating from him, just as Blond Guy stepped forward, his hand extending to slide around her waist.

He never made the connection.

"*What the hell!*" His smile turned to a grimace of shocked pain as Zach grabbed the back of his neck, his fingers digging in deep.

"You lay one finger on her and I'll break every fucking bone in your body."

Six

BETHANY STUMBLED OUT of the club into the smoky night air, her heart racing with equal parts anger and…oh God, she hated to admit it but…*excitement*.

Behind her, she heard Zach's heavy footsteps and Keely's lighter ones, coming after her. She quickened her steps, sucking in desperate breaths.

"Where the fuck do you think you're going?" Zach snapped behind her. She turned to face him and almost wished she hadn't.

This close, his body, his face, stunned and dazzled her into near incoherence.

"I think the better question here is - who the fuck do you think you are, Savage?" Keely, suffering no such debilitating compunction, demanded. "It's a free country. And she's single."

"No. She isn't," he snapped without taking his eyes off Bethany. She stared back at him. Fury, hunger and deep, dark possessiveness blazed from eyes turned almost black with his chaotic emotions.

"Zach," she rasped, then stopped to wet her dry lips. "You can't keep following me around—"

"And you sure as fuck can't go around hitting people, you know," Keely flung at him.

Zach's gaze didn't waver once from Bethany. "Trust me, if I'd hit that asshole, he'd know about it." The menace in his voice was unmistakable.

"Jesus." Keely threw out her arms.

She finally attracted Zach's attention. He faced her, hands on his lean hips, his jaw tight enough to break through concrete. "I trusted you to take care of her. You let me down. As of now, you're relieved from that task."

Keely's mouth dropped open. "Are you kidding me?"

Bethany finally managed to unglue her tongue to string words together. "Wait, what do you mean you trusted her to take care of me?"

Both Keely and Zach stared at her. Guilt flicked over Keely's face, but Zach remained tight-jawed and unapologetic.

Her insides hollowed out. "Someone better answer me, right now. Did you plan tonight with him, Keely?"

Her friend flushed and shook her head. "No. Not exactly."

"Then how...*exactly*?"

"He was just supposed to turn up and wish you happy birthday. At least that's what we agreed to. I had no idea he was going to turn into a homicidal maniac the moment another guy looked at you."

Zach's hands curled into tight fists at his side.

"He was doing a hell of a lot more than looking," he growled, low and dangerous.

Keely stepped back, her eyes widening as her gaze flicked back to Bethany. "Let's go back inside, B."

"No—"

"*Hell, no*," Zach tagged on harshly. "The only place Bethany's going is home with me."

"If you think I'm letting you anywhere near her—"

"I'm going home. *On my own*," Bethany slid in quietly. "Keely, I'll talk to you tomorrow."

"Bethany—" Zach stepped toward her. She turned away sharply. A cab was offloading a couple headed for the club.

The moment the couple alighted, she dived into the back and slammed the door shut.

"Shit, wait!" He lunged for the door but the driver was already pulling away.

Her last glimpse of Zach and Keely showed their astonished faces as the cab sped away.

She lost track of time as her brain reeled from being bombarded with what had just happened. Zach had colluded with Keely to turn up and see her on her birthday. In that moment, Bethany wasn't sure whether she was madder at Zach or at Keely. Or whether she could stop her heart from slamming excitedly against her ribs when she recalled Zach's face. His eyes. God, his hands…

He was waiting when she stepped out of the cab at her apartment. *How the fuck had he gotten here so fast?*

Shock held her immobile for several seconds before the cab driver's impatient prompt pulled her gaze away. She refocused to find Zach slipping him a handful of bills.

Her breath evaporated from her lungs when he turned to face her. "If you do that to me again, I'll put you over my knee and spank the hell out of that tight ass of yours."

"You…God, Zach, what will it take for you to get the message?"

"What will it take for you to understand that I'm going nowhere? That I'm not prepared to let one question and one answer stop us from happening?" he grated out.

His fury hadn't abated. In fact, if anything, it'd escalated. He reached out and grabbed her arms, jerked her forward until she collided into him.

Heat from his body rushed over her burning her from the outside in. He lowered his head until his face was one heart-stopping inch from hers.

"You got into a cab, alone, after fuck knows how many drinks. And after you nearly let another guy *put his hands on you*. Tell me why I shouldn't be hauling you off somewhere to teach you a lesson?"

"Because you don't own me," she yelled. "Because this is my life! Because what you told me is life-changing enough for me to want to reassess whether I let you near me ever again."

He frowned. "Let me near you…what the hell are you saying? That you're afraid *for your life*?" He uttered the words with a shocked breath. A shade of color receded from his face and his eyes widened. "You think I'd *ever deliberately* hurt you?"

He looked so stunned, a wave of shame rushed through her. But then she shook her head. "I won't let you guilt me into defending my feelings, Zach. The reality is I don't know *what* to think. You've given me nothing, and you expect me to just trust you when you don't trust me enough to be open with me. I can't live like that."

He clawed a hand through his hair. "Why can't you trust that if it were up to me, you'd know everything by now?"

"Oh, change the tune, I'm over hearing your excuses. As for the cab thing, I'm a big girl, Zach. A whole quarter of a century old as of," she peered at her phone, "thirty-one minutes ago. As you can see, I'm pretty good at getting myself home in one piece."

"Be that as it may, you're drunk and I'm still seeing you upstairs."

She lurched away from him and walked into her foyer. "Do what you want. It's not going to get you anywhere."

"It's going to give me peace of mind to know you're safe, Bethany. I told you, taking care of you is now my job."

She couldn't stop her heart flipping over as she stabbed the button for the elevator. "If that's supposed to make me all soft and gooey inside, you're outta luck. I don't know if you do it deliberately or if you're just so used to getting your way, you refuse to see or acknowledge anyone else's way, but you don't stop to think twice before you hurt me. So pardon me if I find it hard to believe every word that falls from your mouth."

He stared at her for long seconds, his hot angry eyes raking her from head to toe. Then he sighed. "Baby, I warned you that returning to the real world would be difficult for us. You're not making things easier by showing off that sexy body and letting assholes leer over you. And if you think I'm going to stand by idly and watch that happen, you're seriously deluded."

He turned away and watched the floors count down.

Suddenly she wanted to lash back at him. "What if I liked it, Zach? Other men watching me?"

He stilled, those piercing eyes cutting straight into her. "Are you sure you want to go down that road, Peaches?" he taunted softly.

"Don't call me that."

He raised an eyebrow. "Want me to stop? Come over here and make me."

She actually took a step before she realized his trick. He wanted contact. He knew it would give him the advantage. One touch from him and she would be putty in his hands. She locked her knees and glared at him. "Nice try."

His smile was filled with pure masculine confidence and gritty determination. "I play to win, baby. Never forget that."

The elevator arrived. She stepped in and held her breath as he entered behind her. With a hand she willed not to shake, she pressed the button for her floor and clutched her tiny purse, avoiding eye contact.

He lounged against the opposite wall, his eyes never leaving her. His scent surrounded her, invading her senses, viciously reminding her of the hunger clawing through her belly.

"Peaches," he murmured in a low undertone. The anger still vibrated in his voice but alongside it reeked dark, dirty sex. Pure, lethal Zach Savage, intent on getting his way. "Stop pushing me away."

"No. I can't keep doing this."

"Doing what?"

"Going against my better judgment. Believing that things will turn out okay. I did that with Chris. I refuse to do that again."

His jaw clenched hard. "I'm not fucking Chris, Bethany. If you're saying that to drive me away, I suggest you quit while you're ahead."

Her breath shuddered out. The elevator slid open and she rushed out to her door. Inserting the key, she opened the door and turned to face him. "I'm home now. You can leave."

His eyes narrowed. "I'm not leaving."

"Yes, you are. I have a birthday date with my vibrator and I'm not going to let you keep us apart."

His eyes darkened dramatically. His jaw clenched hard and he breathed in deep. "I can't go. I've been without you for a week. It's driving me fucking insane. You're upset and you're determined to make me suffer. I get it. But I'm not leaving. Not until you tell me you can find it in your heart to give me one hour of your time soon."

Looking at him hurt so much, she turned away abruptly. His low growl, the burn of her skin, told her his gaze had found his favorite part of her body - her ass. The magnetic pull of his gaze threatened to undo her.

Glancing over her shoulder, she sent him a brittle smile.

"Stay. Leave. I don't care. But don't interrupt me," she said with more bravado than she was anywhere near feeling.

With every step she took, her legs shook with the need to reverse her direction. She wanted to run into his arms, jump his bones. But she didn't.

She entered her bedroom and stopped. Breathing in deep, she dug her feet into the carpet, fighting the screaming desire to give in.

No way was she giving in. Zach would get the message eventually. She'd been blind where Chris was concerned. She'd made a fool of herself in Marrakech for Zach. She'd given him her love and he'd thrown it back in her face. He loved to fuck her. But he didn't love her. Would never love her.

His heart belonged to a wife, long dead and buried, and she sure as hell wasn't about to compete with a ghost whose life... *and death* she still had no clue about.

Her hand trembled and she hesitated, then her mouth firmed. *It was her birthday.*

And she had needs, dammit. She'd denied her body's craving for far too long. With an angry jerk, she tugged off her dress and let it drop to the floor, followed quickly by her panties and strapless bra.

She left her jewelry on and sat, naked, on her bed and slid the bedside drawer open. The rabbit Keely had gifted her what felt like a lifetime ago was still wrapped in its package. She ripped it off and flicked it on. The low hum thrummed along her nerves.

Her heart began to pound. Heat raced under her skin, flaring within her at the excitement building inside.

She slid onto the bed and braced her back against the headboard. Her nipples were puckered hard, her breasts heavy and aching as desire rampaged through her. Her bracelets jangled as she slid her hand down her body toward that tight, needy place that throbbed its incessant demand between her legs.

At the first touch, she gasped.

She was wet. God, she was so wet. And hot. And agonizingly hungry for the one thing she wouldn't let herself give in to.

The door she'd left ajar slowly gaped wider.

Zach stood on the threshold, those sizzling intense eyes zeroing in on her with the force and heat of a laser beam.

She froze, her fingers a bare inch from her clit. Her breath panted out as he took another step into the room.

"Don't stop on my account."

"Go away," her voice was a hoarse croak. "I don't want an audience."

His laugh was low and mocking. "Yes, you do. You left the door open deliberately. You knew I'd hear everything you were doing in here." His eyes moved from her face to her breasts, over her stomach to the glistening arousal between her legs. "In fact, you were counting on it. Weren't you? Did the thought make you wet?"

"No."

A tense smile twitched his gorgeous mouth. "Liar."

Her clit swelled and throbbed under his feverish scrutiny. His mouth dropped open and his tongue flicked against his lower lip. "God, how much do you want to punish me, Bethany?"

She slowly slid two fingers on either side of her clit, the sensitive flesh screaming for attention. "Very, very much."

His harsh laugh echoed within the room. "Well this is

extremely effective." He stepped deeper into the room, and kicked the door shut. His hands fisted and released at his sides. His eyes never left her, and his breathing grew harsher by the second.

Seeing the torment in his eyes soothed her bruised heart. Witnessing how much he wanted her satisfied her battered feminine defenses. For as long as she'd known Zachary Savage, this had been her only effective weapon. The urge to hit him where it hurt roared through her.

Keeping her eyes on him, she slid her fingers faster on either side of her clit. The movement was so intensely pleasurable, she groaned. His raw moan echoed around the room but he didn't move from where he'd frozen in the middle of her bedroom. She cupped one breast with her free hand, squeezing and fondling as desire tore through her.

She bit her lip as another moan vibrated through the devastatingly gorgeous man, standing frozen with lust in her bedroom. Wetting her forefinger, she twirled it over her hot and tight nipple. Her breath shuddered out of her, her need growing to astronomical proportions. Feeling her orgasm build, she slid one finger inside her wet and yearning sex. The slick passage immediately closed hungrily over her finger. Pleasure raced up her spine, curving it so her back arched off the bed. But it wasn't enough. She squeezed in another finger and smothered a scream as the climax surged closer.

"Bethany...Jesus, Bethany. Look at you, so wet. So fucking tight." His hand closed over the tent in his trousers and his breath hissed out. "God!"

She squeezed her nipple between her thumb and forefinger. Oh God. Oh...God! Her hips surged off the bed, her fingers plunging faster in and out. She threw her legs open wider and fucked her fingers in desperate lunges.

"Fuck...Peaches."

Her fingers stilled for a second. "Don't call me that," she rasped as pain and pleasure congealed into a tight knot beneath her breastbone.

His fists clenched at his sides, and his nostrils flared. Mouth open, he gulped in desperate breaths. "Do it, baby. Please, don't stop."

She didn't really need that imploration. She *couldn't* stop. Wouldn't have been able to if her life depended on it. She threw her head back but kept her eyes on him. "You're not supposed to be enjoying this." With a shaky hand, she grabbed the rabbit, knowing she was close, so very close.

"I'm in fucking agony. Know that as a certainty, Bethany. But I see how much you need this. And I want you to come before I pass out. Come, Peaches. Come without me inside you. It'll kill me but I'll stay right here."

That was the problem. She hated that he wasn't inside her right that moment. But he was right, she needed this more than she needed her next breath. And there was a different, almost sadistic pleasure coursing through her at the knowledge that he was so very much at her mercy.

She held the rabbit against her clit and screamed as pleasure shot through her.

Zach squeezed himself and gave a pained groan. Stumbling forward, he dropped to his knees. Gripping the edge of the bed, he watched her, his intense grey eyes fixed on her as if she was the one real thing in his universe. He swallowed hard as she rolled her hips, another low moan reverberated through the room.

Through the waves of ecstasy washing through her, she heard him mutter *Fuck, Fuck, Fuck* under his breath. She cried out as bliss crashed over her. She threw her legs wider and buried her two fingers into her soaked heat.

A harder, darker anguished, "Fuck!" roared through the room. The sound of Zach losing it on the floor in her bedroom sent her over the edge. She screamed her climax, gripped her sheet with her free hand, seeking an anchor other than the one she craved. Liquid heat spurted out of her, drenching her sex and soaking the bed. Sweat coated her skin as savage pleasure roared through her.

Minutes later, she collapsed back on the pillows, spent. When she managed to pry her leaden eyelids back open, she couldn't see him. But she knew he was there. She could hear his harsh breathing.

"Jesus, Bethany," he muttered under his breath, but she caught it all the same. She was too attuned to him not to. "What the fuck are you doing to me?"

Seven

MINUTES PASSED IN silence. She wanted to get up, go jump in the shower. But several things stopped her. First, she wasn't sure whether she was capable of walking after that intense orgasm. And second, and most terrifying, she wasn't sure she could walk past Zach without jumping on him, begging him to fuck her pain and confusion away. Because the ache hadn't abated. Not one little bit. Her insides still remained shredded, and her sex just as empty without him. And her body was acting independently of her heart and head.

Slowly, heart thumping enough to drown her hearing, she rose onto her elbows and glanced down at the floor.

Zach lay on his back, his chest rising and falling in rapid breathing, his eyes squeezed shut.

Finally, he rolled upright. His face was taut with held in emotion, his nostrils flared wide as he breathed. The anguish and fierce arousal stamped so severely on his face made her breath catch. His eyes snapped open. Dark, turbulent eyes zeroed in on her, fixing her with that unwavering focus that had never ceased to unnerve her since their first meeting.

"You will come back to me, Bethany."

She shook her head fiercely, holding on to her pain and reminding herself why she couldn't give in to his iron will. He didn't love her. He loved someone else. A *dead* someone else.

"Yes, you will. I won't stop trying until you do," he continued harshly. "And then do you know what's going to happen?"

The aggression in his voice sent a tremor of apprehension up her spine. "What are you going to do, Zach?" She dared him.

His teeth bared in a parody of a smile. "I'm going to punish you for what you're doing to us. I'm going to fuck you raw for days. Until your vocal cords stop working from screaming for mercy. And you know what? I won't stop. Because every day you keep us apart, every minute you maintain this distance, I get that little bit crazier, that little bit out of my fucking head with craving you. And you will pay, Bethany. Dearly. Take a few minutes. Think about that and assess how much you want this thing to drag on. I'm not going anywhere. Now where's your bathroom?"

"My bathroom?"

He looked down at his crotch and back at her, one wry eyebrow lifted. "I blew my load watching you finger fuck that tight, sweet cunt. I'm a fucking mess right now."

There was no hint of embarrassment in his voice. Not a single shred of it. He rose off the floor with a litheness that was beautiful to watch. He took a step toward the bed and raked her naked body with hot, lethal eyes. They burned even hotter when they rested between her legs. She knew the evidence of her climax was pretty hard to miss. Hell, she was drenched with it.

"The cunt that belongs to *me*. That's something else you'll have to pay for, by the way. Bathroom?"

With a shaky hand, she pointed to the closed door to the left of her bedroom. He stepped back from the foot of her bed, his eyes still lingering on her sex. When they finally rose to hers, the condemnation and hunger in the grey depths stopped her breath.

He whirled away, one hand spearing through his hair as he strode to the bathroom and shut the door behind him.

Bethany collapsed back onto the bed, her breath rushing in and out of her in huge, desperate gulps.

She'd wanted to make him suffer. And she had. But by taunting him with what he wanted most, she'd jerked the tail of the tiger. Zachary Savage knew he was in the wrong. He knew he had hurt her - continued to hurt her with his silence. A small part of her even admitted to admiring him for owning up to the fact that he had wronged her. But she had also used the most dangerous weapon of punishment she could think of to show him how badly she was torn apart by the huge issue they grappled with.

How could she crave him like this when he could possibly have committed the most heinous crime?

She clasped her hands over her face and shuddered as she recalled him writhing on her floor. Hell, she'd reduced a proud and dominantly sexual man to coming in his pants like a hormonal teenager.

A horrific little giggle escaped her throat. She clamped her mouth shut when she heard the door opening. He walked in as she was pulling the sheet over her body.

"The shower's all yours," he said. "When you slide that soap all over your hot little body, remember who it belongs to. And who will be claiming it again, very soon."

He walked over and stood staring down at her. His eyes were inscrutable as if he'd washed away every single expression when he used the bathroom.

Slowly, he leaned down and placed a gentle kiss on her forehead.

"Happy birthday, baby," he murmured.

Then he walked out.

❧

She slept heavy and dreamless through the night, not waking until her alarm blared at eight. Slamming her hand over it, she rolled over in bed and was immediately drenched in vivid memory.

God. What had she done? Heat raced up her neck into her face as she recalled her brazen, incredibly dangerous behavior. A part of her remained stunned Zach hadn't annihilated her. He'd been well beyond the boundaries of his endurance.

And for a man who craved sex as much as Zach did to not take what was so temptingly and brazenly laid out in front of him… she shuddered as she recalled him losing it on her floor.

She'd tried to use sex to reach him once. Back in Marrakech, she'd thought the better of it. But last night, she'd been too far gone to think things through properly.

Did she regret it now?

She shut her eyes and admitted that guilt wasn't paramount. But what she'd done had created an even more gnawing hunger in both of them that had become a ticking time bomb.

You will pay...I will punish you...

As much as she tried to be affronted by that threat, she couldn't deny that underneath it all, the thought of being punished severely by Zach made her insides turn over with scorching anticipation. No matter how many sexual toys she went through, Zach Savage's brand of sex would always trump whatever she could come up with in the self-pleasure department.

Her phone rang, jerking her out of her heated daydreams.

"Hey B," Keely greeted her with a tone much more subdued than her usual hyperactive briskness.

"Hey," she replied, refusing to acknowledge that part of her had hoped for someone else, someone with a much deeper voice at the end of the line.

"I fucked up your birthday last night. I'm sorry."

Bethany sighed. "It wasn't all fucked up," she replied. Her face flamed again as she remembered how the night had ended. She'd experienced a seriously intense orgasm and she'd watched one of the most dynamic, sexiest men on the planet lose it on her bedroom floor. "At least now I know what a *Fuck Me Blue* tastes like."

Keely laughed. "Yeah, we must go on a cocktail crawl one of these days. Minus one crazy stalker boyfriend, of course."

A spurt of anger flared up. "He's not a crazy stalker, Keely. He's just…"

"Wants you really, really badly?" Contrite Keely was fast receding and Snarky Keely was reasserting herself.

Bethany's hand gripped her phone harder. "I don't know what he is. Besides, you told him where to find me, remember?"

"Sure, rub it in. But seriously, what are you going to do, B? I get the feeling he's not going away."

I don't want him to. She closed her eyes and swallowed at the fierce power behind the thought. "He wants me to give him an hour. To talk."

"Maybe you should consider that."

"What if he just weaves words around me without really telling me what I need to know?"

"You need to ask yourself what's important to you. Being with him regardless of whether you know about his past or not. Do you think he'll tell you eventually, when he's ready?"

"I don't know. Maybe." Bethany frowned as her memory tweaked. "Last night, he said something about if he had a choice he would tell me."

"When last night?" Keely asked sharply.

"I…he followed me home," she said, then rushed on before Keely could speak, "he wanted to make sure I got home safely. He knew we'd been drinking."

"Right. Okay. So you think he's not divulging his past because something…or someone's holding him back?"

"I didn't ask."

Keely snorted. "Aunt Keely thinks you need to have that talk, baby girl. You're running around in circles chasing your pretty little tail. You're both beginning to drive me crazy. Sort yourself out, then call me. I have some juicy details of my hook up from last night."

Bethany laughed. "You hooked up with someone last night?"

"Of course. After you deserted me, I needed to drown my sorrows. The right guy came along and I went with the flow." A noise echoed down the line, followed by a loud crash. Keely laughed under her breath. "Gotta go. My date is trying to escape his leash."

"Jesus, Keely!"

"Shut up. Don't judge until you try. Oh hey, there's an idea. You can tie Savage to a sturdy post and threaten not to release him until he tells you all his secrets. I can come up with a few—"

"No, thanks," she interjected quickly.

Keely sighed. "You're no fun."

Bethany stretched and eyed the clock. She needed to get up. Her parents would be arriving within the hour. "Heads up before you go, I'm going back to work tomorrow, so no more texts to Sheena."

If not for the sake of earning a pay check, she needed the distraction of work to keep her from losing her mind. Or worse, considering what Zach had suggested last night, that they put the landmine subject of how his wife's death to one side and carry on regardless.

"You sure?" Concern lined Keely's voice, reminding her what a mess she'd been for the last week.

And what a mess she still felt inside.

She sucked in a breath. "I can't quit my job, Keel. And I can't keep hiding in my bedroom hoping everything will right itself."

"Okay. Dinner and drinks on Wednesday?"

"Sure. I'll call."

She rang off and pushed back the sheets. Getting out of bed, she froze for a minute as the memory of Zach in her bedroom hit her full force.

In the light of day, she was even more staggered by his self-control. Had their positions been reversed, she doubted she could've stopped herself from leaping on him.

Their sexual chemistry hadn't diminished one iota - hell it was fiery as ever. And yet he'd respected her wish and kept his distance.

No matter how much she wanted to hate him from keeping her out of the important parts of his life, Zach had a core of integrity that kept her from completely hating him.

If there was really was a reason why he couldn't tell her what had happened between him and Farrah, was she right in pushing him to tell her?

Confusion propelled her into the shower and still stalked through her as she pulled on a pair of light blue capri pants and a white top. She shoved her feet into high heeled wedges just as her doorbell rang.

She let her parents in and accepted a bouquet of flowers from her dad.

Professor Todd Green looked nothing like your typical professor. He favored descriptive T-shirts and loafers rather than tweed coats and bowties. Tall, with a full head of greying dark brown hair, he looked like an overgrown teenager.

"Happy birthday, sweetheart." He kissed Bethany's cheeks, then frowned down at her. "You've lost weight. Are you eating properly?" he asked.

"I'm fine, Dad." She bent her head so he wouldn't see the shadows lurking and hurried to escape into the kitchen. He followed and watched her arrange the flowers in a vase.

"Are you sure?"

"Leave her alone, Todd," her mother waved him away. "How was Paris?"

"Umm, it was great. Lots of fun and…great food." She sent a desperate prayer that the heat building at the back of her neck didn't flare into her face.

Veering away from her parents' prying eyes, she returned to the living room and took her time positioning the flowers on her coffee table.

By the time her parents drifted back in, the smile she'd spent a few minutes practicing in front of the mirror was in place.

"So, Mom, I thought we'd hit a few art galleries around here? There's a new one I think you'd like. Then we'll go to lunch?" she said airily. Her mother was addicted to art galleries, especially ones featuring local artists.

"Sounds great. I've been meaning to find something for the guest bedroom. But it's your birthday, sweetheart. Are you sure that's what you want to do?"

Her father rolled his eyes over his wife's head and made cutthroat signs at Bethany.

"It's fine, Mom. I'm happy to."

Felicity Green pursed her lips. "See, Todd. Not everyone thinks shopping for art is akin to a catching the plague."

Her father flinched. "I'm sure some in-depth research would prove otherwise, dear."

This time Bethany's smile felt less tight as she grabbed her purse and followed her parents out the door. It felt good to be semi-normal again, to bask in her parents' easy banter and affection for each other. She didn't miss her father's concerned glances as they entered the elevator but she carried on smiling, determined to put a brave face on her chaotic emotions.

The sense of déjà vu hit her the moment she crossed the foyer and exited into the sunshine.

The town car was back on the kerb. And she watched, her heart in her throat, as Zach opened the back door and slowly stepped out.

Eight

HER PARENTS' BANTER stopped as she froze on the sidewalk. Her mother followed her stare and her eyes widened as her gaze lit on Zach.

"Sweetheart, is everything okay?" her father demanded.

"I…yes." Her voice emerged in a croak and she cleared her throat.

Zach stepped forward. "Hi."

"Uhh…hi." Despite the avid gaze of her parents and the tempest of emotions crashing through her, she couldn't stop her eyes from devouring him.

Sunlight glinted off his face and hair. A curl had fallen halfway down his forehead and her fingers itched to brush it back.

As usual, even the most casual clothes made his body a work of art that demanded attention and worship. This morning, he wore a simple white T-shirt and jeans. The strong line of his bronzed throat and powerful shoulders made heat pound through her.

He stepped forward and her breath caught as she noticed what he held in his hand.

"I won't keep you. I just wanted to drop this off. Happy birthday." He held out the large white velvet box tied with silky black ribbons.

"Umm…thanks." She took it and cursed herself for her sudden monosyllabic ailment. Her eyes clashed with his and her pulse jumped again. She wanted to stay there, gorge on his beauty. She wanted to run away from the strength of her feelings.

She knew her parents were wondering who he was.

Both her mother and father had known and liked Chris and had been concerned when they broke up. Of course, Bethany had never told them the real reason behind the breakup, but her mother had hinted more than once that she hoped Bethany would patch things up with Chris. Now she saw the keen speculation in her mother's eyes and hurried to speak.

"Mom, Dad, this is Zach." She deliberately withheld his surname. Her parents weren't media hungry but she was sure they knew who Zachary Savage was.

Zach's eyebrow rose at the curt introduction. His eyes also told her he was aware she hadn't mentioned his surname.

Zach held out his hand. "Mrs. Green, Bethany's told me a lot about you. It's great to meet you."

Her mother smiled wide and preened beneath the charm oozing from the man who'd once again caught Bethany completely off guard and turned her brain to mush. "Please, call me Felicity."

Zach smiled and said, "Thank you, Felicity." Her mother melted into a shameless puddle.

Her father was less malleable. His eyes narrowed slightly as he shook hands with Zach. There was no invitation to use his first name but Zach lost none of his charm, nevertheless.

"Can I give you a ride anywhere?"

She forced her brain to track and shook her head. "My parents brought their car. We're driving to The Village."

A hint of disappointment dulled his eyes but he nodded. "Okay. Enjoy your day."

"Thank you."

Her parents said goodbye and headed towards her father's SUV.

Bethany tried to move. Her feet wouldn't comply. Zach seemed incapable of movement either. They stared at each other, his hunger undisguised, her heart clamoring in return.

"Your father's watching me like a hawk." His gaze dropped to her mouth and his tongue touched his lower lip.

The shameless evidence that he wanted very badly to kiss her made heat bloom into her face as she wondered what her parents were seeing as they looked at them.

She licked her tingling lips and his eyes darkened dramatically. "I have to go."

"I'll call you tonight." There was an implacable bite to the statement.

She wanted to refuse but truth be told, she was beginning to recognize that forcing things with Zach would get her nowhere. At least by talking to him on the phone, she could keep her emotions under control and maintain a little distance "Okay."

Pleasure lit his eyes at her simple agreement. He grasped the door and nodded to the present. "I hope you like it."

Bethany glanced at the box in her hand. She'd forgotten about it but now curiosity spiked through her. She wanted to open it there and then but she knew her parents were waiting for her. Also, she couldn't be sure that it would be appropriate for public consumption.

Zach laughed as if he'd read her thoughts. "It's perfectly respectable, Peaches. A little sentimental, even. The naughty stuff will keep for behind closed doors."

She refused to blush. Luckily, her body complied. "Bye, Zach."

She turned and walked away. Her body's acute tingle told her his eyes were firmly fixed on her.

Opening the back door to her father's SUV, she slid in and slammed the door. Her father's searching gaze caught hers in the rear-view mirror.

"Everything okay?" he asked.

"Sure, Dad." She smiled and quickly shoved the box into her purse and pulled on her seatbelt.

"What a charming man. And he looks very familiar. We haven't met him before, have we, Beth?" Her mother asked with a frown.

"No, I don't think so." She couldn't think how anyone who met Zach could forget him but she wasn't about to say that to her mother.

She firmly changed the subject and breathed a sigh of relief when her parents moved on to discuss what was happening in their lives. By the time they reached the busy street where the art galleries were located, Bethany was up to date on everything involving the Green clan, including her grandmother's upcoming hip operation.

As they strolled from gallery to gallery, Bethany tried not to glance at her watch. Or stroke the velvet box burning a hole in her purse. Or think about Zach, wonder what he usually did on a lazy Sunday afternoon.

She knew what he'd been doing two Sundays ago. Round about this time, he'd been frisking her in his office. There's been nothing lazy about that, nor in the days that followed. No, the days had been spent in high octane, world-rocking sizzle and turbulence. The come down from that high was unbearable.

Over lunch, she tried to eat more than a few mouthfuls when she caught her father's concerned frown yet again.

Considering it was her favorite Italian restaurant, she knew anything less than a healthy interest in her food would trigger a full interrogation. Luckily, she managed to avoid it and breathed a sigh of relief when her parents dropped her off back home just after seven in the evening.

She let herself in and leaned back against the door, her fingers already reaching for the velvet box.

Pulling it out, she slowly sank onto her sofa and stared at it. Much like she'd stared at the envelope that had changed her life just over a fortnight ago.

Recalling how she'd felt then, her fingers shook and uncertainly crawled over her. It was hard to believe that a box could change her life. But an indigo envelope had. In such a profound and definitive way she wondered how she'd ever imagined she was alive before she'd met Zach Savage.

She slowly pulled one end of the black ribbon. It fell away, immediately forgotten. Swallowing, she pried it open and her mouth dropped open at the exquisite bracelet propped up on the velvet cushion.

The six linked dime-sized platinum circles were studded with diamonds. In the middle link was a locket that sprang open at her touch.

The clearly expensive jewels weren't what made Bethany gasp in shock. It was the picture inside the locket had been taken as she came across the finish line during the camel race, a huge smile on her face as she punched the air with her hat in triumph. Her face was creased with such open happiness tears sprung into her eyes.

She'd had no idea that her picture had been taken. Had Zach taken it?

What did it say about her that she'd been so far gone, so singularly focused on him that she hadn't even realized these pictures were being taken?

She fingered the charm and tried to keep herself from dissolving into a seething mass of misery.

Her phone rang and she groped through her purse for it.

"Hello," she croaked, then sniffed loudly.

"Bethany, Christ, are you crying?" Zach demanded hoarsely.

"No. Yes!"

"Why?"

She gave a choked laugh. "Because of you, Zach. You're turning my life inside out. And I want to hate you for it, but I can't seem to. I just opened your present, and I…"

"Did you like it?" he asked with a thread of anxiety that made her breath shudder out.

"Yes."

He fell silent for several seconds. "Baby, it'll get better. I promise."

She wiped at her eyes. "I can't see how."

"Just…you have to trust me."

She swallowed and laid her head back against the seat. "It's my birthday. I want you to do something for me."

"Name it."

"I deserve an answer to one question."

His breath hissed out. Silence held a potent mix of hope and despair. "Okay. One question."

"Did you…" she stopped, squeezed her eyes shut and tried again. "Did you mean to kill her?"

A shuddering breath echoed down the line. Ice cascaded down her spine.

"Bethany. I think you know by now that my life isn't that straightforward."

"Just answer me, please."

He hesitated. "I don't want to risk you retreating even more that you are right now."

"I won't if what you tell me is the truth."

"I'd never lie to you. I may not always be in a position to give you full disclosure but I'll never lie. Tell me you believe that?"

"I believe you."

She waited, her insides withering with each passing second. Finally, she couldn't stand it a second longer. "So. Did you?"

"Yes. And no."

"Oh God, what does that even mean?"

"It means…there was a series of events. Events I can't talk about. It was a chaotic time in my life, Bethany. A lot of shit happened. Part of it, hell most of it, was my fault."

"What sort of shit?"

He inhaled raggedly. She could hear a low rhythmic sound as if he was drumming his fingers on a surface. "The usual shit that comes with misguided youth and unlimited funds. Insane partying…sex…drugs."

Her breath caught. "Was that how she died?"

The drumming stopped. "Don't do this, baby. Please. Bottom line is she died. And I was responsible."

Anger clawed through her, blanking out the misery for a few relieved seconds. "You know what I should do? I should be more like you. Just take the wall to wall sex and shut off the emotion."

"You think I'm emotionless?"

"I think as long as you have sex you can survive without getting emotionally invested, yes. Did you learn to block it out? Is that what she did to you?"

"Perhaps it's what I did to myself in order to cope."

"That's what I mean. I should do the same. Then we can be two emotionless people, indulging in mindless sex just for pure relief."

He fell silent for so long she wondered whether he would end the call. But his breathing remained strong and steady.

"The idea is not without merit," he finally said. "As long as the mindless fucking involves each other."

She gasped. "Oh, fuck you, Zach."

"Yes. Soon. Like yesterday." Tension throbbed in his voice. "Last night, watching you…it nearly killed me. I don't know how much more of this I can take."

At the reminder of last night, her anger oozed out of her, leaving behind the sticky mess of misery and arousal. She bit her lip against the need to confess that it nearly killed her too.

"Did you have a good time with your parents?" he asked abruptly as if he found the subject of sex or the lack of it as tormenting as she did.

"It was fun, yes."

"I like them," he said in that snappish voice that told her his tension was still riding high.

"My mother was charmed by you."

He gave a short laugh. "But not your dad?"

"You'll probably find him a tougher sell," she replied and stopped. Zach would most likely never get the opportunity to sell himself to her parents. Lord knew where all of this was going, but there was no way she was exposing him to her parents and have a Chris situation happen all over again. Her mother was already half in love with Zach as it was. She sucked in a breath and tried to think of a safer subject.

"Did you find an apartment yet?"

"Yes. Would you like to see it?" he invited.

She yearned to say yes so badly, her vision blurred. But as bad ideas went, that would top it. Besides, she had no desire to keep piling the anguish on herself and seeing Zach's apartment would trigger a need to wonder what it be like to share the space with him.

"I'm sure it's great but no thanks."

"Ok," he replied.

Perverse hurt scythed through her at his easy acceptance. "Ok?"

"It's not ready to move in yet. Not till the middle of the week. You can come see it then."

"I won't be able to. I'm going back to work tomorrow."

"You can still take a lunch break. Or come after work." That implacable tone was back again. Against her will, thrills of excitement spiked up her spine. "It's not far from where you work. I can have you there and back in an hour."

Again, it struck home hard just how much Zach knew about her life. "It's my first day back. I'll probably be inundated and won't have the time."

"Taking a break shouldn't be an option." She heard the frown in his voice.

"In an ideal world. But I don't mind when there's work to be done."

"Dare I hope that statement applies to us, too?"

"There's a Kenny Rogers song that I could sing to you right now but I'm not sure you'd get the message."

He laughed and her heart turned over at the sound. "I've never heard you sing, baby. Bet you'd be good at that too."

She sighed and shook her head. "I'm getting off this insane rodeo ride, Zach."

"I'll let you, for now. But it's only a matter of time before you're riding me again, baby. So saddle up."

Nine

HER FIRST DAY back at work was frenetic. Sheena Malcolm, her boss, asked about her Aunt Mel, then looked in turn skeptical and anxious when Bethany gave the highly sketchy details of her aunt's phantom illness.

Sheena tugged on the sleeves of her Prada suit and lingered outside Bethany's cubicle. "You won't need to return there anytime soon, will you?" she asked with a thin sniff.

The pain that had found permanent residence beneath her breastbone kicked her hard. "No, I imagine not. Aunt Mel is expected to make a full recovery." Keeping her fingers crossed behind her back that karma would be kind to her, she held her breath until Sheena retreated to her glass-walled office.

At lunchtime, she grabbed a sandwich from the deli on the first floor and returned to her desk to pick at it. Her phone beeped intermittently with messages from Zach but she ignored them. She needed all her concentration to get through the pile of work on her desk.

By four, she'd planned a Michelin culinary crawl for corporate heads of a Wall Street investment giant, chased down the last RSVP for an art gallery opening, and sent out the itinerary for a Napa wine tasting stag event she was organizing for an Internet mogul.

Her feet ached, her back ached and her heart ached from tripping over itself every time she heard the faint beep of another incoming message.

At six, she finally gave herself permission to read Zach's messages. They contained more of the same, relentless pleas.

Persistent. She had to give him points for his persistence.

She was reading through the last message and fighting not to blush at the blatant description of what he intended to do to her once their hiatus was over, when the phone blared to life, causing her to nearly drop it.

"Have you finished for the day?" The deep, sexy voice attacked her senses without mercy.

She swallowed hard before she could speak. "Just about. And hello to you too, Zach."

"Hey, Peaches. Come downstairs. I'll give you a ride home."

She jumped up and nearly toppled over when she tripped over her discarded shoes. "You're here? Why?" she blurted.

"I was in the neighborhood," he answered vaguely. "I'm double parked so you need to be quick."

She floundered. The nearest window that overlooked the street twenty floors below was in Sheena's office and no way was she going in there to find out if Zach was really double parked or whether, as she suspected, he was bluffing.

She also wanted to tell him she didn't need a ride home but the words stuck in her throat.

As if sensing her battle, he sighed. "Come down or I'll have to come upstairs and get you. I don't think you'll want that."

"Blackmail, Zach?"

"Friendly suggestion. Now tell me you're on your way."

Her belly flipped over. "I'm on my way."

"Good girl."

She stepped into her shoes and gathered up her stuff. Gary Wright, the other partner of Neon, walked past as she turned off her computer.

Normally, he was aloof and avoided eye contact with the staff, leaving Sheena to do all the hiring, firing and general ball breaking.

This evening, he stopped and slanted her an *almost* smile.

"Good to have you back, Bethany."

She glanced at him in surprise. "Umm…thanks."

He nodded and she could swear she saw his gaze assessing her briefly before he looked towards Sheena's office.

As if she was on some silent bat signal, Sheena burst out of her office at that moment. The large plant at the side of Bethany's desk precluded Sheena from seeing her until she was almost at her cubicle. "Gary, we have an appointment at ten tomor—" she said excitedly, only to stop when she saw Bethany. "I didn't know you were still here, Bethany." She exchanged glances with Gary.

"I was just leaving."

Sheena nodded. "Well, have a great evening. And see you tomorrow."

Bethany was still mulling over the strange scene when she walked through the revolving doors and exited into the warm July evening.

Zach was indeed double-parked on the busy street. In the driver's seat, Philip kept the engine running.

The sight of him made her footsteps falter. He leaned against the side of his town car without a care in the world. Black designer slacks caressed his lean hips and his dress shirt and dark lightweight jacket emphasized his mouth-watering torso and broad shoulders.

The casual kerchief tucked into his breast pocket gave him a debonair air that was so jaw-droppingly powerful, a full body shudder raked her.

He really had no right to be so insanely gorgeous. His rugged good looks were attracting every single passing female glance. Jealousy tore through her as she noticed one particularly brazen female actually stop, stare, and smile a come-fuck-me-hard smile that made Bethany want rip her face off.

"Are you going to stand there all night, slaying passers by with your eyes?" he drawled.

She was in no mood for his mockery. "You should've stayed in the car. Then I wouldn't have to deal with your female appreciation sidewalk traffic jam."

He straightened and held the door open for her. She found it infinitesimally gratifying that his gaze never once strayed from its intense focus on her. "Your grouchiness is cute. Step into my cave and I'll see if I can make it better."

A reluctant smile twitched her mouth.

She slid in and he followed quickly. He slammed and locked the doors. The glance he sliced her held a touch of anxiety, as if he was afraid she'd bolt. It was certainly something she'd considered when she'd stepped out of the building and seen him again.

His ability to capture and hold her attention to the exclusion of all else had always bothered her. Being with Zach was like holding a live electric wire. It was only a matter of time before she experienced another profound shock.

Right now though, with the soft seats beneath her and the cool air-condition of the plush car washing over, moving her exhausted body would've taken some effort.

She slid her shoes off as they moved into traffic.

Zach's gaze fell to her exposed feet and back to hers. Before she could guess what he intended, he lifted one foot into his lap and pressed his thumbs deep into her throbbing muscles. Memories of her Shanghai foot massage washed over her and she just managed to smother a moan.

"Feel good?"

"You know it does," she accused darkly.

His smile held a trace of satisfaction and that healthy dose of anxiety. He continued to massage her soles, his fingers moving expertly over her tight, stretched muscles.

Bethany found herself easing back into the seat. When she sighed, he looked over at her.

"Everything okay at work?"

She eyed him. "Sure. Why do you ask?"

"You looked slightly bemused as you stepped out."

"Oh, that. Yeah, Gary, my other boss who has barely said a word to me since I started working there, actually engaged in conversation with me tonight. *And* he actually said something nice. And Sheena was acting weird too." She shrugged.

Zach's hands stilled for a moment before they resumed the massage. "Did they say anything in particular?"

She relaxed deeper into the soft leather seat and sighed as the air-conditioning cooled her skin. "Not really. It was just weird, is all." She laughed. "Maybe they missed me. The amount of work waiting for me certainly indicates so."

"Don't sound so surprised. You're a valuable asset to any company, I'm sure."

"Hmm, a foot massage and compliments. Anyone would think you wanted something, Savage."

His answering smile looked a little strained. He shifted in his seat. Her foot settled deeper in his lap and she understood why.

Zach was hard. And hot and straining his pants. The car swayed into a turn and her heel grazed his length. He hissed out a breath.

Molten grey eyes connected with hers. Slowly, his hand slid from her sole to her ankle, caressing up her leg.

"Zach," her protest was feeble enough to be completely useless.

"I want to make you feel good, baby. Let me." His hand slid higher, cupped her calf and massaged her bare skin.

Heat scythed through her. Her pussy clenched hard, her need so acute it became a pain lodged between her legs. He reached the sensitive area at the back of her knees then pressed his fingers deep.

She jerked but when she tried to withdraw he held on.

"Up." He indicated her other foot.

She considered refusing. Then she considered how unhappy her foot would be if it didn't get the same boneless relief her other foot had just received. It was really a no brainer. Besides, she was fully clothed, in a moving car in the busiest city in the world.

Yeah, keep deluding yourself.

Zach's smile grew even tighter around the edges when she raised her other foot and placed it in his lap. His erection was granite-hard, and his chest rose and fell in harsh breaths.

Bethany wanted to ask why he was torturing himself so much, then thought the better of it. She knew why. She was suffering the same deep, dark hunger. Their chemistry defied reason and she'd known the moment she'd entered the car that a version of this would play out.

They watched each other, their breaths growing more frantic with each passing second as his caress deepened and slowed.

When his hands slid under her black skirt, her whole body shuddered in response.

Sure, expert fingers grazed her inner thighs. Her nipples peaked and throbbed painfully as her breasts swelled against her pink shirt.

Wetness oozed between her thighs, soaked her panties and infused the air between them. She knew the moment Zach smelled her arousal.

He shuddered and gritted his teeth. "God, I need to make you come!" He brushed her skirt higher. "Will you let me?"

"Zach…" Another feeble protest barely worth the effort.

But he took it seriously. He slammed his head against the headrest, squeezed his eyes shut and gripped her thigh hard enough to leave marks in the morning.

"You should know, I can't even jack myself off anymore. You've ruined me for everything, Bethany. Even my fucking masturbation. I hope you're pleased with yourself."

Against her will, she felt laughter bubbling up her throat. She pressed the curves of her feet over his erection and was rewarded with a dark, hungry growl. "I'm glad you didn't jack it until it fell off."

He grunted a half laugh, then immediately sobered. "You're cracking jokes. Dare I hope that this is a step forward for us?" he probed gently. His eyes were full of hope and the grip on her thigh trembled slightly as he stared at her.

"This isn't really funny, Zach. This last week wasn't a walk in the park for me. I hurt. Very much. It's been…the pain has been unbearable," she whispered. A part of her wondered why she was opening herself up to him like this, making herself even more vulnerable than she already was.

But then hadn't she been like this with Zach right from the beginning? Being this close to him was like walking around with her nerves exposed. She felt raw. She'd felt naked with him from the moment she'd laid eyes on him.

She stared at his gorgeous, haunted face and tears welled up in her eyes.

"Bethany! Shit, baby, don't cry."

He scooped her up and placed her in his lap. His mouth grazing her cheek triggered faster tears. "You're shutting me out of the important bits of your life, and I can't...I can't take it. God, I'm so pathetic."

"You're not pathetic and they're not the most important bits. You are."

"If they're not then why won't you talk about them?"

"Because some parts of it are not mine to tell."

"But they're a part of who you are. That shouldn't be a secret."

He sighed, then gripped her waist hard, before he raised her face to his. "They won't be. Not for much longer."

"Do you give me your word?"

He stared back at her for a long, hard moment. Then he nodded. "Yes."

Her breath shuddered out. "So what happens until then?"

Molten grey eyes slid over her face, dropped to her mouth and stayed. "Until then...you use me for sex?"

She started to snort, then realized he wasn't laughing. In fact, his face, his eyes, his whole body was tense with a poised expectation as he waited for her answer.

"God, you really mean that, don't you?" she gasped.

"I haven't fucked you in ten days. Trust me when I say, I'd jump in a fucking volcano right now for another taste of your pussy. Then I'd walk back for a chance to bury my cock in your tight heat." He crooned his need in a voice so husky with lust, she could barely hear him over the dark rumbled in her own ears.

"That sound like…fiery work."

He smiled that tight, I-wanna-fuck-you-so-bad smile. "You don't know the half of it, baby."

His cock swelled beneath her ass as he shifted.

"I think I can feel…some of it."

He laughed. "More jokes, Peaches? Maybe I should tell Philip to keep driving. I could be buried deep inside you come morning."

The reminder had her glancing out the window for the first time since she got into the car. She didn't know whether to be relieved or disappointed that they were approaching her neighborhood.

Surprise rocked through her as the car glided to a stop in front of her favorite Italian take out.

"How did you know?" she asked as Philip got out and headed into the restaurant.

He shrugged. "You mentioned it when we were together. I haven't forgotten a single thing of our time together, baby. I just did some research and hit the jackpot."

She had a feeling it was more than luck on his part. For the first time since he crashed back into her life, Bethany allowed herself to touch him.

His face, stubbled and sexy as hell, felt warm beneath her fingers. Her hand drifted down his cheek and he turned to kiss her fingertips.

"I'm scared that this won't work out. That to keep doing this is asking to be hurt even more."

"Are you willing to let me go?"

Quaking inside and out, she shook her head. "Not willingly. But—"

He placed a finger across her lips. "No buts. I'm not going to let you go either. Which means the only way forward is to fight through this."

Philip returned to the car and placed the take out on the front seat.

Zach kept her firmly in his lap as the car rolled smoothly back into traffic. When they reached her apartment, he opened the door and helped her out. The window slid down and Zach reached in for her food. In silence, he passed it to her and gazed down at her.

Expecting him to push his way up to her apartment the way he'd done on Saturday night, she was acutely disappointed when he just said, "See you tomorrow."

The stark emotions coursing through her made her snap, "I don't need a ride home every night, Zach."

His smile was enigmatic enough to cause tingles down her spine. She'd learned to her cost that when he smiled like that, it meant something was up.

"I didn't say anything about rides home, Bethany."

Before she could ask what he meant, he was back in the car and the door was shutting.

Long after his car had disappeared from view, she stood on the sidewalk, staring into the empty space.

Ten

Zach watched the LED lights count up the floor numbers and tried to stem the unease swirling inside him as he waited for the elevator rushing up from the ground floor.

The next hour would determine whether what he'd planned would succeed or backfire horribly.

The past few days had been an exercise in panic-management. He'd never known anything like it. Not even with Farrah had indecision consumed him so completely.

After his conversation with Bethany in his car, he'd nearly called off this meeting. He'd felt as if they'd made progress; that she would give them a chance while he tried to get over the hurdle of his erstwhile brother-in-law and the piece of paper that now stood between him and the woman he was coming to realize he couldn't live without.

The idea that he could lose Bethany was what had made him keep this appointment. Come hell or high water, he intended to hang on to her. This was merely another angle…

She may not like what was coming next…hell, he was pretty sure she would have a thing or two to say about it…but he was damned if he would let the chance slip by to keep her with him until such time as he could come completely clean.

The elevator door pinged open.

He saw her first. Dark humor lit within him as he silently mocked himself. Hell, when didn't he see her first? She was like a laser beam attuned to his radar. Wherever she was, his senses zeroed in on her.

And today, as always, the sight of her knocked the breath from his lungs. Jesus, but she was fucking gorgeous.

Her hair was tied away from her face in a loose knot that caressed her nape. Her navy pinstripe jacket covered a cute pink flowered shirt, and her skirt ended at her knee, leaving her knockout legs exposed. Delicate studs adorned her ears and a single pearl string necklace rested against her collarbone.

She looked prim and proper.

He wanted to mess her up. Tousle her well and good, leave her glossy mouth and other equally captivating parts of her, used and bruised.

He barely managed to tear his eyes away when Sheena Malcolm stepped out first, followed by Gary Wright.

He hurried through the handshakes and glanced back at Bethany.

Shock, surprise, then uncertainty streaked across her face. Before hurt and anger flashed through her eyes.

His blood thrummed at the anticipation of fireworks even as he wondered whether he'd chosen the right path.

"Mr Savage, this is Bethany Green, our very talented assistant," Sheena said.

Zach stepped forward. "Miss Green. Very pleased to meet you."

Bethany remained frozen against the elevator wall, her throat working as she watched him. He kept himself firmly in the elevator entrance to prevent her bolting. And he could see in her eyes that she was considering it.

He held out his hand and cocked an eyebrow.

Her eyes flashed as she glanced down at his hand and back at him. When the silence threatened to strayed into awkward territory, she finally stepped forward.

"Mr Savage. It's an *honor* to meet you, I'm sure."

The bite in the word made his lips twitch but the hurt and wariness in her eyes didn't prolong the humor. Bethany wouldn't take this situation lying down. And he had to play his cards right.

But the moment her hand slid into his, the belief that he was doing the right thing reasserted itself. He was not willing to live without her.

He held her hand for as long as it was appropriate without raising questions from the two Neon executives behind him. Then he reluctantly let her go.

Jeff, who'd flown in that morning from San Francisco, was waiting in the newly set up meeting room. Introductions were made and coffee served.

Zach made sure Bethany was seated first before he took the seat next to her. He caught her hastily indrawn breath as he quickly squeezed her bare thigh under the table.

She began to ravage her lower lip with her teeth and heat surged into his groin faster than he could process the reaction.

God, please. Soon. He was dying of blue balls.

Sheena Malcolm cleared her throat and smiled a brittle smile from across the table.

"Mr Savage, Gary and I can't express our appreciation at being given this opportunity to spotlight your company. I will be your first point of contact on anything to do with the Indigo Lounge, of course, but Gary and I—"

Zach forced himself to concentrate on the meeting and not on the urge to flatten Bethany to the nearest surface and fuck her until the world stopped turning.

"You made a PR bid for the Indigo Lounge last year, did you not?"

Sheena nodded eagerly. "Yes, but we've had even more exciting ideas about profiling your company since then, and like we mentioned yesterday, we have a portfolio of clients who would be perfect for your New York events. The package we've put together is edgy and exciting—"

He felt Bethany tense next to him and his neck grew hotter. Time to bring this thing to an end before she exploded. "Who spearheaded your initial research last year?"

Bethany tensed further. Again, he slipped his hand onto her thigh. She froze but didn't move away. Zach chose to take it as a good sign even though her face was set in a quietly furious look.

He'd have his work cut out to win brownie points after this stunt. But he was well up to the task. His hand slid higher, the need to connect with her clawing through his gut.

She clamped her thighs shut, stalling his upward movement but also imprisoning his hand against her warm flesh. He barely managed to suppress a smile.

Sheena exchanged a glance with her partner before her gaze moved to Bethany. "Well, Bethany was tasked with digging up the pertinent information about your company but putting the package together was a group effort."

"If I decide to go ahead with Neon, I'd like Miss Green to take point, guided by you two, of course. But before I make a decision I'd like to hear about the sort of New York clients you intend to attract and what fresh ideas you can bring to the table entertainment wise."

"Of course. We can do that," Sheena replied quickly, hiding her surprise at his directive.

Zach nodded to Jeff, who picked up the remote on the table and aimed it at the screen on the far wall. It flickered to life, revealing the familiar indigo jet with the custom trim. "This is the latest IL plane. It arrived two weeks ahead of schedule so we're planning an extra IL trip before the scheduled trips commence."

Zach continued. "We already have a waiting list to fill the slot if needs be, but I'd like to give Neon the opportunity to stage this event. You have three days to put a package together—"

"Three *days*?" Bethany snapped, her eyes firing livid blue flames in his direction. "Are you serious?"

Jeff's eyes widened. Sheena's mouth dropped open. Gary Wright looked downright displeased. Zach didn't give a damn about any of them. All he cared about was the fact that Bethany was engaging with him. "

"Is that a problem, Miss Green?" He raised an eyebrow and her blue eyes flashed. She looked as if she was contemplating tackling him right there and then.

His blood thrummed faster with anticipation. She read his

reaction he didn't bother to hide and her nostrils flared.

Her mouth thinned into a prim line and her eyes slid from his. "Well, normally three days is *ridiculously* short notice, but I'm sure we can come up with something more than suitable for your launch."

Gary, who'd been poised to intervene, relaxed. "Shall we come up with an itinerary for the trip or will your office provide us with one?"

"I concede Miss Green's point that this is somewhat short notice. Neon can take care of the first two stops and my people will arrange something else for the last two. Call it a collaboration. Also for the sake of clarity, Neon's guests will only be on board for the first two stops. After which they will be expected to disembark."

Gary frowned. "I'm not sure how our clients will take an abbreviated tour, Mr Savage."

Zach narrowed his eyes. "It's your job to sell it to them. Or I'm happy to pass the whole thing to my people."

Sheena hastily shook her head, shooting her partner an evil glare. "That will not be necessary. We'll make this work."

"Miss Green? Do you think you can make it work too?"

Her eyes met his. Electricity zapped through him at the heaven and hell he glimpsed in her eyes. Her mouth compressed in further mutiny and he grazed his thumb across the top of her thigh.

Her tiny jerk sent a pulse of heat and delight through him.

"Yes," she replied huskily. "We can make it work."

"Great."

Her bosses breathed a sigh of relief and everyone started to relax.

Jeff grabbed the remote again and pressed another button. "The next slides show you the full extent of the various compartments of the plane—"

"Jeff, I'll leave you to show the slide to Sheena and Gary. I want to speak to Miss Green in private, if you don't mind?" He raised a cursory eyebrow at the rest of the table and rose.

Speculation quickly followed surprise on the faces of the occupants around the meeting table.

He ignored the looks and stood, staring down at Bethany's bent head. He was prepared to drag her out if need be. As if she heard his thoughts, her head snapped up.

"Miss Green?"

"Sure. Excuse me, please." Her smile was stiff as she stood and followed him out of the room.

He managed to stop himself reaching for her until they were in the hallway. Then his hands closed over that trim waist and half carried her into his living room.

"Zach! What the hell…put me down." Her voice was a fierce, husky, whispered demand, but he heard the catch nevertheless.

He kicked the large door shut behind him, set her on her feet, and gave her a chance to face him before he propelled her backward into the wall.

"No!" she protested.

"Yes. Hell, yes."

Starved and desperate for her, he slanted his mouth over hers, taking full and merciless advantage of her shocked gasp.

His tongue surged against hers, demanding and achieving entry. Wet and erotic, her tongue met his in a series of bold flicks that told him she hadn't forgotten how he liked to be kissed. He surged deeper, eager to drown in her taste and touch.

He pressed closer, imprinting his body on hers as his craving escalated. His cock found the cradle of her hips, that sweet curve he was so desperate to rediscover.

She whimpered and wriggled against his hold. His hands tightened, holding her still as he rocked his erection deeper into her pelvis. Once he was satisfied she could feel him, all of him, he let go of her waist and slid his hands upwards.

Her full, covered breasts filled his hands, her nipples tight buds against his seeking thumbs. He gorged on her mouth until the need to breathe caused stars to dance behind his closed eyelids.

Even then, he would gladly have suffocated in the kiss if the hands clamped in his hair hadn't pulled desperately.

Easy...he cautioned himself. For now.

He broke the connection and stared down at her. Wide blue eyes locked on his as she sucked in air. His gaze dropped from her bruised lips to her heaving chest. She breathed in and her gorgeous breasts filled his hands once more.

He groaned as his cock stiffened to stone.

"You feel so fucking lush, Peaches. And so damned fuckable in that prim suit." A tremor rocked through him as he continued to deny the forceful urge to rip her clothes off and do what he desperately yearned to do. "Jesus, baby, I want to fuck you so damn badly."

A long sigh shuddered out of her as he mercilessly kissed his way down her throat and barely resisted the urge to bite her supple, silky skin. He'd raised enough questions for one day. Although he personally didn't care who knew, he cared too much about Bethany to leave her to explain a giant hickey on her neck to her bosses.

But there were other, equally enthralling parts of her body he could explore.

Sliding his hand beneath her skirt, he touched her between her legs. Hot dampness met his fingers. Tugging aside her panties, he plunged one finger into her tight heat, groaning deeper when her flesh closed greedily over his knuckle.

Her shocked cry made him grin.

"You naughty girl. Did you get wet imagining me having you here like this?" he crooned in her ear.

She gave a jerky shake of her head. "Uhhn...No."

He laughed. "Well, something got you wet and hot. So what was it?"

"I don't...let me go, Zach."

He leaned even closer. "No way."

Her throat moved in a convulsive swallow. "Why? Why are you doing this?"

"Because I know what you're thinking."

"No. Trust me, you have no clue what I'm thinking."

"Yes, I do. You have a plan. You've made up your mind about what happens next. But you forget, Bethany. I'm a much better negotiator than you could ever be. And for me, there's only one way this ends. You. Becoming mine. In every way."

"So you planned this. All of it," she accused, her voice breaking as he pushed deeper inside her. "You met with Sheena and Gary yesterday, didn't you? That's why they were acting so weird at work."

"Yes." He may have had some doubts before about what he was doing. But now he'd kissed her again, now her sweet, wet pussy pulsed around his finger, he regretted nothing.

"Why?"

"Access."

"Access? To me?"

He bit lightly on her earlobe and delighted in her shudder. "Of course."

"But like this? How could you?" The raw hurt finally penetrated his fog of lust. He drew back and looked down at her.

Confusion and a hint of despair grappled with her desire, causing her eyes to darken. He hated seeing that.

"You told me you'd never lie to me." Her voice was dark with accusation.

He tensed. "How have I lied to you?" he demanded.

"What the hell do you call this? Barreling your way into my work life just to get what you want?"

He slid another finger in, felt her stretch deliciously around him. Jesus, at this rate he would blow his load as shamelessly as he'd blown it the other night on her bedroom floor. He fought the tightening in his groin. No way was he losing control that quickly again.

"I call it the extra edge. With perhaps a little manipulation thrown in. But no lies."

He watched her toss that in her mind for a few seconds. Then she shook her head, even as her thighs spread that little bit wider, and her hips slowly undulated against his hand.

"This isn't okay, Zach. It's nowhere near okay. This is my *professional life* you're messing with."

"On the contrary, I'm seeking to enrich it. Besides, we discussed this, back in Paris, remember?"

"What?" Gratifyingly lust-glazed blue eyes met his.

"I said I'd find a way to make it work in the real world. This is me making it work." He flexed his fingers and her pouty lips dropped open on a gasp.

"If we discussed it then, why couldn't you discuss it with me now?"

"Because it's partly business. Believe it or not, if Neon hadn't been a good fit, this meeting wouldn't have happened. Now the only thing that needs clarification is whether you feel you can work with it, or if you want to refuse Neon the opportunity of a lifetime."

"Are you really saying that if I don't come with the package, this doesn't happen?"

He shrugged. "A little hardball to get what I want, Bethany. That's all this is. Now if you don't want those panties shredded, be a good girl and hold them to one side for me so I can see to your needs."

Alluring blue eyes met his and he watched her struggle to take a breath. "Zach…"

"Do it, Bethany. You're not leaving this room until I make you come. I can bend you over the sofa or we can do it this way. This way I can control your screams, but it's totally your choice."

Her lips parted wider and a hot little breath burst through them. He licked her lower lip and felt another shaky sigh spill from between kiss-swollen lips.

Her fingers grasped her hemline and slowly lifted the skirt up to her hips. He caught sight of her panties and his breath stopped.

Indigo lace.

"Jesus. You fucking know what this color on you does to me, Peaches."

"I didn't even know I was coming here until an hour ago…"

His hand left her breast to tug her chin upward. "But you were wearing it anyway. When you saw me it made you wet, didn't it? Knowing you were wearing my color against your sweet cunt?" He hardened his tone, not prepared to accept anything less than total honesty.

"Yes," she sighed.

He dropped his head until his forehead touched hers. Withdrawing his fingers, he plunged them deep, deeper until his middle finger grazed her sweet spot.

Her hips jerked against his ruthless invasion. Liquid heat oozed between his fingers, sliding down into his palm. "Fuck, baby." He could barely breathe. She was so hot, so fucking incredible.

How could he ever let her go?

They both watched, fascinated and breathless as he finger-fucked her. Dirty, decadent sounds of suction filled the room as he plunged in and out of her, pushed her to the brink of her endurance. She bit back a cry as her orgasm drew closer. More than anything he wanted to hear her scream her climax but he was mindful that there was an audience next door.

"You like this, baby?" he growled down at her. "Watching what I do to you?"

She didn't look up, her attention totally engrossed in the precisely timed pull and thrust of his fingers.

"Bethany?"

She gave a jerky nod, her fingers tightening convulsively over her skirt.

"I want to hear it," he demanded harshly. He'd missed her vocal celebration of what he did to her; was as starved for it as he was starved for her body. "Tell me!"

"Yes, I like it," she whimpered. Her back arched and her thighs widened, giving him better access.

He greedily took it. Catching her nape to steady her, he angled his fingers and executed a series of fast, hard thrusts that slammed her over the edge. He swallowed her throaty groan as she came. Hot liquid gushed into his palm and dripped between his fingers. Her body jerked against his as sensations buffeted her. He soothed her down with kisses until she quietened, then slowly withdrew his fingers.

Her whimper of protest was joyful to his ears.

She started to slide her panties into place and lower her skirt. Before the thought was fully formed in his mind, he'd hooked his fingers into the lace and ripped her panties off.

"Zach!"

He knew his grimace fell short of contrite. "Sorry." He wiped her slickness from his hands and stuffed the soaked panties in his pocket. "I want nothing more than to taste you right now but if I start eating you now, you won't get out of here any time soon. This will have to serve as a peace offering."

Biting her lip, she straightened and pulled down her skirt. Her eyes met his and slid away. He caught a glimpse of the hurt and his insides shredded.

God, he hated that look.

"Can you show me where the bathroom is, please?" she asked in a low voice.

He wanted to kiss her again, reassure her that things would get better but he knew she would see them as just words. After all, he'd been saying that for the better part of a week and half now.

The only thing he could do now was to use the only weapon in his arsenal to keep her with him until the right time came to share his sordid past with her.

Swallowing a growl of frustration, he took her hand and led her down the hall. He saw her glance around her for the first time, take in that décor around her. He wondered if she liked it.

Wondered what she would think about the room he'd created especially for her.

The toy room was much more extensive than the one he'd introduced her to in Morocco. He wanted to tell her about the room but he cautioned himself against it. They weren't out of the woods yet. Far from it. She may have allowed him to make her come but that didn't mean their issues were anywhere near resolved.

On top of everything else, she was still hurt and confused by the stunt he'd pulled today. He had a long way to go before Bethany opened up herself again the way she had on that last night in Marrakech.

But no way was he giving up.

Eleven

"Oh, God!" Bethany muttered again under her breath as the cool water gushed over her hands.

The enormity of what she'd just done escalated in her mind until it was a huge, insurmountable obelisk. She dried her hands, smoothed one hand over her skirt and the other over her hair. But she couldn't stop the shaking that raked through her insides every few seconds. The languorous post-climactic feeling made her semi-drowsy even as her heart hammered fast enough to scare the shit of her.

"What the hell am I doing?" She'd tried her best to repair the damage in the bathroom but one look into her feverish eyes and flushed face told her she was rocking the I've-just-come-really-hard look. Which was why she was avoiding her reflection. Although she didn't really need a second look.

Her lipstick was chewed off and her jawline was slightly grazed from Zach's stubble when he'd growled those heated demands in her ears.

Demands she'd granted like some helpless, sex-starved chick…

Oh, who was she kidding? She was helpless when it came to Zach. And his brand of sex always left her starving for more.

Mortification rocked through her at how fast she'd lost her panties along with her willpower. "God," she groaned again.

A hard knock rattled the bathroom door. "Baby, are you okay?"

They were far enough away from the meeting room on the other side of the apartment for them not to be overheard but her heart lurched at the husky endearment anyway.

Springing for the door, she opened it. "Can you not call me

that with my bosses within earshot, please?" she whispered fiercely.

Zach ignored her, his eyes raking her face and body with that insane intensity she was beginning to think would never abate. "What's wrong?" he demanded.

She closed her eyes and sucked in a will-sustaining breath. "Are you really this blind, or do you really not care about anything except what you want?"

"We want the same thing so I fail to see where this conversation is going."

Lazily, he slid a strand of silky hair through his fingers. She tried to bat his hand away. He caught her fingers in his and started to bring them to his mouth.

She snatched them away as mortification reddened her face. "God, my lipstick is in my bag. My bag is in the conference room. They'll take a look at me and know what I've…what we've been doing?"

Satisfaction oozed through the smile he sent down at her. "So?"

"The fact that you ask me that just makes me want to throttle you."

"Peaches, it's only a matter of time before the whole world knows I'm nuts about you. If I had my way, it would be sooner. Much sooner."

Her mouth dropped open in shock and a full body shudder raked her from head to toe before she could catch herself.

No matter how much she told herself to get used to it, she would never get used to the way Zach spun her senses with his words.

"What happened to protecting your privacy?" she blurted.

"My privacy is no fucking use to me without you in my life," he replied through gritted teeth.

More words to render her speechless.

"But if this bothers you that much, I can find a way to excuse your absence. You can leave after your bosses are gone. I'm sure I can come up with a satisfactory excuse."

"So *now* you care about my professional reputation?"

Grey eyes locked on hers. "I care about your happiness."

"If you did, you wouldn't have dragged me out of that meeting room in full sight of my bosses. And you sure as hell wouldn't have manipulated me here in the first place."

Again that careless shrug. Only this time, she knew just how much she'd underestimated him. And how so not careless that shrug really was. "I had to get through to you once and for all. I want you. I'll do anything to have you."

He turned and started heading for the meeting room. With no choice but to follow or risk even more questions if he returned without her, she followed. "So what was Monday night all about? I thought we made progress." She'd gone to bed believing they'd taken a small step forward; that they'd made progress during the ride home. Being proven wrong again made her wonder if she'd ever even come close to guessing how Zachary Savage ticked.

"This was added insurance I put in place before our conversation on Monday night."

"Yeah, I kinda guessed that from earlier. But you still didn't see the need to call it off?" she asked, unable to stop the tiny spurt of excitement from sprouting within her.

Zach paused with a hand on the meeting room door. "You mentioned Sheena gave you a hard time after you failed to come up with the goods last year. I looked into Neon and I liked what I saw. I'm killing several birds with one stone."

She licked her lips. "So this is real? You want us to work on the IL project?" A tiny wave of excitement rushed through her, escalating before she could stem it.

"As long as your ideas pass muster, the deal is yours," he murmured. "But don't think that just because the boss has a soft spot for you that you'll be given an easy ride. I intend to ride you very hard. And often." He winked shamelessly and threw the door open.

She was still trying to catch her breath when she took her seat. In total, she guessed they'd been gone less than twenty minutes but it felt like hours. When she looked up and encountered the speculative faces around the table, Bethany's mortification grew. Heat continued to thrum through her pelvis, making her very much aware that she was without panties.

"We all good?" Jeff asked as he looked from Zach to her.

Zach sat back, a small smile playing on his lips. "Miss Green survived the grilling so I'm satisfied our working relationship will thrive." He cast her a glance and she caught the possessive heat in his eyes. She glanced away quickly, her eyes dropping to his chest, only to nearly choke when she spotted her panties peeking from his jacket pocket where he'd stashed it.

Grabbing the glass of water on the table, she tried to cover her flustering by taking a huge gulp.

"Everything okay your end?" Zach batted the question across the table.

She saw Sheena's glance narrow further before she smiled at Zach. "Yes. I've passed a preliminary list to Jeff. Once we've whittled it down to the desired numbers, with your approval of course, we'll get started on the actual event coordination."

"Good. Have Miss Green report to me tomorrow with her ideas for the first two destinations, and we'll take it from there." He stood, signaling an end to the meeting.

Sheena picked up her sleek leather case and rose with Gary. She rounded the table, her eyes zeroing on Zach with a keen intent that made Bethany's nape tingle with apprehension and acute irritation.

"I was thinking, a tour of the actual plane would be beneficial. I believe that hands on knowledge of the product would help us profile it more effectively."

Zach's brow rose. "Really? You do realize that the only way to truly experience the Indigo Lounge is to take a trip and indulge in everything it has to offer? Are you saying that the best way you can stage this event is to participate, Miss Malcolm?"

Sheena Malcolm, the renowned ball-breaker known for reducing her interns to tears within minutes of their first day, flushed a deep crimson.

For a brief moment, Bethany actually felt sorry for her. Until she recalled the look in Sheena's eyes as she'd looked at Zach.

Her Zach.

"Umm, no…what I meant, of course, was a private tour…of the plane…without the guests—"

Gary cleared his throat loudly and Sheena subsided into silence.

"Since the plane is already here, I can arrange a tour for tomorrow morning if that suits before I fly back to California?" Jeff offered into the awkward silence.

"I would prefer it if Miss Green starts on the event planning straight away. But by all means, arrange a tour for any Neon staff you think need it. Would it be better for Miss Green to work from here?"

Bethany shook her head immediately. "No, my office is adequate for liaising purposes. I don't need to relocate here, Mr Savage. Thanks all the same."

Zach's jaw tightened for a second but thankfully, he let the matter go.

When his gaze flicked to hers, she caught the steely determination in his eyes. She raised her chin and flashed back the same warning.

"If that's all for now?" she pressed, eager to be away from his electric presence. She needed to think. To focus and regroup after what had happened in the last hour.

Further plans were made for a tour of the IL plane. Goodbyes were said, and she made the appropriate responses. But all she could think of was Zach's scent in her nostrils, his dark promises in her ears and the fact that she was now exposed to him in a way that saw no outlet from the emotions he wrought inside her.

They were now linked professionally unless she could come up with a hell of an explanation as to why she would refuse to work on the IL event planning.

She had no doubt that Zach would pull his offer from Neon should she in any way try to back out whether the company was a fit or not. Neon were small fry in the PR and event organizing world. He could have two dozen companies lining up to snap up the offer in a heartbeat.

She entered the lift and held her breath when he followed. The rest of the group crowded in. With no choice but to squeeze up against him in the small space, she was once again bombarded by the charged sphere surrounding him. His aftershave, spicy and alluring as hell, wove around her as the elevator whisked them downward. Jeff made small talk, which the others joined in. Zach remained silent, his nostrils slightly flared and his face set in that aloof mask she'd come to recognize as his resting expression when dealing with employees.

But when the lift started to part on the ground floor, he turned his head toward her. Eyes, dark and stormy, clashed with hers.

"Four o'clock tomorrow, Miss Green. I'll send a car for you."

She gaped at him. "I didn't think I'd need to attend another meeting, Z…Mr Savage. I can email you my ideas or we can video conference."

"I prefer a face to face meeting. Make yourself available, please." His tone suffered no argument. With a curt nod to Sheena and Gary, he walked away with Jeff.

Bethany watched, dumbfounded, as the two men got into the back of his town car. Philip shut the door behind them and slid behind the wheel. Within seconds, Zach was gone.

Sheena's expression was a cross between shock and affront as she walked on four-inch heels to the door. In the back of the cab, she exchanged glances with Gary, then glanced at Bethany.

"I've heard Zach Savage was…eccentric but I had no idea he was downright rude."

Bethany attempted a shrug, her whole concentration centered on keeping her mouth shut against the urge to spring to Zach's defense.

Bottom line was that in the need to have his way, he'd nearly blown their connection wide open.

"And why on earth would he insist on having you as the front person on this project?"

Bethany jerked back into focus at the clear insult in Sheena's voice. "If you don't think I'm up to the task, feel free to allocate it to somebody else."

Sheena's mouth compressed. "We both know that's not an option. So you have no idea why he's adamant to have you on board?"

The way Zach was going, it was only a matter of time before the cat was out of the bag about their connection. But there was no reason for her to reveal anything just yet.

The revelation that one of America's richest, sexiest, most dynamic men was super keen to get back into her pants would be huge enough when the time came. She hadn't given it much thought at the time when Zach had mentioned it in Paris, but now she knew without a shadow of a doubt that any revelation would be overwhelming.

"No. Absolutely none," she lied through her teeth.

Sheena's light hazel eyes narrowed. "I suppose, he does have a point. You played a lead role in the research last year so I guess this ought to be your baby. I hope though that I don't need to point out how big this could be for us. And for you. That means, whatever Zach Savage wants, he gets."

Bethany barely stopped herself from snorting. "Sure. Understood." She'd been doing that willingly, and sometimes unwillingly, since she walked into a certain VIP Lounge in Newark two weeks ago.

For the rest of the afternoon, Bethany cleared her desk of all other work in preparation of the brainstorm session Sheena had arranged for five pm. At first, she was thankful her phone stayed silent but as the hours crept on, a mixture of anxiety and anticipation mired through her belly.

Gritting her teeth, she pushed the feeling aside and concentrated on her work.

Jeff had given them a much meatier info file on the Indigo Lounge. Clients were chosen after a strict vetting session done by an elite in-house investigation company under the Savage Inc. umbrella.

With such a team at his disposal, it came as no surprise that Zach knew her life inside and out.

His team could turn around investigations within twenty-four hours. Which meant any guests chosen could be vetted quickly and efficiently. When she re-read the IL policy for zero tolerance on drugs, she paused.

Zach had mentioned a life of drugs and partying in his younger days. She suspected that something had happened with drugs that involved Farrah. Had she overdosed? Dear God, had he supplied the drugs that killed her?

A slither of ice eased down her spine. If it turned out that that was what Zach was guilty of, could she live with it?

She shook her head and pushed the thought away. There was no use torturing herself when she had no facts to base her theory on. She stared at her computer screen for several minutes before she started typing the variation of the info she'd first typed into her search engine a week ago.

A touch of shame crawled over her, but she pushed that feeling too away. If Zach wasn't above playing dirty, she could too.

Zach Savage and Farrah marital connection.

She hit return but already knew there would be nothing there. She'd trawled through over three hundred pages of links before she'd given up in the first few days of her miserable spiral last week.

Besides, if there was some deep, dark reason why Zach couldn't tell her, she was sure he'd have taken steps to have any information removed from public record. It'd taken her a while to grasp the full implications of just who she'd become involved with but she now knew Zach Savage the billionaire wielded power and influence the same way lesser mortals breathed.

Her phone rang, startling her into gasping. She answered it, and felt a heavy twinge of disappointment when the dark, sexy voice she expected didn't respond.

"I thought we were going to make plans for dinner and drinks tonight?" Keely demanded.

"I need a rain check. Have to work late tonight." She scrolled through the twentieth page of her search, hoping to catch something she'd missed.

"Fuck. Is Sheena getting back at you for taking all that time off? I can call her and drop a few mild threats…"

Bethany laughed. "Stand down, Xena Warrior Princess. I have to work late because I've been put in charge of a new event."

"Oh. Okay, cool. Anything exciting?"

Bethany hesitated. Although there was an implicit confidentiality in the early stage of her work, she and Keely had shared info on their various projects before. She trusted her friend with her life. But she wasn't sure how Keely would take the fact that Zach had inveigled his way into her work life too. Keely was still bent out of shape over the *Shades* incident, and Bethany wasn't sure how much reserves she had left where the whole Zach situation was concerned.

"Potentially. We only got the commission today and it's a fast turnaround so it's a bit hectic over here. I'll fill you in when I can, 'kay?" she said breezily.

"Fine. Guess, I'll have to find a way to amuse myself," Keely grumbled. Bethany smiled, confident in the knowledge that her best friend would have other plans before she hung up.

After ending the call, she stared at her computer screen, her mind screeching back to Zach and the enigma that surrounded his life.

Could she wait until he divulged his secrets to her? And could she work with him in the meantime and not delve deeper into the despair she could feel swallowing her whenever she thought back to that last night in Marrakech?

There was a way she could get out of their professional relationship, but she'd discarded that line of thought before it'd even fully formed earlier today. There was no way she would do a bad job and lose Neon the commission.

Even if she wanted to, her pride in her work wouldn't let her take that route.

Footsteps clicked along the corridor towards her desk. "You ready to get started?" Sheena quipped.

Bethany gathered the information she'd put together in the last hour. Glancing at the search page one last time, she clicked it shut and breathed out. "Yes."

Twelve

PHILIP ARRIVED AT four o'clock on the button the next afternoon. Again Bethany felt a sharp twinge when she noticed the back seat was empty. All day, she'd nervously dangled on tenterhooks as the hours crept by and her phone remained silent.

The pendulous swing from fielding his calls several times an hour to nothing in almost thirty-six hours played havoc with her nerves.

Those nerves escalated as she slid into the backseat and secured her seatbelt. With a small nod, Philip steered the car into traffic and headed for the Upper East Side.

Yesterday when she'd arrived with Sheena and Gary for the mysterious interview, she'd been too curious as to the details of the meeting to pay much attention to her surroundings.

Today, knowing this was Zach's place for however long he chose to remain in New York, her interest heightened as she walked into the plush lobby of the condo whose address constantly appeared on glossy property magazines.

White oak hardwood floors and Venetian papered walls dominated the entry hallway and the discreet concierge service tucked into a neat corner was staffed by a uniformed couple who looked like they'd just stepped off a photo shoot.

Philip rode up the elevator with her and accessed Zach's condo with his own key card. Expecting him to step in beside her for the ride up, she looked up in surprise when he nodded and withdrew.

"Mr Savage will be waiting for you. Good evening, ma'am."

With that, the burly man silently retreated.

Steel butterflies battered her insides as the elevator whisked her upward. Turning her head, she stared at her reflection in the mirrored interior of the gilt framed elevator and groaned silently when she caught sight of the feverish excitement in her eyes.

She looked away quickly, her hand closing convulsively over her leather document case as her pulse spiked frantically and her breathing altered.

He was waiting for her when the elevator opened.

Fierce grey eyes bore into her, the narrow eyed look focused on her in that unnerving way that caused nervousness and excitement to war within her.

"Bethany."

God, the way he said her name. Like a prayer. Like a decadent invitation to sin. All wrapped in a wicked, husky rasp that had the power to stop her breath.

She forced herself to move, to not stand there like a gaping idiot, intent on devouring him with her eyes. But despite cautioning herself against it, she couldn't help but notice how delicious he looked. His white sleeves were rolled up, exposing strong, muscled arms and his dark grey trousers streamlined lean hips and strong thighs in a way that would've made most male models drool.

He didn't move when she reached him. He seemed content to stare at her, one hand braced on the elevator door to keep it from sliding shut.

"I wasn't sure whether you would come," he said finally. His voice held a hint of uncertainty even as his gaze roved possessively over her.

"I work for you now. I don't have a choice."

A dark forbidding look gleamed in his eyes before it disappeared a second later. Reaching out, he caught her hand and pulled her forward. "Whatever the circumstances, I'm glad you're here." He kissed the back of her hand and tugged her along the wide, exquisitely designed hallway.

She glanced up into his gorgeous face as she walked beside him. "Even if I'm not totally happy with the circumstances?"

His jaw tightened. "What would it take, besides the obvious, to make you happy?"

She looked away and bit her tongue against the urge to ask why he hadn't called her in the last day and half. She wasn't that pathetic...yet.

"There's nothing you can do, Zach."

He sucked in a harsh breath as he steered her into the living room. "I refuse to accept that. Take your jacket off."

Setting her case down, she shrugged out of her lightweight jacket that matched her knee-length business dress and forced herself to look round; to at least pretend that there was something else in the room that held her interest besides Zach.

The décor in his New York condo was a world removed from his Marrakech palace but no less decadent or jaw-dropping. Pieces of art that would make her mother gape in awe and envy graced the walls, including a painting she was willing to bet was an original Klimt.

Four large cream sofas were spread out over the vast floor, each large enough to almost double up as a day bed. Rugs warmed highly polished parquet floors and a coffee table made of a solid slab of roughly carved white stone sat in the middle of the large, sun-filled space.

She took it all in in seconds. Then her attention veered back to the man who'd stalked closer to stand behind her. His warm, masculine scent enveloped her, making her remember just how much she'd loved to breathe him in. She stood, frozen and completely captivated as light fingers brushed aside the hair she'd left loose and trailed down her nape. She could no more stop the full body electric shudder cascading over her body than she could stop her heart from beating.

Swallowing hard, she forced her brain to function.

What did he just say?

I refuse to accept that...

"You manipulated yourself back into my life when we agreed that I needed time. Don't act surprised that I'm not playing ball, Zach."

His sigh pushed a warm breath over her nape. "What would it take for you to play ball?"

"Nothing."

His low growl was bitten off abruptly and a hard kiss landed on her first vertebrae. She gasped and jerked around, but he was moving toward the drinks cabinet at the far side of the room.

"Wine spritzer?" he asked with a raised brow.

Her nod was clumsy and her fingers unsteady as she clawed them through her hair. She watched him fix her drink, his shoulders tense and unyielding.

Drink in hand, he walked back to her, those eyes fixed once more on her in a way that made her throat dry. Silently, he held out her glass.

"Thank you."

He stood watching as she took a sip. She licked her lips and his eyes darkened, a raw hunger tightening his features.

"Shall we get down to business?" she suggested into the strained atmosphere.

"Not yet. I'll show you around first," he replied. Tension still raked through his frame and this watchfulness had ramped up another thousand degrees.

Bethany had last seen that look the first time they met, in his office at the Newark Airport. He'd proceeded to annihilate her senses in a way that she was still reeling from.

She wanted to refuse him. Wanted to set the glass down, grab her case and run out of there as fast as her shaky legs would carry her.

But she stayed put. Because Zach continued to captivate her. Because her feelings for him were as chaotic and as beautifully complicated as ever. And no matter what had happened since that momentous night in Marrakech, she had a feeling she and Zach were far from over.

She also had a feeling she wouldn't get more than a step before he nuked any plans she had to flee.

He slid an arm around her waist and propelled her toward the door. In the hallway, his hand tightened.

"You've seen the meeting room. Next to that is my office." He opened the door and she caught a glimpse of an imposing desk, bare except for the large laptop, Tiffany lamp and silver phone gracing its glossy surface. A large screen faced the desk and another immense leather sofa faced floor to ceiling windows overlooking the spectacular view.

He tugged her down the hallway to the dining room, another breath-taking room decorated with top of the line pieces which blended comfort with unspeakable luxury. The tour of the kitchen was cursory as was the extensive library.

Exiting the library, he led her to a door with a keypad fixed next to the handle. He keyed in a code and it swung open to reveal stairs leading upstairs.

"After you," he murmured in a husky rasp.

Again memories of Newark assailed her. Her legs were shaved this time but her tight dress did nothing to hide her ass from his avid stare. The heat of it branded her skin as she went ahead of him and the constricting skirt of her dress reduced her steps to tiny, ridiculously faltering moves.

Over the hammering of her heart, Bethany wondered whether she'd imagined the same hiss of arousal she'd heard that first time too.

Drowning in déjà vu, she quickly hurried up the stairs and turned to face him.

Molten eyes stared down at her as he raked a hand through his hair. "You've lost weight, sweetheart. I don't like it."

Not what she'd been expecting. "Drowning in angst will do that to a girl," she quipped.

His mouth tightened but he said nothing as he led her down another, smaller hallway. A bathroom and smaller office veered off the eastern corner of the condo. Double doors opened onto an entryway beyond which a large pool stretched the length under stylish, gleaming lights. Residual sensations of her phobia and memories from Marrakech clashed as she watched the shimmering water.

Gently, Zach slid his hand around her waist. "We have more work to do with your water issues but not today. Come."

He steered her back into the main hallway.

Off the west, three doors led to stylishly decorated bedrooms, two of which were clearly guest bedrooms.

By the time he brought her to a stop in front of the last door, Bethany's pulse was beating so rapidly, her head swam.

His eyes pinned to her face, he threw the door open and pushed her inside.

She stumbled in and drew to a halt. All Bethany saw was the bed. Huge, imposing and built for sex, the bed was made of solid oak with an intricate headboard that rose almost halfway up the bedroom wall. Decadent white cotton sheets and countless pillows brought into stunning relief the thick indigo and black spread gracing the lower half of the bed.

Once again, he stalked closer and stopped behind her. "Bathroom's through there. Double dressing room is next to it."

She tore her gaze from the bed. "And that last room?" she asked, although a part of her suspected the answer. The way heat shot through her body, there could only be one answer.

"It's your new toy room, Bethany. I had it made especially for you," he whispered in her ear. "Do you want to see it?"

Adrenaline and excitement surged through her body, jerking her around to face him. "No thanks. I have all the toys I need."

His face darkened and he shook his head. Dark hair flopped onto his forehead, giving him a rakish look that was far too sinful for words.

"No, Peaches. From now on, I'm in charge of your orgasms. You got a free pass the other night in the self-pleasuring department because you needed to get your head straight. No more. Until my heart stops beating, you won't come again without me because I intend to take an active role in all your orgasms. Are we clear?"

She detested the electric shiver that amped through her at his powerful words. "For fuck's sake. How exactly do you intend to police my orgasms? And how will you even know?"

His sensual mouth twitched in a semblance of a smile. "You forget I know how you look when you come. I know how soft and languid you feel after a climax. You use any gadget on that sweet pussy without me, and I will take a paddle to your gorgeous ass."

"God, Zach." She closed her eyes and shook her head to get some semblance of clarity. When she opened them again, her eyes widened. "What are you doing?" she croaked.

Eyes fixed on her, he continued to pull his shirt from his trousers and began to unbutton it. Slowly. Button after button popped through its hole as he kicked the door shut with an ominous thud behind him.

"We're going to fuck, baby. Right now. Because I'm at the end of my fucking tether."

Thirteen

BETHANY'S MOUTH DRIED and fire flashed through her belly as she watched his wide, sculpted chest slide into view.

Heaven help her, he was as breath-taking as ever. She caught sight of one flat bronze nipple and her thighs began to tremble.

"Do I get a say in any of this? At all?" she asked.

A taut smile slashed across his face. "You can decide whether you want to be fucked from behind, on the floor or up against the wall. I'm fine with whatever surface you prefer. As long as I'm inside your tight cunt inside the next five minutes."

He moved towards her and she slammed out her hands.

"No!" Her cry was hoarse and agony-filled.

He stopped immediately, shock colliding with the lust on his face. "Jesus, Bethany, what's wrong?"

"You overwhelm me, Zach. I can't think straight when you do this. I don't want to hate you for it, but I don't like this…this out of control feeling when you brush my feelings aside and carry on regardless."

His jaw clenched tight and he frowned. "I'd never force you to do anything you didn't want. You know that, don't you?"

She laughed, the sound scraping her throat raw. "We both know it's not that simple."

Sizzling eyes pinned her in place, searching, assessing. "Tell me how I can make this work. Would it help if you were in charge?" he rasped.

Her breath jerked out. She noted the distinct lack of his agreement to her *no*. "In charge?"

He nodded. "Wait here."

Striding to the farthest door in his bedroom, he entered the room he'd just spoken about. Dark, tormenting curiosity warred with the need to stay sane in this furiously escalating sensual ride that she'd once again found herself on.

There were so many things wrong with her presence here in Zach's bedroom. But for the life of her, Bethany couldn't move, couldn't lift a single finger to halt what she knew was coming.

A part of her wept with just how overpowering Zach's will was over her. He smothered her protests with just a look. When he touched her, her brain ceased to function. She loved it and hated the unique way he could command her emotions.

She was silently shaking her head in despair when he returned. He walked slowly to where she stood, his throat moving in a swallow. As impossible and unconscionable as it seemed, Bethany was shocked to realize he was nervous.

She guessed why when she saw what he held in his hands.

"I know my silence hurts and frustrates you. And you're well within your rights to punish me. Tonight you're in charge. You can do whatever you want. As long as it involves my cock, your tight cunt and hot, wet, vigorous fucking. Do it to us, baby. No matter how angry you are with me, you can't deny we both need it."

Her eyes widened as he held out the large silver handcuffs to her.

"Zach—"

He pushed them at her, his breath shuddering out of his chest. "Take them, Bethany. God, please use them. I've been without you for far too long." He raked a hand through his hair, his eyes dark with tortured heat. "I won't survive another day. If this way makes you feel a little bit in control, then I'm okay with it."

She took the handcuffs and slowly turned the key in the tiny lock and watched the cuffs spring open. They were made of solid steel, well able to withstand Zach's imposing strength. Dark excitement fizzed into her bloodstream. "Aren't you afraid I'll abuse my power?" she enquired huskily.

His dark laughter sent fresh tingles dancing down her spine. "Fuck, I'm hoping you will."

"God, even in this, why do I get the feeling you're getting exactly what you want?"

Abruptly, he knelt at her feet and slid one shoe off. "I like to think we're both getting what we want."

He stared up at her, gently caressing her instep before setting her foot down and doing the same with her other foot. Memories of their first meeting sliced across her unguarded senses, making her breath catch roughly.

His bold hands crept up her ankle to her calves. He squeezed them, using the action to draw her closer until his mouth was one hot inch from her pelvis.

Slowly, he shut his eyes and laid his cheek against her belly. Warmth from his skin seeped into her, rose to cradle her heart.

"I'm on my knees, Bethany. I'll beg if you want me to."

A powerful shudder rocked her. She was certain it would've propelled her from her feet had he not been holding her.

She stared down at his dark head resting against her and trembled against the feelings cascading through her.

In Marrakech, she'd told this man she loved him. Although those feelings were buried beneath the pain still residing like a hard stone in her chest, they were there nonetheless, eating at her, demanding she acknowledge them one way or the other. She hated that she was too afraid to look too deep into her heart right now. The probability that she would accept anything Zach chose to offer loomed far too large in her mind.

But this…what was happening between them right now, she understood.

She had no idea what tomorrow would bring but the sex between had always been honest and true. It was the one thing that held no ambivalence whatsoever. Ironically, it was the one thing she could count on when it came to Zach.

"Are you going to take that shirt off or do I need to rip it off you?"

His head jerked up. A second later, he surged up to tower over her, his shirt a useless heap on the floor. Up close and intensely mouth-watering, his broad chest just begged to be touched.

She slid the thin side of the handcuff over his skin and felt his deep shudder as the cold steel grazed his nipple. "Fuck!"

Power surged through her. She repeated the action on his other nipple and bit her lip when his flesh puckered beautifully.

Starved for him, she lowered her head and tasted him.

Desperate fingers speared into her hair, holding her to her task. "God, yes, baby!"

Exercising the prerogative he'd handed her, she bit him, glorying in his hissed, guttural response. "Let me go, Zach."

He released her immediately, his chest rising and falling agitatedly as he stared down at her. Deep excitement flared in his eyes as he watched her trail the handcuff down between his pecs to his waist.

She paused just above the rigid swell in his pants. "I own you tonight. Will I need to remind you again?"

His nostrils flared and he licked his lower lip. "You've owned me since the second I saw you. I don't need reminding."

Her breath faltered. Tears brimmed her eyes and threatened to fall. He cupped her cheeks and started to brush them away.

She turned away abruptly and walked to the huge, imposing bed. Taking her time, she removed the key from the cuffs and dropped them on his bedside table. With one finger, she dangled the handcuffs in front of her. "I'm going to have a lot of fun with these."

A hint of uncertainty crossed his face but it was gone a second later. "Tell me what you want me to do, baby."

Her eyes devoured him from head to toe and back to his crotch. Hunger clawed through her belly with a viciousness that made her wonder if this was how addicts felt when confronted with their favorite drug. She could barely think straight, never mind speak through the need that pounded through her.

"Undress for me. I want you naked."

He complied with a fevered enthusiasm that would've made her smile had she not been caught up in a similar overwhelming turmoil of need.

Zach shucked out of his clothes and roughly kicked them aside. Without waiting for permission he strode to where she perched on the edge of the bed.

The handcuffs slid off her finger onto her lap, unheeded. She breathed him in and fought the heady scent of his heated body and unique scent of his arousal.

His huge cock bobbed with each heartbeat. Unable to resist, she grasped him in both hands. He was rock hard and hot, thick and so incredibly tempting, she wetted her lips.

"Shit!"

She glanced up him through drowsy eyes and saw flared nostrils and high color slashed across his cheeks. Power, sweet and potent surged through her. But at the same time, she recognized that she was equally enthralled by him, equally at his mercy.

But wasn't about to give up her power just yet. She caressed him harder, watched his face grow more taut, more tormented. "Do you want me to suck you, Zach? Do you want to feel the back of my throat?"

"More than I want to breathe," he replied tersely.

She tilted her head and blinked slowly. "What if I wanted to do something else first?"

A thicker wave of tension washed over him. "Something like what?" he croaked.

"I don't know. I'm thinking…" She slid her tongue over her lips once more and felt him shudder in response.

"Torture, Peaches?"

"Not necessarily. It may be something you enjoy immensely."

"Or I could be dead by the time you make up your mind. Then we both lose. Think about that." The gravelly plea didn't diminish the determined bite in his voice. Her answering smile was as tight as the need knotting inside her.

She caressed him again from root to tip, then cupped his heavy balls in one hand. Deliciously sensitive to her touch, he groaned deep but his eyes remained fixed on her, watching every single thing she did to him.

Leaning forward, she trailed her lips above his groin, nipping and licking her way up his pelvis. She saw his hands twitch at his side, knew he was resisting the urge to spear his hands into her hair and keep her locked against him.

"You want to do something with those big hands?" she teased.

"Hmm," he rasped.

She tongued one nipple and nearly passed out from the pleasure overload. "Undo my zipper," she managed to instruct.

Unsteady fingers eased her long zipper. Cool air washed over her heated skin, exposing her bra and the top of her matching thong.

His heartfelt, "Christ," told her he'd noticed the color.

She withheld the urge to tell him every piece of lingerie in her underwear drawer had been changed to indigo, the impulsive online shopping madness having struck her that day he'd been caught up in video conference meetings in Marrakech.

Hearing him now, she was glad she hadn't resisted the urge to return every scrap of lace and satin the day she'd returned to New York.

"Let me take off your dress," he requested.

She nodded against his chest and let go of his cock long enough for her arms to free her dress. It slithered over her hips and dropped to the floor.

Eagerly, she grasped him again as her mouth drifted up his strong throat. Feeling his pulse underneath her tongue, she licked the strong flutter, then bit him hard enough to leave a mark.

Dark laughter rumbled through his chest. "Marking your territory, Peaches?"

She didn't respond. His mouth was too close. Too tempting to resist. Rising on tiptoes, she kissed him.

Strong hands closed around her immediately, holding her tight enough to strangle her breath. With her hands on his cock, locked between them, she felt every pulse through his hard erection. Wet heat oozed between her thighs as her clit pounded with need.

His tongue invaded her mouth and she flicked hers against it, earning herself a deep groan. Fused and desperate, they devoured each other, stopping every few minutes to breathe.

Her bra came off somewhere along the process, and she just managed to pull back when his hand knotted in her panties, ready to rip them off.

"No," she protested raggedly.

Hard, demanding eyes clashed with hers and his hand tightened in her thong, pulling it tight against her heated sex. "Baby, you know that's not my favorite word."

"What happened to me being in charge tonight?"

His mouth firmed into a thin line of displeasure. Slowly, he loosened his grip and closed his hands over her ass instead. He squeezed the tight globes and his clenched jaw told her he was reaching the end of his rope. She stemmed the urge to appease him and gripped his cock harder.

With a sustaining breath, she stepped back and picked up the handcuffs. "Lie down," she instructed.

His hand tightened on her ass for a few seconds before he let go. He levered one knee on the bed, his body sleek and predatory as he drew back the sheets and discarded all but two pillows.

With his eyes on her, he arranged himself in the middle of the bed. One hand gripped the steel and wood carving of the headboard, the other rested on his groin, just above his thick erection.

Looking at his sculpted perfection made her throat dry and her heart pound with incessant need. She swallowed and forced herself to concentrate.

"Both hands up, please."

Releasing a rough breath, he raised his other hand to grip the headboard.

The high expansive bed meant Bethany had to get up and close to secure the handcuffs. Which meant bringing her body close to the predatory beast beneath her. She barely managed to secure one wrist before his head surged off the pillow and his hot, hungry mouth closed over her tight nipple.

She gasped as pleasure shot fiery darts through her. "Zach!"

He rolled her nipple in his mouth, groaning deep and long as her flesh puckered tighter. Then he bit her flesh and sucked some more. Her hands shook so badly, she gripped his wrists to steady herself.

He was unapologetically derailing her every intention. And she was letting him. With a pained groan, she pulled back. He lurched for her other breast and caught the second peak just as she slapped the second cuff in place. He laved her once, twice, before she found the strength to move away and scoot down the bed.

He stared at her, his eyes imploring and demanding at the same time. "Come back, baby. I can make you feel—Oh, fuck!"

Her mouth closed over his cock, her greedy and desperate suction making his hips surge clean off the bed. With all her strength, she pushed him down and took him as deep as she could, his thickness filling her to discomfort. Her wet, slippery tongue slid along the underside of his engorged length and felt the thick vein pulse against her lips.

His biceps bulged against his restraints, his eyes darkening to a molten grey as pleasure washed over him. She released him and flicked the tip of her tongue over him. He panted out thick, coarse words of pleasure.

"You like that?"

"Fuck. Yeah." He shuddered.

His hips twitched again and his thighs brushed her sensitive nipples. Suddenly a memory cut through her thoughts. Slowly she licked him one last time and pulled away.

He watched her leave the bed with something akin to horror and outrage. "Where the fuck do you think you're going?" he roared.

She raised a brow and earned herself another dark look. Turning on her heel, she slowly lowered her panties and kicked them away. Then she looked at him over her shoulder. "Be a good boy and be patient, Zach. It'll be worth it, I promise."

His eyes remained on her ass, his breathing rough and harsh. "God help you, Peaches because when I get my hands on you, I will fuck you until you break in half. Then I'll fuck you back together again." The dark promise sent sensation skittering over her skin as she headed for the room he'd retrieved the cuffs from what felt like ages ago now.

She opened the door, stepped in and gasped.

As it had in Marrakech, the sight of the extensive toy room made a fierce blush suffuse her body. The smell of leather and steel had never been so heady. Nor had she felt so very turned on by the sight of so many pleasure-giving gadgets collected in one room. She turned in a full circle, noting the cock-chair, the gurney and the collar and nipple clamp combo and the bigger St Andrews Cross taking up the whole of the opposite wall.

Of course, there wasn't a chastity belt in sight. But there was a tall gadget that looked like a rocking horse, complete with a double saddle, stirrups and bridle.

Bethany shivered as she walked past it, her mind frenzy with images of what Zach could do to her on that thing.

She went to the large chest of drawers and searched until she found the bottle she needed.

His gaze found hers the moment she walked back into the bedroom. Then it flicked to what she held. "Did you like your toy room?"

"I've seen it. A rocking horse, Zach? Really?"

"Just say the word, baby, and I'll give you the ride of your life."

"You're depraved."

He caught her shiver and laughed. "And you love it. What are you going to do with that?" Dark anticipation coated his voice.

She climbed back onto the bed, flicked the top of the bottle and tipped it over her chest. "I'm going to drive you out of your mind."

Liquid dripped down her midriff to pool in her belly button. Dropping the bottle containing the most heavenly scented oil, she smoothed her hands over her breasts and then over his erection.

Intense grey eyes watched her every move, her every stroke. "Holy fuck."

She stared up at him and smiled. "Too much, Zach? I can be gentle if you ask nicely."

"That sassy mouth is going to get your ass pink, Peaches. Count on it. Now do it."

She pouted and pretended to hesitate. His growl warned her into action. Bending low, she cupped her breasts around his cock, trapped him in her cleavage, and began to rub him up and down.

Zach being Zach, he took over within seconds, fucking himself between her breasts with long, sure strokes that drove them both close to the edge.

Just when she believed she would come just from being tit-fucked alone, he jerked away. "Your pussy, baby. I need it. Now."

She was too far gone to remind him that she was in charge. Besides, she needed to feel his possession as much as he yearned to be inside her.

She rose and stared down at the beautiful, breath-taking man bound and ready for her. Something hot, hard and painful clenched in her chest.

Tears she believed were dried pricked her eyes.

Emotions she thought were buried for tonight threatened to break free.

Abruptly she turned away from him and straddled him, her back to his front. He hissed in surprise but she was already grasping him, angling him toward where she craved him most.

His thick crown probed her entrance. It would hurt, she knew that. She'd been too long without him. But she didn't care.

With a deep groan of anticipation, she slammed down on him.

Fourteen

"Fuck...God!"
"Oh, Zach!"

The sound of his name on her lips threatened to fry his brain. Zach struggled to breathe through the intense, unique feeling of once more being inside Bethany.

At long fucking last.

His heart pounded and sweat broke out on his brow as he stared down at her sweet ass bearing down on him, her tight cunt struggling to accommodate him.

He felt thicker than he'd ever been before, probably on account of all his blood surging happily to one place. She pulled up and his cock glistened with her slickness.

Jesus, how the hell had he managed to stay sane without this?

A mocking laugh echoed in his head. He hadn't stayed sane. He'd climbed walls and resorted to underhanded tactics to get this woman back into his life and into his bed. But she was here now.

And good Lord, she was fucking him like her life depended on it. Like...she was fucking him goodbye.

His brain scrambled to think through what was happening here but her wet heat was threatening to send him into orbit. Something told him he ought to be afraid, that he needed to get to the bottom of her intentions.

But...*God*...She slid down, her cunt slicker but no less tight. She whimpered and he felt her thighs tremble. Her back arched, giving him a view like no other. Drowning in bliss, he started to reach for her tiny waist, to drive himself deeper, and groaned as his wrists protested against the restraint.

Fuck. He'd forgotten about the handcuffs. Why the hell had he suggested them anyway? He'd foolishly believed not touching her wouldn't be unbearable.

Now he knew different.

Watching that insanely delectable ass bounce over his cock made him realize just how much more he wanted. He was greedy for her, for all of her. He was insatiable with the need.

She whimpered again as she fucked him deeper, her snug channel taking another inch of him. She threw back her head and gasped, her silky hair sliding all over her back and ass. Zach gritted his teeth and groaned.

"Fuck, baby, you look so hot."

"Hmm…" Her breath panted out as she began to increase the pace.

His balls tightened and he fought the urge to give up, to roar his climax. He was nowhere near ready to come but for the first time in his life, he wasn't in complete control. Desperately he tried to slam the brakes on his runaway libido.

"Bethany." His voice was barely coherent.

She continued to bounce up and down on his cock. The sight of her, so beautiful, so damned sexy, tripled his already thundering heartbeat. He could've come there and then. But he wanted something else. Something more. His desperate hands tugged harder against the restraints. But like everything in the toy room, they were made for a specific purpose. They held him easily, much to his frustration.

"Bethany," he rasped louder.

"Hmm?" she responded but she didn't turn around. She readjusted her stance, leaned back, her hands on either side of his waist. Her hair caressed his chest as she began to work him from a different angle.

Holy fucking hell.

When he'd thought about what would happen when she got here today, this hadn't been the scenario he'd imagined. But hell if it didn't blow his mind.

"Christ." She fucked him faster, her tight sheath milking him with sure, excruciatingly intense strokes. But still he wanted more. "Baby, turn around. I want…I need to see you when you come."

His heart jerked wildly as he accepted the veracity of that statement.

He *needed* to see her.

He was addicted to the look in her eyes as she came. He needed to see that look, that helpless surrendering that smashed through before she lost her mind for him. He was hooked on it; had dreamed of nothing else for the last ten days.

She looked over her shoulder but her eyes stayed on his chest as she continued to fuck him.

Frustration pounded through him. His hand jerked at the restraints, his wrists protesting at the raw pain. His whole body throbbed with the need for that last demand to be met.

"Peaches. God, please. Turn around."

"I thought you loved my ass, Zach," she gasped as she worked her hips in a dirty little circle over him.

Jesus.

"I do." He brought up his knees and jerked his hips upward, eager to experience that delicious slap of her wet cunt against his balls. "I love every single inch of your body. But I want to see your face, baby. I need it."

She shook her head wildly, and he began to panic. He was close. So fucking close. Blood pounded through him with enough force to knock out a horse.

"I…I like it this way," she replied huskily. But he heard the caginess in her voice, and his panic escalated.

God, what was going on here?

Before he could bark out an even more desperate demand, she stretched back further over him, until she was almost prone over him with her arms almost touching his biceps. Not once did she lose her rhythm. Her hips continued to work over him with a cadence that reminded him this sexy woman who owned him was once a trained ballerina. Her body undulated with a sinuousness that was so fucking beautiful his throat closed up and his eyes stung.

"Christ, Bethany." His voice was a rough imploration. He wasn't sure whether he wanted the intensely mind-blowing release that clawed inside him or whether he wanted this sensation to carry on forever.

"Come for me, Zach," she gasped hoarsely.

"Yes, baby. So hard. So fucking hard for you." He was a slave to her needs. Of course he was. He'd been without her for too long. Unable to hold back, he surged high, felt his semen shoot hot and endless inside her. He filled her with everything he had, everything he couldn't say out loud.

All the mistakes he'd made in his past. All the mistakes he was terrified of making with her. The past week and a half had shown him just how precious Bethany was to him. Just how impossible living without her would be.

She bucked one last time over his still hard and throbbing cock, then let out a sweet cry of ecstasy. Unbelievably, it prolonged his own release.

With another roar, he jerked out the last of his come as she collapsed on top of him, her back as slick and hot with sweat as his body was.

More than anything, he wanted to hold her, cradle her sweet body against his. But he couldn't move, and he couldn't find any more words that wouldn't shatter the profound beauty of the moment.

So he closed his eyes and simply breathed her name. "Bethany."

His heart lurched when she turned her head and gifted him a single kiss along his jaw.

When she turned away a second later, his gut tightened. The knowledge that she was avoiding eye contact with him made his chest raw with a feeling he didn't want to contemplate too closely.

Bethany was hurting. No matter how much she loved sex with

him, she needed more. He hadn't given her what she craved.

He'd seen the interest in her eyes when he mentioned using him for sex on the ride home on Monday. Although he'd joked about it, and told himself it didn't hurt that she was considering it, a part of him had reeled a little.

He should be pleased that she hadn't ruled out the idea out of hand. He should be pleased to have any tiny part of Bethany that she was willing to give him. But the simple truth was he was a fucking greedy bastard. He wanted her in every way. Everything he could lay his hands on.

More than anything, he wanted to hear her say she loved him, like she had in Marrakech. It was unfair as all hell but he'd never played by the rules. And he of all people knew life wasn't fair.

She moved on top of him and renewed hunger crawled through him. He knew he could never be satisfied with any less than total devotion and passion from Bethany. Just as he knew he would have to work damn hard to win her back. Because as much as he loved fucking her, sex without eye contact with Bethany wasn't an option he ever wanted to consider again.

That last surrender was too beautiful to forgo. And he felt too damned scared at what the consequences would be without it.

She moved again. He began to harden inside her.

She groaned, turned her head and kissed his neck again. "Zach," she whispered, his name a husky sound loaded with pain and ecstasy.

His eyes prickled again.

Fuck. He was so much more screwed than he thought.

ᝍ

"Release me, baby."

Although the words were a gruff entreaty, she didn't miss the steely demand behind them.

Bethany kept her face buried in his throat a little while longer, a light trembling seizing her body as she recalled the power of her orgasm. She'd always thought being taken so possessively and completely by Zach was what had taken her bliss to a whole new level. Now she knew that no matter how the sex came, it was the man who enthralled and captivated her that brought that extra edge to their sexual encounters.

"Peaches, it's time to take the cuffs off," he said again.

She shivered. The animal within him was waking. Zach Savage was no longer content to let her have the upper hand in bed. Not that he'd ever been fully content with it.

He'd done it because he'd been afraid she'd bolt. He'd been panicked enough to let her have a little control.

Her heart lurched. Surely that meant something?

It wasn't just sex.

And the thing with asking her to turn around? She knew Zach loved watching her come. She hadn't thought he would miss it until she'd heard his desperation. Her heart gave a little foolish leap.

It wasn't just sex. Was it?

"I know you haven't gone to sleep because your cunt is tightening around me again. So get up and release me, baby. It's time."

"Time for what?"

His stubble scratched against her cheek as he smiled. "Time to make you feel even better."

"Are we going to even pretend that I came here to work tonight?"

"Sure we are. I'll take a look at what you've got. As soon as I take care of you. And you want me to take care of you, don't you? You came without me petting your plump little clit. Or getting your pretty tits sucked properly."

She groaned and moved on him. "Are you saying I got the Volkswagen service instead of the Rolls Royce service?"

He laughed. "You got the abbreviated Savage service. Now it's time for the full works."

"Maybe nowadays I prefer less horse power and a little less revving."

He bucked, his body powerful enough to dislodge her, should

he choose. "Not if I have anything to do with it. You get nothing but the very best. Get up, Bethany."

She slowly rose, felt him thick and hard inside her and fought the need to ride him hard again. He would probably let her but she had a feeling Zach needed to prove a point. Most likely stamp his possession all over her again.

The more she withheld herself from him that way, the more agitation and merciless he would be.

Reaching for the key, she levered herself over him, supremely conscious that his eyes were on her. She released the handcuffs and gasped as she saw the red welts on his wrist. Abruptly she recalled him jerking hard at the handcuffs as she'd fucked him. Her heart lurched.

"Oh God, Zach…"

"Forget about it, baby. It's nothing." Lowering his hands, he grasped her waist and flipped her beneath him. "Now, where were we?"

His hair flopped over his forehead and he looked so utterly gorgeous her heart cracked with the beauty of him. Struggling to breathe, she tried to think. "I was just about to head to the bathroom. I'm…dripping." Her face flamed.

Sure fingers slid into her soaking heat and his face grew rigid with dark purpose. "You're not going anywhere. Besides, I love you wet and filled with my come." His eyes darkened further. "Every time you take me inside you, I want to leave a piece of my soul inside you. I'm hoping that if I do it again and again, you won't forget me when we're apart," he whispered raggedly.

Her heart tore wide open. "Forget you? You make it so damn impossible. But what about me, Zach. Do you feel a piece of me inside you when we're apart?"

"Always. I can't breathe when you're not with me. I can't think straight." He removed his hands and slid his cock slowly inside her. He groaned deep and long. "God, I've missed you so much, baby. You fucking missed me too, didn't you?" The sheer assuredness behind his words sparked a futile rebellion inside her.

"No, I didn't."

His eyes narrowed as he surged deep and left her gasping. "Give it up, Peaches. Your cunt says different."

Her eyes rolled with her escalating ecstasy. "Shut up and fuck me, Zach."

He caught her mouth in a wild, merciless kiss. "Talk like that will only get you into trouble. Remember, you still owe me for the last ten days. Now, I prefer your ass peachy and pretty but don't think I'll hesitate to make it cherry red if you keep holding yourself back from me like that. Or maybe you like the idea of being spanked, naughty girl? Does the idea of going over my knee make you hot?" He fucked himself deeper and held himself still.

"Yes," she blurted before she could stop herself.

His brow slowly rose. "Good, now we're getting somewhere." He just stared down at her and didn't move.

Desperately she wriggled, eager to feel the delicious friction.

"Do you want me to move, Peaches?" he rasped.

"Yes. God, yes, please."

"Then look at me."

"Zach—"

"Look at me or you won't get fucked."

Sucking in a deep breath, she schooled her features and forced her gaze upward. His features were taut with the strain of holding himself steady above her. Another layer of sweat sheened his skin and his eyes were dark and turbulent. "You reminded me how flexible you are when you went to town on me just now. So, raise your legs high for me."

She complied immediately, nearly insane with desperation. But he shook his head.

"Higher."

She raised her legs until her feet touched the headboard.

"Good girl. Now, tell me you missed me."

Fifteen

ZACH WOKE WITH a start and glared at the empty space beside him. Bethany was sliding out of bed, her back to him. That distance he'd sensed was still there. Hell, if anything, it was escalating by the second. More than anything, he wanted to grab her, keep her pinned until she acknowledged him, accepted that they were meant to be.

He struggled to stay put. He'd done enough imposing last night. He may have ceded power to her in the beginning but by the time they'd fallen asleep, exhausted in each other's arms in the early hours, she'd known who was in control. Had eagerly participated and granted his every demand.

And yet, through it all, he'd sensed her reticence. And more than that, he'd seen her determination as she'd given herself wholeheartedly and demanded more in return.

It wasn't until that last mind-bending fucking that he'd guessed her intention. Panic had resurged a hundred-fold but he'd stemmed it.

Now, he watched the curve of her waist, her sleek torso as she raised her hand to shrug into the dressing gown he'd provided for her and hid a determined smile. She thought they were done. Last night, she'd fucked him with a purpose he'd been thrilled to receive. Now he knew it for what it was.

"Good morning, Peaches."

She tensed but didn't turn around. His pulse shot up as the urge to get off the bed and make her face him smashed through him. "How do you feel?" He struggled to keep his voice even. A part of him wondered why he was so stunned that she turned him inside out without even lifting a finger. It was the same realization that had staggered him in Marrakech. That feeling that she meant more to him than everyone or anything in his life.

It was what also terrified him that any further revelations about his past would drive her away for good.

"Great. I feel great." She fiddled with her belt for a few minutes. Then caught a strand of hair between her fingers. Zach was content to let the thick silence continue. He was perfectly content where he was, watching her fidget. This woman confused the hell out of him enough for him not to feel lenient toward her this morning.

After another minute, she looked up. "Zach, I need to go to work."

"No you don't. You're working from here today. I've cleared it with Sheena."

She rounded on him. "You've *what*?"

He stood and walked over to her. Her color was heightened with her anger but her eyes were adorably drowsy from sleep and sex. And he'd never craved her more. "We never got round to discussing what you've come up with for the project. I thought we could discuss it this morning."

"That will take about an hour. Then what the hell will I do for the rest of the day?" she snapped, her eyes blazing blue hell at him.

He couldn't stop his grin at her exasperation. She was getting animated. Good. He preferred that to her silent scheming on how to leave him.

"I'm pretty sure we can come up with something."

She closed her eyes. "I can't spend what's supposed to be my work day here with you—"

"Fucking my brains out? I beg to differ. Wasn't that what the marathon fucking last night was all about?"

Her frown held a world of wariness. "What are you talking about?"

He shook his head, unwilling to embrace his fears. Last night had been getting him out of her system. A fuck before the fuck off. Little did she know his mission had been the opposite. He'd tried being a gentleman. He'd tried begging. Hell, he'd even tried blackmailing.

Now he intended to fuck himself back into her system. But he couldn't risk frightening her off by coming on any stronger.

Pulling her close, he slanted his mouth over hers. His dread lessened a fraction when she responded by opening her mouth and participating wholeheartedly in the kiss. When her hands slid around his waist, he breathed even easier. Her eyes were dreamy with need when he raised his head and stared down at her.

"Let's try this again. Good morning, Peaches."

"It's not a good morning for me when you try and derail my day before it's even started, Zach," she complained.

She tried to pull away but he held on. More and more, he felt like he was trying to hold on to her while she pulled away from him. Slowly, he glided his thumb over her bottom lip, felt it quiver beneath his touch.

"That's not what I'm trying to do. I thought I'd save you time by cutting out your commute into work."

"You don't get it. I'm a grown up. I can arrange my own work day. I know you don't care whether Sheena finds out about us but I do. Can you try and respect that?" Blue eyes glowered at him but there was also a hint of sadness in them that shredded him.

Something had to give here. And soon. "Forgive me, baby. I just wanted you here with me today."

She continued to stare at him for another minute, then she nodded. "But we're definitely working, got it? I want to give Sheena a progress report by close of play."

"We'll be done by lunchtime. Then I'll take you to lunch. If you want," he tagged on quickly when her brow started to rise. "Or we can prolong work and call it a business lunch."

She shook her head in exasperation. "Do you not have...I don't know, other work to do?"

"My work day is...fluid." He had nothing planned in his immediate future beyond doing everything in his power to hang onto her.

Her eyes met his and slowly a wary speculation grew in the mesmerizing depths.

"How long do you think you can keep this up, Zach?" Again that sadness, that soul-deep echo of pain that cut a jagged path through him.

"Fight to keep from losing you? As long as I have breath in my body."

Her own breath caught but she began to pull away.

"Bethany—"

"I need a shower," she said, her tone more than suggesting that she didn't need company.

He dug his feet into the carpet to keep from stalking after her when she headed for the bathroom. Shucking a hand through his hair, he calculated the time difference on the West Coast and exhaled noisily. He was beginning to realize that even if his attorney managed to get the non-disclosure clause lifted he would have to tell Bethany a lot more about his life than Farrah and what had led to the incident six years ago.

For one thing, there was also the issue of his mother and her lifestyle.

Compared to the parenting he'd been through growing up, Bethany's parents were saints. Saints who wouldn't want him around their daughter when they learned of his depraved past. Of his mother's proclivities.

He'd seen the way Bethany had been cut up about her asshole ex, and the way she'd reacted to his bombshell. How would she react if he told her his mother had done worse, and continued to do so?

The sound of running water hit his ears. He paced to the bathroom door and sucked in a sustaining breath. He needed to give her space. Give her a minute to collect her thoughts—

Fuck that. He needed her. Being around her made him forget what a fucked up life he'd led until tragedy had propelled him into sickened numbness.

He entered the bathroom and stopped at the sight of her. Jesus, she was fucking magnificent. Stupid to feel jealous of the water running down her body but *rational* had flown out the window where Bethany was concerned a long time ago.

She'd secured her long hair on top of her head and was leaning forward so the water hit the top of her spine. With her hands braced on the wall, he was reminded of their first shower in Paris when he'd lost control and come all over her ass.

He grew hard within seconds. He must have made a sound because she turned sharply.

The haunted sadness in her eyes made him grit his teeth. "Shit, Bethany, I can't stand that look in your eyes," he rasped.

"Then fix it," she replied. Hearing the tears clogging her voice made his chest tighten. "Do you trust me, Zach? Even a little?"

"I do trust you."

She shook her head. "Not enough, obviously."

He stalked to the vanity, aware that her eyes followed him. Leaning against it, he crossed his arms. "I signed a non-disclosure clause agreeing never to talk about what happened six years ago. My attorney is working to overturn it."

Her eyes widened. "You mean you can't legally talk about how she died?"

He nodded. "I've been trying but her family aren't cooperating." His jaw tightened. "And deep down, I don't blame them."

"Why not?"

His chest filled with regret, pain and a desperate panic that he was skidding towards saying something that would cost him the beautiful woman in front of him. But he couldn't seem to stem the flow of his words. "Because, she was doomed the moment she met me."

"God, Zach…"

Ice speared into his soul, throwing him back to a time he could never forget. "She was innocent, Bethany. She had no fucking clue what the real world was like. She was a virgin for heaven's sake. I fucked her up so badly, even I could barely recognize her in the end."

She flinched at his harsh tone and fought to pull back from the brink he was skating toward. He speared a hand through his hair and tried to breathe. Absently, he heard the shower shut off. A moment later, she stood in front of him.

"Did you force her to do anything against her will?" she asked.

He frowned, his thoughts a jumbled chaos. "Did I…? Probably. Possibly. I was pretty full of myself back then. I had life by the balls and I was squeezing it for all it was worth. I was pretty damn capable of anything. I knew it and made sure everyone around me knew it too. I think I hammered that point home with Farrah most of all."

She took another step closer. "How?"

He tried to shrug but his shoulders wouldn't move. "She trusted me. I made sure she knew what the consequences would be if she ever betrayed that trust. I…made her choose between her family and me. She chose me. And ended up paying the ultimate price for it." Pain seared his insides, followed swiftly by a damning ice that threatened to freeze his heart.

She touched his arm and immediately the ice started to recede. "Zach, I'm sorry."

He grabbed her hand and tugged her closer. Her body was drenched from the shower but she was warm, and soft and everything he yearned for, despite knowing deep in his soul that he didn't deserve her.

Her arms circled his shoulders and she buried her face in his neck. His breath shuddered out as she held him tight.

God, he never wanted to let her go. Never.

"Is that why you're afraid to trust me? Why you keep pushing me away?" she whispered raggedly.

"I'm terrified of what you'd see if I open up. That you'd see someone you don't want to be with."

"The person you think you are, did he start and end with Farrah?" Her question cut to the heart of his every fear.

For several minutes he couldn't speak. "No," he finally admitted.

"But she was the reason you've closed yourself off, isn't she?"

"I've had to. I can't risk putting anyone else through that. Her family are still grieving over what I did, Bethany. What I can never undo."

She leaned back and looked at him. "So you're going to spend the rest of your life punishing yourself, paying the price by never risking happiness?"

"I don't deserve to be happy."

Pain clouded her eyes. "Then what am I doing here?"

The bottom fell out of his world. Numbly, he shook his head. "I…don't deserve it. That doesn't mean I don't crave it."

She pulled back another inch. "So you want me to do all the work while you hide behind whatever guilt is consuming you?" Her voice shamed him. Completely and utterly. But still he held on. Letting go was not an option.

"I'm trying. I'm willing to work for it. Work for you. You told me you loved me in Morocco. I want to deserve that love." Desperation clawed through him when her expression didn't change. "Tell me you love me, Bethany."

Her eyes darkened and she sucked in a breath. "I…can't."

Pain seared deeper. The earth shifted beneath his feet as pure terror took hold. "Why the hell not? You said it once, I don't think you can take it back."

"I think you were right. I said it too early. You didn't want to hear it then, remember?"

"I want to hear it now! Have you changed your mind? Is that it? You've caught a glimpse of the monster underneath and you're beating a hasty retreat?"

She jerked out of his arms. "Shut up, Zach. Once again you're presuming you know what's in my heart and mind. I'm here. Despite what you told me, I'm here with you. Why can't you trust in that?"

"Because I look into your eyes and I see the sadness. I see the pain. I can already feel you slipping through my fingers. You say you won't run but you sure as hell can retreat. You're already doing that."

She shook her head and glanced down at her feet. He'd thought looking into her eyes hurt. But not seeing her expression hurt even more.

"You were right. The real world is kicking our asses pretty hard."

His bark of laughter ricocheted around the bathroom. "Just say the word and we can get on a plane and head to Bora Bora."

"We can't run away from our problems, Zach."

"We won't be running if we're together. We'd just be facing them with a much better view."

"I can't step away from my life. Or my job. As much as the sound of Bora Bora thrills me."

"So what do you suggest?" he asked before he could think better of it.

She turned and plucked a towel from the heated rail. Watching her cover her incredible body made him swallow hard and fight to keep from ripping away the piece of cloth.

"We agreed on a question a day in Marrakech. I want that back on the table."

His chest burned but he nodded. "Okay."

A sheen of tears filmed her eyes. "Thank you." She turned away.

When she reached for the doorknob, he jerked upright and crossed to her. Once again, that feeling of unraveling assailed him. His heart pounded with despair and desperation.

Catching her wrist, he stopped her from leaving the bathroom. "Baby?" His hands slid up her arms to cup her shoulders.

"Hmm?"

He breathed in then exhaled noisily. "Don't let the love die. When the time comes, when I earn it, I want to hear you say you love me like you did in Marrakech. If it's not too much, can you promise me that?"

"Yes. I promise."

His breath shuddered out and he trailed his mouth down her neck. "Thank you." He stepped closer and heard her breath catch. "God…thank you."

He slid one arm around her shoulders and pulled her back into him. She smelled heavenly of soap and warm, alluring woman. His cock jerked against her ass and she gasped.

"Jesus, Zach, how can you be hard even now?"

He laughed against her smooth throat. "You have no fucking clue how hot you are if you don't understand that I can't help being hard when you're close."

Sixteen

They worked through lunch and ended up ordering from the executive Michelin starred chef who came as part of the building's concierge services.

He picked through Bethany's initial plans, firing questions at her as they ploughed their way through a double-grilled steak with fries and salad and a chilled glass of Chablis.

He tried to keep things business-like but the knowledge that she wasn't wearing any panties beneath the suit dress she'd insisted on wearing again, played havoc with his thought processes every time he allowed himself to dwell on it. Which was every three seconds.

"Zach?"

He fought to refocus. "Hmm?"

"I asked what you thought of Romania for the second trip."

"Not at this time of year."

"Okay. How about Rio?" she ventured.

"How about Reykjavik?" he said.

"How about Rome?"

He grinned. "Do names beginning with R turn you on, Peaches? Or do you just like the idea of getting down and dirty in the Holy City?"

A cute little blush reddened her cheeks. "Stay on point, Zach. Besides, there won't be any down and dirtying since I'll be right here in New York."

"Ah, I hate to burst your bubble but you're coming on the trip."

Her eyes widened. "I'm what?"

He struggled not to lean forward and kiss the surprised O from her swollen mouth. "Part of the contract terms stated one member of Neon had to be present on the trip. I asked for you."

She stared at him in silence. His nape began to prickle. "And where will you be during this time?" she asked quietly.

He noted a hopeful wariness in her eyes and dared to think she wanted him to answer one way only. "I'll be right there with you."

Her breath shuddered out. His heart soared.

"Does that please you, baby?"

She wrinkled her nose but he was happy to see the shadows retreating. "Technically, it shouldn't. Business and pleasure. Bad idea."

"Fuck technical. And don't pigeonhole us. We're unique."

She laughed and he raised a brow. "It's the second time I've been called that this week," she supplied.

"Really."

"Don't give me that look. I'm a unique little snowflake."

A dark feeling rushed through his gut. He plucked his reading glasses from his face and tossed them onto the table.

"Who called you unique?" he asked, struggling to keep his voice even. He must have succeeded because she smiled, popped a fry in her mouth and chewed.

"The guest list coordinator at *Shades*."

"Right."

She slowly stopped chewing. "You're jealous? For fuck's sake, Zach, he was gay." He started to relax. "I think."

His stomach clenched hard. "Christ. If this were the Middle Ages I'd keep you chained in my tower so no other man could see you," he half joked.

She laughed. The sound filled him with a joy that knocked the breath out of him. "So you think you can tame me? Maybe I'd be the one to keep you chained up. And naked for my use whenever the urge takes me."

God, why did that idea make him so damned hard?

He shifted to adjust his crotch and laughed under his breath at the futility of trying to control his body around her. "I like the idea of you as a marauding warrior princess. I like the idea of being exclusively yours even better," he added.

Laughter slowly faded from her eyes. The atmosphere thickened with hope and pain and sex and desperation.

Christ.

She glanced down at the papers spread on the table and cleared her throat. "So Rome gets your approval?"

"Throw in a quick stop to the Amalfi Coast and it's a go. I have a place there. We can stop in for lunch."

She nodded and made quick notes, studiously avoiding his eyes. "Okay. Next stop…how about Kenya? Your guests can watch heartless predators rip their prey to shreds. We'll call it nature at its worst or the circle of life tour or something?" Her voice was dark with anguish.

"Bethany."

"Sorry, bad joke." She chewed on her lower lip for several seconds. "I still think Kenya would be awesome."

"Okay. If you like." His shoulders moved restlessly.

She started to argue but pressed her lips together and made some more notes.

"Or we can do Thailand instead?"

"The islands or Bangkok?" he asked, hoping she would look at him.

She kept her gaze on her notes. "I'll work on both, the guests may prefer bright lights to laid back, especially since the tour is abbreviated."

He thought for a moment. "Source out events for both. We'll let the guests decide which they prefer."

"Great. It's settled then. Are you sure you don't want me to work on the other trips?"

"I'm sure. It's already taken care of." Whether Bethany would like what he had planned for them on those remaining trips was something he didn't want to think about just yet.

"I'll liaise with our contacts in Italy to get a few venues sorted out." She positioned her laptop on her thighs and fired it up. "Kenya and Thailand I'll have to plan from the ground up."

He picked up his glass and drained the last mouthful of wine, grimacing at the suddenly sour taste. He knew very well the taste wasn't the problem. The wine had tasted exquisite only minutes ago, when his blood buzzed with contentment at just being with her and trading jokes.

That his body was psychosomatically reacting to Bethany was no surprise. She was under his skin. In his blood. Embedded in his mind in a way that made him reel inwardly thinking about it.

"Bethany," he found himself saying her name just to feel that intense connection again.

"Just a second. I'm checking to see if Sheena has sent the list of guests."

"Bethany," he murmured again.

"Zach, please. Just…let me do my work." The husky plea shredded him.

He forced himself to stay silent but his gaze didn't stray from her. After several minutes, she lowered the laptop shut. "Thirty-six guests have accepted the invitation. We need to narrow it down to the required twelve. I've sent the details to your tablet."

Setting his glass down he rose. "I'll take a look tonight." He held out his hand. "Right now, we're taking a break."

Ten minutes later, after she'd brushed her hair and against his protests, pulled on her underwear, he met her in the hallway, ushered her into the elevator and hit the RT button.

She glanced from the lit button to his face. "We're going up? I thought yours was the Penthouse?"

He smiled. "It is."

"So…"

He kissed her as the elevator stopped and the doors slid open. In the mid-afternoon sunshine, the helicopter gleamed black and indigo.

Bethany jerked to a stop. "You have a private chopper at your beck and call?"

"You should know by now that I love my toys, Peaches."

She rolled her eyes and he threaded his fingers through hers, insanely pleased that she was once again looking at him.

They would work through this. As long as she stayed with him, he had to believe they would succeed.

He helped her into the back of the chopper, and secured her seatbelt as she looked around the plush, cream interior. Her eyes flashed with excitement and he found himself grinning.

"You like what you see?"

"What's not to like?" She caressed the soft leather next to her thigh and he mock frowned.

After securing his own belt, he picked up her hand and put it on his thigh. "You know, we can see the pilot but he can't see us. Wanna make out?"

Her immediate blush made his senses leap. "You're really determined not to stop until you get us both arrested, aren't you?"

He leaned in close as the rotors began to whir, and whispered in her ear, "You've already had me in handcuffs, Peaches. It's a downward slope from here on in."

She shook her head with another alluring laugh. "Tell me where we're going."

"To Newark, to tour the new plane. Then I'm taking you out to dinner."

※

Bethany tried not to stare in awe at her surrounding and the view below her window but she failed at both.

And with Zach so close and so mesmerizing, it was a futile task anyway. Every time she turned, his gaze met hers and he smiled that heart-stopping smile she was sure was specifically designed to batter her resistance to pieces.

And damn, if it wasn't working. Her insides shook every time she met his eyes. Her heart swelled every time he smiled at her. She may very well have patted herself on the shoulder for refusing to say she loved him and even believed her reasons for saying so, but she knew the feelings were there, alive and stronger than ever. Especially after that revelation in his bathroom this morning.

Recalling his anguish, her chest tightened. Whatever had happened between him and Farrah, Bethany was beginning to believe deep in her heart that there had been exigent circumstances. The man next to her bore many flaws, but her instincts were fairly set on believing he wasn't a heartless predator with pre-meditative intentions.

The chopper banked around Ellis Island and she glanced at him again. She followed his chiseled profile to his strong neck and broad shoulders masked by his long-sleeved indigo T-shirt. Just like he liked his favorite color on her, she loved seeing him in indigo. His mouth-watering chest rose and fell in an even breath and her gaze travelled lower, past his ripped abs to the legs encased in Armani casuals.

Her belly heated as her gaze became trapped at his crotch. Even soft, his bulge was impressive and extremely noteworthy. He shifted and she glanced up, met his electric gaze. In silence, he curved his arm around her shoulders and pulled her into his body.

Resting her head on his chest, she slid her arms around his waist.

The sound-proof interior meant they could chat easily but they fell into a comfortable silence she was content to keep for the moment.

She had no doubt there would be even more turbulent times ahead; times when they violently disagreed, or times when his arrogance and blatant disregard for propriety made her see red. And yes, there would be times when she would refuse to let the secrets of his past remain dark and distant.

But for now, she let herself be content.

Seventeen

The latest Indigo Lounge aircraft was the last word in aviation perfection. Even to her untrained eye, the plane had been built to a stunning specification that made her want to caress it.

"Wow." A sense of déjà vu washed over her as she stared up at the indigo-trimmed plane. Was it really a mere three weeks ago since she'd arrived here and placed herself in Zach's intense sphere?

"What are you thinking?" he rasped in her ear.

She turned to face him in the cavernous private hangar. Even in the large space, she felt a sharp connection with him. The crew who were working on readying the plane studiously avoided them, hurrying about their duties.

He stared down at her with a mixture of possessiveness, blatant sexual interest and that touch of anxiety she felt deep within her own soul.

"I'm checking out your plane. And reliving the moment we met three weeks ago."

His fingers curled over her nape, and she settled her hands on his chest. His heartbeat was just as erratic as hers.

"Do you have any regrets about that day?" The anxiety had risen a notch.

Before the incident in his bathroom this morning when she'd witnessed a different Zach, she would've been torn about her answer. "No," she replied. "No regrets."

She realized he'd been holding his breath when he exhaled noisily. Tugging her closer, he touched his forehead to hers, his eyes dark and turbulent with intense feelings. "You don't know how happy I am to hear that."

Unable to resist, she pressed her mouth to his. "I think I can probably guess."

He deepened the kiss for a few seconds before he lifted his head. "Time for your tour." He tugged her to the bottom of the steps and motioned her ahead of him. "After you."

She raised a brow. "Are you sure?"

"Am I sure I'll survive watching your sexy ass bounce in front of me? Probably not. But I can't think of a better way to die."

She laughed and took the first step. Looking over her shoulder, she took the next step with an exaggerated sway of her hips.

His dark laugh followed a groan. "Revel in your power, Peaches. You've more than earned it."

The moment she stepped onto the plane a different kind of pleasure permeated her senses. If she'd thought the previous Indigo Lounge plane was breath taking, the vision spread before her took that concept to a whole new level.

The reception area was much larger than before, but with the same indigo theme that stamped its authority and brand over the space.

Stylish, strategically placed LED and chrome lights shone from the towering ceiling, casting subtle light and shade over the luxurious silk and leather seats and gleaming surfaces. Even though it was large enough to hold fifty people, the area had an intimate ambience that immediately set a guest at ease.

The central suspended glass staircase leading to the upper floor had a glassed off area, over which a solid see-through glass bar had been set.

She reached the top of the stairs, turned around and gasped. On both sides of the bar, balconies with short poles protruded from the walls from which hung restraining hooks and leather-studded cuffs.

With a hand on her back, Zach guided her forward to one of the hooks. She reached out and traced a finger over one cuff.

She felt Zach's breath on her ear before he spoke. "For those with a voyeuristic bent. Which rules us out. I'd maim anyone who attempted to see you naked."

She shivered at his dark tone but couldn't pull her gaze from the hooks and leather. The idea that people wanted to be seen fucking both repulsed and excited her at the same time. She didn't think she would ever be brave enough to even contemplate it for a second.

"What are you thinking?" he asked.

"That human sexuality is an intriguing thing. It's amazing how a bunch of chemicals can cause such a strong reaction."

She heard his breath catch but when she looked up, his face was expressionless. "Or it could be as simple as being in the right place at the right time to find your right person."

"People spend lifetimes trying to find the right person. Most people fail or end up with the wrong person."

"I'm not going to dwell on the intrigue or delve into the human psyche, baby. I think we both know I have enough demons in my closet. I've found my right person. The rest is just white noise."

There was a hard bite to his tone that made Bethany frown. "Something wrong?"

"No. Come on, I'll show you the rest." His hand slid around her waist and they moved from the balcony, through a short arch into another open space.

This was a chill out lounge area like nothing she'd ever seen. It was like something from the set of a Tim Burton movie, with six bright colored *chaise longues*, and each seat had an indigo place card with a ribbon tied around it. Through the ribbon had been threaded two rings, one for a larger male finger and one for a smaller feminine one.

She picked up the nearest card. "What are these for?"

"They're…parlor games, if you like."

Her eyes widened. "How does it work?"

"A question is asked. Everyone involved in the game is given the opportunity to answer their own way. The person who poses the question get to pick which answer he or she likes the most. And things take off from there."

"So…like a swing party but framed like a quiz show?"

He laughed and the last of his puzzling tension evaporated. "I guess."

"And the rings?"

"They have tiny digital timers on them with a minimum time guests are allowed to play before leaving the lounge." He touched a panel and shaded screens dropped from the ceiling over one seat, blocking it completely from view.

She slowly set the card and rings down and stared at the gold and indigo screen. It was beautifully etched with intricate swirls that together formed sensual images. "Wow."

He lifted a brow. "Did I just impress you, baby?"

She glanced up. "No, but I'd love to have your designer on speed dial."

That earned her a sharp smack on her ass before he motioned her forward. The sky lounge was like the one on the first plane but since they were grounded, the view beyond the wide windows wasn't as impressive. But she recalled Zach's husky suggestion to fuck her as they raced for the stars and a blush crept up her neck.

"Naughty thoughts, Peaches?"

"Considering where I am, I think I'll give myself a free pass," she answered.

"Hmm." He tugged on their linked fingers, bringing her flush against his hard, warm body. "Just so we're clear, during the trip, I'll be with you each time you leave our suite. And if anyone so much as looks at you sideways they will be shoved out the nearest airlock without a parachute."

"God, you're such a Neanderthal!"

"I like that you smile when you say that." He laughed when she punched him in the arm.

They left the sky lounge through a side door and went down

another hallway. Bethany's mind was beginning to boggle at the sheer vastness of the place. But she'd studied the layout Jeff had given Neon and knew Zach's designers had used every available space to make the Indigo Lounge a stunning experience.

They reached a black door and Zach stopped. A different kind of excitement leapt off him in a way that intrigued her.

He entered a code and the door slid back with a sigh. At first the room was dark. Zach passed a hand over a wall panel and indigo and bright lights beamed over the space.

A single, huge throne-like armchair faced away from the door. That was intriguing enough but it was the other central feature that held her attention.

A pole, strong and sturdy, rose from a staged platform. Tiny, spotlights ringed the two short steps to the platform, drawing the eye to the silver pole.

Zach's keep stare swung from the pole to her and Bethany found herself drawn like a magnet towards the platform in the middle of the room.

She jumped as a loud ring smashed through the thick atmosphere. Zach barely flinched but his nostrils flared in annoyance. The phone continued to ring as he walked beside her to the middle of the room.

"Any reason you're not answering your phone?"

"Yes. I don't want us to be interrupted."

It rang a few more times then stopped. Seconds later, it rang again. Zach cursed.

"Take it. I really don't mind."

With an impatient huff, he drew the phone from his pocket. "Savage," he barked.

She smiled to herself and wished the person at the end of the line well as she walked towards the pole. Stepping up onto the platform, she grasped the cool steel and felt its sturdy strength beneath her fingers. After making sure her heels weren't scuffing the surface of the platform, she walked slowly round the pole, conscious of Zach's eyes on her as he spoke on the phone.

Taking a firmer hold with both hands, she swung off her feet in a perfect three-sixty, before landing back down with her legs in a scissored walk back around the pole. She repeated the move, then went one better and twined her legs round the pole.

Zach made a hoarse sound, then with a brusque, "I'll have to call you back," he ended the call.

Poised three feet above the ground, she read the naked intent in his eyes and her core blazed with desire.

She slid slowly back down, her hands a sensual slide that he followed with avid attention.

Her gaze flicked to the oval windows, conscious of the workers outside.

"Privacy windows," he rasped without taking his eyes off her. "Sound proof room."

The implication that any pending frenzied screams of pleasure wouldn't go beyond this room made her blush. Thankfully the lights were too low for him to see, although his avid gaze had probably picked up her soaring pulse rate.

When she began to walk around the pole again, he stalked closer. Without stopping her sure stride, she reached behind her and took her time to lower her zipper. She stopped long enough to kick her dress away and looked up to find him narrow-eyed, his chest expanding on an uneven breath.

His eyes raked her semi-nude state. "You wouldn't have made it this far if I knew you were braless underneath that dress."

She turned so her back was braced against the pole, its cool steel sliding between her crack. Her only accessories were her earrings and shoes. And she' never felt sexier in her life. "There was a reason I kept that to myself."

Fevered eyes raking her body, his hands went for his belt. Freeing it, he undid his button and lowered his zipper.

"Ready to see how flexible I can be?"

"Fuck. More than ready. Dance for me, baby." He reefed his shirt over his head and flung it away. Walking backward, he sank into the seat and leaned forward, elbows on his knees.

A spurt of trepidation pierced her composure. Zach loved her body, she knew that. But when she'd performed in his ballroom in Marrakech she hadn't been aware he was watching. And this sort of dancing was a whole world of difference from what she'd been trained to do.

She bit her lip.

Zach stared at her. Then he slowly reached to the right side of the chair and pressed a button.

A slow, seductive slide of a violin string pierced the air, followed by a few more. Music throbbed through the room, infusing her body. The tempo increased with a steady beat of a drum until the loud cacophony sent vibrations through her feet. Keeping her legs closed and her hands gripping the steel, she slid down the pole and back up, twirling her hips to the music. She performed the action again to ground herself, then turned to face the pole.

She swung herself high and around, then abruptly ended her momentum with her legs crossed. Her thighs screamed at the vice-like hold on the steel as she let go with her hands. Her loose hair formed a seductive curtain around her, sliding over her breasts as she leaned forward. Her cleavage touched the warming steel and her nipples immediately puckered.

She flung her head back, and gripped the pole with one hand. Slowly, she arched her back and rocked her hips against the pole, still suspended high.

"Fuck!"

She looked over, her thighs beginning to burn from supporting most of her weight but the look on Zach's face was worth the discomfort. Arching her back even further until her body was curved in a perfect C, she reached for the base of the pole and executed a perfect scissored landing.

Gliding her hands back up, she jumped and kicked her legs apart, then twined them around the pole as they came together. She laid her cheek against the steel, her heart racing as she looked over to see Zach's reaction.

His tongue rested against his lower lip and his eyes burned with volcanic heat.

Power roared through her veins, lending her insane confidence to perform a series of risqué moves that had him jerking to his feet and striding toward her.

The moment she landed, he grabbed her around the waist and slammed her into his body.

"Jesus, how is it that just when I think you can't be more incredible, you prove me wrong?" he asked hoarsely.

She stared up at his breathtaking face, feeling flushed and so turned on, she could barely breathe. "I take it you liked my dancing?"

He barked out a strained laugh and his hands slid up to cup her breasts. He tweaked her nipples hard, and her knees turned to jelly.

"God, baby, I'm going to fuck you so hard."

The idea that had been budding in her mind bloomed to undeniable life. She forced herself to speak before her mind turned to oatmeal.

"What other delights have you got hiding in that chair?"

His gaze never wavered from her face. "Everything your naughty little heart desires, I'm sure."

It took almost superhuman strength to free herself from him long enough to walk to the chair.

After examining it for a few minutes to see how it worked, she pressed a button. A deep drawer sprang free. A saucy smile curled her lips as she drew out the black rope.

She turned and walked back up onto the platform. Deep excitement leapt within and she was gratified to see it echoed in his eyes.

"You tied me to a cross. I'm tying you to a pole. Fair's fair, Zach."

Eighteen

His throat moved on a powerful swallow, his neck taut with pent-up emotion. "You wanna tie me up again, Peaches?"

She had a lot more in mind. So much that the thoughts made her blush but she held her nerve. "Yes."

One shoulder lifted. "If it makes you happy, I'm okay with that," he croaked.

She had a feeling Zach would be okay with anything that involved her body and the promise of mindless sex. She tried not to let the thought that this was all it would ever be, wreck the moment. She held onto what had transpired in the bathroom this morning as a beacon of hope.

Zach was working on making things right. She could give them both this while that happened.

And who knew, perhaps sex, like food for some men, was the way to Zach's heart.

"You're thinking too hard, Bethany. Should I be terrified?" That note of anxiety was back.

Another thing she found intriguing; that a man as powerful and influential as Zach could be anxious about her reactions.

She strode toward him and stopped as the tips of her breasts brushed his chest. His inhalation was gratifyingly jagged. "It'll be good, I promise."

Flames leapt in his grey eyes, turning them mesmerizing gunmetal. "I know it will. But after this, the bondage swings your way again."

The hot little shiver went through her as she recalled being tied up on Zach's cross. The raw, chaotic emotions that had triggered her surrender still had the power to knock the breath out of her lungs.

But then she recalled his reaction when she said she loved him and her shiver turned cold. She may have been too quick to offer it, but he'd still rejected her love. No matter how she sliced it, it hurt to think about it.

"Baby?" He started to reach for her.

She pulled away quickly and stepped behind him before he could change his mind and grab her. His head followed her movement but he remained in place, even sliding his hands behind his hips to give her access.

Binding his hands took more expertise than she'd anticipated. And her hands shook as she contemplated what she was doing.

Less than a month ago, she'd lived in a vanilla world that most people were content to bask in. Now here she was, tying up one of the world's most powerful men in an elaborate knot that made the tiny dominatrix in her roar.

When she was satisfied he wouldn't get away, she glided her hands up his powerful bicep and gloried in the rippling of his muscles.

"I love the way you react to my touch," she confessed before she could stop herself.

His chest expanded on a breath. "That's because you own me, Peaches."

The pain that lurked sharpened. "I own you *sexually*."

He shook his head. "You own *everything*. I may be too terrified to bare myself completely to you but believe that you own me. I'm not going anywhere in this lifetime."

Her hands reached his shoulders and curved over his nape. His pulse beat strong and rapid at his throat, vitality surging beneath his skin as he breathed through his mouth.

Slowly she walked round until she faced him. The lights gleamed over his jet-black hair, face and sculpted chest. With his legs planted wide, he looked like a proud, chiseled statue come to life.

Her heart tripped over. "You really are magnificent, Zach."

A corner of his mouth lifted. "No, baby. You are. Inside and out. Tell me you won't give up on me." The abrupt stark need for reassurance burned his eyes.

She rested her hand on his stomach and felt his hard muscles quiver. "No, Zach. I won't make a promise I may not be able to keep. What happens to us from here on in is up to you. You let me in a little this morning. I'm still here. I don't scare as easily as you seem to convince yourself I do. But I'm willing to give you a little time to believe you can trust me."

He gave a single, grateful nod.

"And in the meantime…" she let her voice trail off.

"Yes?"

Her hand slid lower to the opening in his trousers. Working her way in, she grasped his thickness in her hand and pulled him free. A drop of pre-cum glistened at his wide crown. The sight of it made her mouth water.

God, he was so beautiful.

"Are you going to suck me off, Peaches?"

"Hmm, you're so hard and gorgeous; it'd be a shame not to." She fisted him harder, felt him jerk within her hold.

"Jesus…kiss me, please," he pleaded, his lips parting to draw in breath as his eyes devoured her mouth.

She leaned up and kissed him, hot and deep. His tongue immediately slid into her mouth, her dominant, virile man unable to accede control even when he was tied up. They kissed until her mouth felt raw and swollen. Then they kissed some more.

When she found the strength to pull away, her insides shook with trying to grapple with how emotionally charged just kissing him made her.

Stepping back, she shakily tugged her panties down. And them, simply because she didn't want to cause any unwitting damage, she stepped out of her heels. On her bare feet, she padded, naked back to him.

Zach watched her with hungry, desperate eyes. Slowly sinking onto her knees, she tugged down his pants and boxers and freed him from his clothes and shoes.

Gloriously naked and all hers. She trailed her nail up his inner thighs and smiled at his pained groan. Cupping his balls, she squeezed and watched his stomach clench hard. With one hand, she traced a vein that arrowed down into his groin. Then going one better, she licked her way down until her chin brushed his cock.

"Suck me, baby. God, please blow me."

His plea was well-timed because she was equally desperate for him.

Settling herself on her knees, she opened her mouth and licked the underside of his broad head. Salty and hot, he tasted glorious.

"Open wider," he groaned. Wetting her lips, she complied. He guided himself in, ramming home at the last moment with a muted roar. She barely managed to control her gag before he was coming back at her.

Clawing back her dwindling control, she gripped the base of his cock and sucked him long and hard.

"Oh, Christ. I love your mouth. So fucking perfect. More, baby. Please."

She gave him more, until he coated her tongue with more pre-cum. Then reluctantly, she pulled back and rose.

The slick heat between her legs should've shamed her but she was long past shame when it came to Zach.

As if he knew exactly his effect on her, his gaze dropped to where she ached most. "Are you wet, Peaches?"

Biting her lip, she nodded. "So wet."

His nostrils flared. "I want to taste. Untie me."

She shook her head. He groaned and his biceps clenched.

Stepping forward, she gripped his shoulders. "Don't fret, Tiger. I have an idea."

His brow quirked. "Tiger?"

She laughed, leaned close to his ear and whispered. "I'm going to climb you like a tree and let you eat me. Then I'm going to climb back down and take your beautiful thick cock deep inside me."

His mouth dropped open and his eyes darkened to near black, his breathing heavy. He gave a slight shake of his head and stared down at her.

"Is that a *no*, Zach?"

His biceps strained along with his cock. Tendons stood out in his neck as he growled, "It's a *hell yes*." He lowered his body and bent his knees. "Whatever you need, baby. Take it." Dark anticipation throbbed in his voice.

Gripping his shoulders tighter, she stepped up onto his strong thighs. He made a rough sound of encouragement and gazed up at her. Letting go of him she grabbed the pole, rose higher and hooked one knee over his shoulder.

"Fuck, Peaches. You're so wet, so fucking ready for me." He licked his lips and groaned as she hooked her other knee over him.

From her elevated position, she looked down and began to tremble.

His face was bare inches from her core. She watched as his lips puckered and he blew a cool breath on her clit.

Her body jerked. His head reared back and dark eyes speared hers in warning.

"I'm tied up so I won't be able to catch you if you fall. So. Do. Not. Fucking. Fall. Understand?"

She nodded shakily.

"I'm gonna blow on you again. Can you take it?" he demanded.

She tightened her grip on the pole until her fingers ached and trembled. "Yes."

His gaze left hers, drifted down her body to her wet core once again. Gently, he blew. She gasped as her body vibrated with insane pleasure.

Lowering his mouth further, he placed a soft kiss on her core.

He was testing her reaction but she was desperate for him. "More."

He opened his mouth wider and his tongue flicked against her clit. Her insides clenched greedily with anticipation. He flicked that wicked tongue again, his eyes keenly watching her reaction.

When he was satisfied she wasn't about to let go, he deepened the kiss, starting a steady, heady rhythm that fractured her thoughts.

Bethany rolled her hips closer to that sweet torture, her body a vessel of pure sensation that lived for the chaos Zach was creating between her legs.

He feasted on her like a voracious predator and she loved it.

She loved him.

Accepting that had grown a little easier. But the realization that she couldn't live without this man - that she might have to live with never knowing him inside and out as he seemed to know her, grew with each second he possessed her with his tongue until it consumed her.

Would she be able to live with that?

She shuddered and pain and pleasure darted up her spine. Tears stung her eyes and she squeezed them shut, unable to process the torrent of emotions rushing through her.

His teeth grazed her clit and she screamed. He sucked her fold deep into his mouth, then impaled her on his stiff tongue.

"Oh. Oh!" Bliss roared through her as she came, hard and fast.

His deep groan echoed through her as he lapped her up. Several minutes later, he pulled away after one last lingering kiss. "Slide down and take me, baby. I'm dying for you."

Trembling from head to toe, she eased her legs down and released her grip on the pole. Straddling his hips, she clutched his shoulders, very much aware of that focused gaze on her face. She kissed him, tasted her essence on his lips and lost even more of her mind. She was so lost in the kiss, she didn't realize she was no longer in control until he surged upward, hard and fast inside her.

"Ah!" Pleasure cannoned through her and she buried her face in his throat as he filled her, stretched her to breaking point and held himself deep inside her.

"Fuck. So incredible, baby. God." He surged up another unbelievable inch until pleasure caressed pain. Her fingernails dug into his flesh as she struggled to hang on.

From then on, the world ceased to make sense. Only pure bliss ruled. Despite being tied up, Zach fucked her like she was his captive, his thrusts relentless and deep to deliver the ultimate pleasure.

She closed her eyes as sensation rode her hard, tearing a sob from her throat as her orgasm gathered speed, rushed toward her with unstoppable force. "I can't...oh God, Zach."

His head jerked toward her, the one thing he couldn't achieve - propelling her gaze to his - making his voice rough. "Baby, look at me."

She buried her face deeper, and bit his neck where his pulse pounded. A primitive roar ripped through the room.

"Bethany!"

She bit him harder and felt him swell even larger inside her. God, was there no end to this man's pleasure stream? She was thankful that he was so hot for her, that everything they did seemed to turn him on harder.

She arched her back so his thrusts hit her at a different angle. It must have done something incredible to him too because he groaned, long and deep.

"Christ, you're shredding me. I can't hold on much longer, baby. Are you close?" he grated out roughly.

"Yes! Please...I...can't bear it."

"Yes, you can!" He slid lower down the pole, so she was more seated on him, so he could drive even deeper.

She began to spasm around him.

"Tell me you love me, Bethany," he demanded, his voice ragged and raw.

Drowning with polarizing sensations of pain and pleasure,

heartache and joy, she desperately shook her head. Feeling him about to punish her for her denial, she ground her hips into his rock hard cock.

She screamed and came in shameless abandon.

His dark roar of pleasure followed a minute later, triggering a longer climax for her. He panted, his teeth bared against her cheek as she milked him dry.

With shaky hands, she reached behind him and untied his hands.

Strong arms banded around her immediately, holding her so tight she couldn't breathe.

"You will tell me."

"Yes, I will. When the time is right."

But would she ever hear it back?

Nineteen

HE TOOK HER out to dinner at an Indian restaurant near the Flatiron District after giving in to her pleas for a change of clothes. After their sweaty sex escapade, she'd also needed a shower.

After slipping into a simple cream, floaty summer dress that left her shoulders and bare, she'd hurriedly caught her hair up in a loose bun and added long silver dangly earrings that brushed against her neck when she moved. Matching silver looped chains and three-inch wedges completed the look and she'd seen Zach's very masculine appreciation when she'd returned to the car after her mad dash to get ready.

Now he fed her fragrant rice with his fingers and didn't care that he was making a mess.

The journey back from Newark had been as quiet as the journey but this time, Zach's profile held a concentration that indicated he was weighing up serious issues. She'd wanted to ask if those issues involved them, but she'd been too raw from the charged experience to risk the choppy waters of Zach's unreasonable demands.

Zachary Savage was used to getting what he wanted. And he'd decided he wanted her love, even after admitting he didn't deserve it.

She shook her head to clear the jumbled thoughts. Tearing off a piece of peshwari nan, she dipped it in spicy sauce and held it out to him. He opened it his mouth and took the offering, then nipped her fingers with his teeth.

His eyes sparkled with mirth and her heart turned over. Of the many facets of Zach, his playful side rarely shone through but when it did, she was overwhelmed all over again but how much her heart yearned for him.

They ploughed through several courses, their appetites voracious. Easy banter accompanied the beer and good food and his husky, deep laugh drew more than a few glanced throughout dinner.

After the waiter cleared away the warm water, soap and hand towels he'd indulgently brought for them to clean up, Zach took another swig of his beer and settled the tab.

"You're coming back to the Penthouse with me." It wasn't a question and he didn't bother framing it as such.

"Zach"

He shook his head. "I don't want to spend another night without you." A trace of tension returned.

She sighed and twisted her napkin in her fingers. "Zach, don't take this the wrong way but you wear me out."

One corner of his mouth lifted. "And you love it."

"Yes, I do," there was no point denying it. "But I really want to do a good job on the IL project. To do that I need to pay some solid attention to what I'm doing. I can't do that with you around."

"I distract you," he said slowly after he drained the last of his beer and set the bottle down.

She snorted. "Is that a serious question?"

He frowned and looked genuinely hurt. Well. Go figure.

"You distract me too but you don't see me asking for time off. Come back with me. I'll set you up in the library and I promise I'll keep my inappropriate thoughts and hands to myself. I'm sure you can do the same."

"I don't have inappropriate thoughts," she lied brazenly.

"You don't need to. Your whole fucking tight body is an inappropriate thought."

"Zach!"

His grin was wide and unashamed, the tension gone. She had

no doubt it would return. And soon. For one thing, she couldn't avoid his heated demands to look at him when they fucked for much longer. She'd learned very early on what it meant to him to look into her eyes when he possessed her. She'd got away with it twice. She was almost certain there wouldn't be a third time.

For another thing, the time was creeping up for her next question. And she had a suspicious feeling he wouldn't like the question burning at the back of her mind.

In the car, he pulled her close and slung an arm over her shoulders. She leaned in and breathed him in. He smelled of heat, and sandalwood and pure, unadulterated male. She glanced up at him and saw the teeth marks she'd left on his neck earlier. Then she glanced down and saw the faint bruising on his wrists.

"Admiring your handiwork, Peaches?" he teased.

Mortification drenched her. She kissed his neck, and traced her fingers over his wrist. "I…does it hurt?"

"For what I got in return, I'd take this and worse."

"That would probably please me if I had a pain fetish. But I don't. So I'm sorry."

He tilted her face to his, serious eyes studying her. "I don't want you to apologise for anything we do in bed, or out of it. We're finding our way and I don't care how we do it. As long as we do it together. Understand?" He waited until she nodded, then placed a hard kiss on her lips and tucked her head under his chin.

They remained silent for a few minutes. She closed her eyes and just listened to his steady heartbeat.

Then she sighed. "I still want to go back to my place, Zach."

He stiffened. "Christ, Bethany. Do I need to fuck a *yes* out of you?" he growled.

She opened her eyes and met his intensely irritated gaze. "You could just try *saying* yes?" she ventured, trying to appeal to his rapidly diminishing reasonable side. "It would make me happy," she added.

His eyes darkened and he sucked in a long, harsh breath. "I ought to take serious issue with you even suggesting you would happy to be without me for one night."

"But?"

"I'll try to be accommodating."

"Thank you. I also need the final guest list. Have the investigative reports come back yet?"

"The first one, yes."

She frowned. "How many did you order?"

"Normally? Two. This time…a few more."

She knew why. "Because of me."

"I'm not taking risks with you, baby."

"I can take care of myself, Zach."

"Sure you can. But I prefer to lend an active hand."

She wasn't going to win. So she gave up. "You'll let me have the list as soon as it's ready?"

"If it'll help you finish your work quicker and get back into my bed, yes, dammit. You'll have it in the next couple of hours."

Smiling, she started to lean up to kiss the corner of his mouth. He turned and took over and didn't stop until her mouth burned with the power of his kiss.

He pressed the intercom and informed Philip of the change of plan, then instructed him to take the most traffic-heavy route.

Bethany rolled her eyes. "Is that your idea of being accommodating?"

He shrugged unapologetically. "The best route takes thirty-five minutes. This way gives us a full hour before we get to your place. Not nearly enough but it'll have to do." He released his seatbelt, pulled her into his lap and started lowering her thin straps.

Then he proceeded to work an all-night-long's worth of sex into a single hour.

≈

The moment she closed her door after her, Bethany wondered whether she'd made the right choice.

She missed Zach like crazy and it'd only been ten minutes. Her phone buzzing with Sheena requesting a Skype call check in an hour propelled her out of her sorry state and into a semblance of work mode.

Ten minutes after she fired up her laptop, her phone buzzed with a FaceTime request from Zach. Biting her lip, she decided to ignore it. She was hopelessly addicted to the man. She knew it. But she needed a tiny bit of independence from him or she would become hopelessly lost in him. Turning her phone to silent, she worked steadily for the next hour and a half.

By the time she logged on with Sheena she had enough to report on not to feel total shame that she'd spent half the day fucking Zach Savage instead of working.

"Where are we on the guests shortlist?" Sheena asked after perusing the report Bethany had emailed her.

"Z...Mr Savage is sending it shortly."

Sheena nodded. "Excellent. I see he's chosen Rome, Kenya and/or Thailand. You're using our people to arrange entertainment on the ground?"

"Yes. But I'm also sourcing a few contingent ones in case we need a back up plan."

"Good thinking. Let me have the guest list as soon as you receive it."

Vague wondering why Sheena had requested a Skype call if this was all she wanted to talk about, Bethany nodded and prepared to sign off.

Her phone vibrated again, and another tingle fluttered through her. Zach had been calling almost incessantly in the last half hour. Irritation rose to mingle with the tingling. Despite missing him like crazy, she would need to have a serious conversation with him about holding up his end of a bargain to give her a little space.

"...so nothing can go wrong—am I boring you, Bethany?" Sheena interrupted sharply.

Bethany refocused and noticed Sheena's flushed face for the first time. She also toyed with the stem of a half-glass of red wine, which she picked up and swigged from as she waited for Bethany to answer her.

"Umm…no. Of course not. I'm giving this commission my full attention."

"Yeah, I'm sure you are," Sheena murmured. The snark in her tone was unmistakeable but there was also a wariness in her eyes that made Bethany frown.

"Is there something going on I should know about?" Bethany asked.

Sheena smirked. "You tell me." She took another sip and slid a hand through her strawberry blonde hair, tousling it into comical disarray. "You're the one who's landed the big fish. Trust me, I'm all for it if it brings Neon other fat commissions. You better not think about jumping ship anytime soon." The mild threat was delivered after another gulp of her wine.

Bethany frowned. "What are you talking about?" Trepidation started beating an erratic tattoo in her chest.

"Your *picture*, dear. It's doing the rounds on social media."

"*My picture?*" she screeched.

Sheena nodded. "I don't blame you, really. Zach Savage is the fucking hottest thing since…God, since the history of the world. All that animalistic vibes he throws around." She leaned forward and Bethany could almost smell the wine on her breath. "I have to know. Is he a beast in the sack?"

Bethany froze, her body going from warm to icy within a millisecond. "*Excuse me?*" It couldn't be…Zach had assured her the windows on the plane where they'd made love were mirrored. And surely, she hadn't been too far-gone to notice a camera flash, had she? Yes, she had.

Her body grew icier.

Sheena shrugged a bony shoulder. "I get it now why he demanded that we have you on the project. And like I said, I really don't mind. I'd do it too in your shoes. In less than a heartbeat." She drank some more, gave a little giggle, then notice Bethany's cold silence. "Hey, if you don't want to share, that's fine. But I you really can't blame a girl for trying."

Bethany's phone buzzed again.

Zach.

There was a photo floating around on the Internet. A photo to do with them.

She now understood why he was calling. Her fingers itched to grab her phone but she stopped herself and returned Sheena's blatant stare.

Ideally, she didn't want to lose her job before she'd taken her next Indigo Lounge trip. Most likely, Zach would still take her with him if she were fired. But still she bit her tongue against the anger roiling through her.

She realised she didn't mind being fired if it meant putting this bitch in her place. "Are we done here, Sheena? Because I don't believe requesting inappropriate details about my sex life is part of my job description," she enquired frostily.

For the first time since she started working at Neon, Bethany witnessed a touch of embarrassment flicker over her boss's face. Followed closed by a dart of envy.

"Sure…we're done." She seemed to realise what had just happened, and the fact that their exchange had been recorded. "Umm…Bethany," she said, leaning forward.

"See you at work tomorrow, Sheena." She ended the call and realised she was trembling from head to toe.

She quickly accessed her search engine and exhaled when the mysterious picture popped up.

Except it wasn't mysterious anymore. It was very current; as in less than six hours old. And the article that went with it was accurate enough.

Her phone buzzed. She leaped for it.

"Zach, I know someone took our photo—"

"No, it's *not* Zach. But I guess that tells me everything I need to know. What the fuck, B?" Keely's voice held a world of hurt.

Twenty

BETHANY GRIPPED THE phone harder. She'd been putting off telling Keely about her renewed reconnection with Zach. Now it was too late.

"I meant to tell you. I really did."

"Right, you had your chance when I asked you what you were working on. Obviously you chose not to share that you were working on a commission for the Indigo Lounge and for none other than Zach Savage, the man you're *obviously* banging again."

Bethany cringed. "I wasn't…I didn't know how things would pan out. I still don't…I'm sorry."

"Fuck sorry. You think I would've interfered, is that it?"

Guilt assailed her when she silently admitted the truth to herself. "I didn't know what I was thinking myself but I wanted to make any decisions without…" she stopped and bit her lip.

"Without Pushy Keely's influence?"

"No. I like Pushy Keely. But I was scared Kick-Zach-In-The-Nuts Keely would hurt my man."

"Oh right, he's *your man* now, is he?" Keely's voice rose.

Bethany sighed. "We're trying to work through it. Like you suggested."

Keely remained silent for several seconds. Then she sniffed. "I fucking hate that you shut me out. I don't want to lose you, B."

"You won't."

"You say that but you're already keeping things from me. Next you'll be telling me you're flying off again with billionaire lover boy to some exotic paradise."

Bethany's heart flipped over with more guilt as her silence

damned her.

"Fuck, Bethany!"

"It's for work, Keely."

"Sure, you keep on believing that. Because of all the event planning outfits in New York Zach Savage could've picked, he just happened to pick the one where you worked," she drawled.

"Okay, maybe it's also to get away from things like this photo," she flicked her finger against her computer screen, but her gaze was riveted on the picture of her and Zach, taken at the exact moment before he'd kissed her on the forehead in the aircraft hangar.

At least it wasn't a picture taken on the inside of the plane. She cringed harder at the thought of that happening.

Nevertheless, this picture was equally as potent. The look on Zach's face...the look on hers.

"The way he's looking at you, B," Keely whispered raggedly, so perfectly in tune with Bethany's racing thoughts. "It scares me how much he wants you. Especially when you still don't know shit about his past."

Bethany shivered. She yearned to reassure her friend, to spill what Zach had told her this morning in his bathroom. They'd never kept secrets from each other in the past. But this was the kind of secret she couldn't tell. Even if it came to nothing, Keely was the type of friend who'd fight to the death for her, whether Bethany wanted her to or not. And if there were legal implications to what Zach would eventually reveal, then no way could she jeopardize his safety by betraying his trust.

"I'll be okay, Keely. He won't...he won't hurt me that way. I mean physically."

"How do you know? Did he say something?" she snapped.

"No, not exactly. I really can't talk about it." Bethany could feel Keely's hurt as if she stood in front of her. She closed her eyes and swallowed. "I'm sorry."

"Not as sorry as I am. I'll see you around, B." The line went dead.

Crap!

She blinked back the tears that welled and stared blindly at the picture that was currently trending on Twitter.

A New Prey In Savage's Lair?

The caption would've been ridiculous if it wasn't ridiculously accurate. There was no room for ambivalence in the picture whatsoever. Zach was staring at her as if he wanted to devour her. And she was staring back as if she yearned to be his next meal.

Another shiver ripped through her. God.

If the whole world could see how she felt about him, what hope did she have of denying him what he wanted from her?

When her phone went again, she forced herself to check the caller ID. Seeing who it was, she answered with shaking fingers.

"I really need to teach you a lesson in answering your phone immediately when I call." His voice held a hard, savage bite, tinged with a boatload of anxiety.

"I'm sorry…I was online with Sheena. Then Keely called…" her voice fractured.

"What's wrong?" he demanded sharply.

"She's mad at me."

"Because of me?"

"Because of us. She thinks she's losing me."

"You have two demanding alphas in your life. One has to win eventually, baby." His tone spelled out clearly that he intended to be the victor. And damned if she didn't want it to be him.

"I want you both."

"Then we'll find a way to make it work." He spoke with such conviction that it immediately set her anxiety at ease.

"Thank you."

"You're welcome. Did you see the photo?" he asked warily.

"Yes," she answered simply. "It's…"

"Revealing? Yes. It is."

"Do you know who took it?"

"Yes," his voice turned deadly sharp, "and that problem's been taken care of."

Her breath shuddered out. "Is there another problem?" She didn't know if she could bear it if this picture became yet another thing between them.

"I'm working on it. We'll talk about it when I get there."

Surprise arrowed through her. "You're on your way here?"

His silence told her how he felt about her question.

"Sorry, I just didn't think…"

"No you didn't. I'll be there in five minutes. You know what to do." He hung up.

She got up from her tiny desk and went to the door to buzz down to the front desk. "Vlad, I have a friend coming over."

"Yes, Miss Green. He's already here. He's on his way up."

When Zach exited the elevator a minute later, his face was set in grim lines. She realized he'd tried to moderate his tone on the phone. Seeing him, watching the tension twisting through his frame and the way he moved, she swallowed.

"Is it that bad?" She asked after he set her free following a searing kiss.

He shut the front door and followed her into the living room. "It could be," he clipped out. He stared at her for a long moment, then he began to pace the room.

"Don't shut me out. You're worried. Tell me why," she said.

He stopped and jerked a hand through his hair. "I didn't want certain parties finding out about us. Just yet."

She winced inwardly at the dart of pain that lanced beneath her breastbone.

"Certain parties."

"Farrah's family," he replied. "I don't care that they know about you, but I don't want to give them any more ammunition to stall them providing their consent."

Her pain eased. "Oh. I see."

His gaze sharpened. "What are you thinking? Or should I ask what *were* you thinking a moment ago?"

"I thought…you were…ashamed for them to know about me."

He inhaled deep and long. "Ashamed. Jesus, on top of

everything else going on, do I have to take the time to show you again how much you mean to me? How incredibly fucking blessed I feel to have you in my life?"

Her heart did that crazy gooey shit again. "I…No," she said hurriedly. "I'm good."

He put his hands on his hips and glared at her. "You better be. A reminder fuck would take too long."

She couldn't stop her smirk. "You have somewhere else to be?"

"No, but I don't want to be accused of *distracting* you. I sent you the final list by the way," he threw at her, then he resumed pacing.

She wanted to tell him she'd finished her work for the evening, but she had a feeling sex would very quickly climb back up the menu if she confessed that. And more than anything, she wanted to establish a connection with him some other way.

"So what are you going to do about the photo?"

"My attorney is dealing with it. I can't have direct contact with her family."

Her eyebrows rose. "They filed a restraining order against you?"

He reefed his fingers through his hair. "No. We just agreed that it would be better that way."

"God, just what the hell happened?" When he stopped pacing, she raised her hands. "I know you can't talk about the actual event but tell me something…anything! How did you and Farrah meet?" she asked in a rush before he could tell her something inane that told her nothing.

He stared off into the distance and swallowed.

Her breath caught in terror in her throat, she walked slowly toward him. "Would you like a drink?"

Turbulent grey eyes refocused, stared down at her for an age and finally nodded. She went into the kitchen, got a couple of glasses and a corkscrew, and grabbed a bottle of red from her alcove. He was seated when she returned, albeit leaning forward with elbows on knees and thrumming with tension.

He took the bottle from her, and patted the seat next to him.

When she sat, he worked the foil loose and held out his hand for the corkscrew. He poured and handed her a glass before pouring his own.

Setting back, he pulled her into his side, his fingers sliding into her hair to gently caress her scalp. For several minutes he stayed like that. And although outwardly he may have looked calm and assured, she heard the erratic beating of his heart.

Remembering Marrakech when she'd been sick with jealousy that he was dreaming of another woman, she fought to hide the acid bite of envy that a woman could create such a powerful reaction within him.

The feeling grew and grew until she wanted to block her ears when he finally started to speak.

"We met in grad school. You know she's Moroccan. She grew up there. Her parents were very wealthy, very influential. She was…very beautiful."

She winced and his fingers convulsed in her hair. He pulled her head back and stared down at her in a narrowed-eyed way that questioned whether she was okay.

When she nodded quickly, he exhaled and continued.

"I said that because her parents were very strict and she told me it was partly because of her looks. They were right, I guess. She turned heads whenever she went." He stopped and drank.

"Grad school was the first time she knew any real independence. She was completely innocent and beyond naïve. Hell, she could barely meet my eyes when we first met."

Her heart squeezed tight. "Is that why you liked her, because she was submissive?"

His bitter laughter ricocheted around the room. "Trust me, she wasn't submissive for very long. Once the culture shock wore off, she fully embraced her inner wild child, right along with the wild partying. Even changed her PhD to reflect her new outlook on life."

She frowned. "What was she studying?"

His mouth twisted. "I don't remember what her initial course was - a doctorate of some sort - but she changed it to sexual psychology."

"Great. She started studying sex. Right after she met a sex god." The bitter acid in her gut rose higher.

"Bethany." His voice was a low warning.

She took a sip of wine and tried to keep from choking on her feelings.

He slid a hand around her nape and began massaging her knotted muscles. "Are you going to be okay with this?" he demanded.

Hell no. "Yes," she muttered.

His eyes told her he wasn't sure about her answer but his hard kiss heated her from the inside, sparking an immediate yearning that had her clutching him when he pulled away.

"Let's get this over with. Then you can have your way with me. Yes?"

The heat cooled. "Did it occur to you that I may not want to after you tell me about how you once felt about another woman?"

"You'll want to."

She rolled her eyes at his sheer arrogance but decided not to challenge him. Challenging Zach always got her in trouble. That kind that usually included getting fucked to within an inch of her life. "So she embraced her inner wild child. Then what?"

He closed his eyes and his chest expanded on a ragged inhale. "Then she found drugs."

Her breath caught.

"It was soft stuff at first. I didn't think anything of it because I…I was using too." His hand tightened on her nape and his eyes searched hers frantically. Understanding. He wanted understanding.

Her hand slid around his waist. When she nodded, he exhaled.

"Even after she started the hard core stuff, I never thought twice about it. I was already making serious money from my business ventures. I was young, a bit of an arrogant dick and independently wealthy enough to have a fucking posse. They kept me supplied with enough drugs to keep everyone happy but right from the start, it was very much recreational for me. I could stop whenever I wanted so I foolishly believed she could too."

"But she couldn't?"

He shook his head. "Her parents began to get suspicious when she stopped calling and refused to return home between semesters. When they threatened to cut her off and sent her brother after her - he's everything you can possibly imagine: a tyrannical, asshole of an older brother - she panicked and for a while she stopped using. I checked her into rehab to get her clean properly. She even went home for a couple of weeks. But within a week of returning for our last semester, she was using again." He closed his eyes and leaned his head against the sofa. "I tried to get her clean again."

"Because you felt responsible."

Stormy grey eyes met her, and her heart squeezed at the raging torment in the bottomless depths.

"I *was* responsible. I introduced her to that world, to that life. Hell, I rolled up and put her first joint in her hand!"

Twenty-One

A SHUDDER OF revulsion scoured his insides and Zach felt her hand tighten around his waist. When the shaking didn't stop, he drained his wine and willed his unraveling control back into his body.

"Zach, there was no possible way you could know that things would end up that way. Thousands of people experiment one way or the other when they're young. Not everyone turns into a raging addict."

He winced and saw contrition cloud her eyes.

"Sorry, I didn't mean it that harshly."

He shook his head. Only Bethany would state the blatant truth then apologise for the delivery. "Did you?"

"Did I what?"

"Did you experiment?"

Her gaze slid away and she shook her head. When he winced again, those blue eyes slammed back into his. "Not because I was some goody two shoes. The only reason I didn't try anything was because one whiff gave me a violent headache." She gave a mocking laugh and shrugged. "My body was warning me not to mess with it. And I was too chicken to disobey it."

"You weren't chicken. You were being sensible." He gazed down into her stunning face, amazed all over again by how incredibly gorgeous she was, inside and out. How incredibly lucky he was to be sitting here with her. To shamelessly let her sooth away the sharp knife of memory that threatened to slash his insides to shreds.

"What's going on in that head of yours, Zach?" she asked softly.

He slid his hand from her nape to her jaw and down to her plump lips. "I'm thinking If only I'd met you then, instead of…" he stopped himself for the futile wish even as another jab kicked his heart into his gut again.

What sort of bastard was he, wishing a woman whose life he'd messed up and ended out of existence? "God, you must think I'm a fucking A-hole by now."

She gave a soft gasp. "No. We all wish things to be different in hindsight. I wish I'd fought harder when I was being held under water and I thought I was about to die. I wish I'd told my parents what a fucked up individual he really was. I wish I'd confronted Chris about my suspicions that he was cheating long before he pulled the rug from underneath me. It's natural to want a different outcome after the fact. The best we can do is to make life the way we want it right now."

"You're fucking incredible, you know that?"

"I know."

A laugh jerked out of his constricted chest. She leaned forward and offered her mouth, and greedy bastard that he was, he took it, groaning at the goodness and pleasure that just kissing her brought him. He cursed under his breath when she started to pull away before he'd had nearly enough.

"Tell me the rest."

Tension whipped up a storm inside him. "The cycle continued. She would get clean for a while, then relapse. The month before grad school ended, I'd almost gotten the first Indigo Lounge blueprint finished. She was excited by the concept, even helped with some great ideas about the whole thing."

He felt Bethany begin to tense beneath his touch and he silently cursed. He knew he would be climbing the walls by now if it was her telling him about an ex.

Sliding a hand under her thighs, he picked her up and repositioned her in his lap. He trapped her to him with a hand on her hip and felt her relax a little into him.

Breathing easier, he forced himself to continue. "A couple of weeks before the maiden Indigo Lounge flight, her family started pressuring her to return home."

"She didn't want to return, of course," Bethany stated.

He glanced at her. There was nothing but simple understanding in her eyes as if she knew exactly what had motivated Farrah. "She was in love with you."

Pain seared his chest and burned from the inside out as he recalled just how messed up things had been back then. "I guess you could call it that."

Bethany's gaze dropped and her breath shuddered out. His hand tightened on her hip, desperate to hang onto the connection he felt when he looked into her eyes. "Baby?"

"It's okay," she muttered. Her eyes lashes fluttered before she glanced back at him. "I'm okay. So you felt the same way about her, I guess?"

"I liked her. I enjoyed her company…when she was sober."

Her beautiful mouth compressed. "Don't trivialise your feelings for my sake, Zach."

"I…fine, I was into her. She was smart and funny when she wasn't using. When she was using…it was a different story."

"But the sex was great. Right?" she whispered.

He held his tongue and forced himself to just breath.

She slowly stiffened and he felt her withdrawing from him. His fingers dug into her hip and he cursed.

"Fuck, Bethany. Don't you dare compare yourself to her. Because she would lose. Every time. But I told you I would never lie to you. I like sex. You know that. And yes, we were compatible in the sack." He released her hip and gripped her chin. When she raised her gaze, her eyes shimmered with pain. "But nothing comes close to what you do to me. No one has ever made me feel what you do, and no one else will. Believe that or I will be forced to prove it to you."

When her eyes raked his face and paused at his mouth, he forced himself not to abandon this insane confession and just rip their clothes off and make good on his threat.

"Tell me you believe me."

"I believe you."

Relief poured through him. Her body gradually relaxed against his, her soft curves settling into his harder ones. She still wore the sexy, floaty number she'd worn to dinner, and he gave in to the need to lift her hem and slid his hand between her warm thighs.

Her breath hitched beautifully and her eyelids fluttered again. "Zach…"

"It's okay. We're not straying off subject. Not yet anyway. But I get to exercise my right to touch you."

Her head settled on his shoulder and he breathed a little easier. "Okay."

A part of him wished she would fight him so he could abandon talking and let his body take over. Cowardly, he knew, but reliving what had happened six years ago had never been easy for him. He trailed his hand down and back up, struggling to find the right words.

"A week before the launch, her brother called, told her he was coming to get her. She freaked out. At first, I didn't really see the big deal. She was only going home for a while, just to show her parents she was okay. I even offered to go with her."

Bethany frowned. "What was the problem?"

"She flatly refused to go. I'd been keeping an eye on her and knew she wasn't using. So I knew she wasn't just being high and irrational. I called her brother and tried to get to the bottom of what was going on. Turned out her family had arranged for her to marry some guy she grew up with." Residual rage filled his vision for a moment before he blinked it away. "Remember how I told you what an unstoppable dick I was back then?"

Wide blue eyes held his, sympathy softening the vivid depths. "She was with you. It couldn't have been easy to hear she was promised to someone else."

His grip tightened and his chest filled with awe at her complete understanding. "It wasn't. My dickish behaviour really emerged then. I may have told her whole family to go fuck themselves. Even though a part of me knew she would be better off back in Marrakech where her access to drugs would be hugely minimised and she had a chance of getting clean once and for all, I still took the stubborn prick approach. She was mine and I wasn't letting her go."

She looked down and shut her eyes and he fought not to be swallowed by panic. "Bethany?"

"It's okay. I just need a minute," her voice was barely above a whisper.

His hand crept higher, brushed her between her legs and her eyes flew open.

"I can't stand it when I can't see your eyes, baby. When you look at me, even when you're seriously pissed at me, I feel I can cope." Unable to help himself, he pressed harder. His cock thickened when his fingers met her dampness. Her shudder echoed within him. When her hips twitched against his hand, he sighed.

"The IL trip was a five-stopper, starting from Vegas. The morning we were supposed to leave, Farrah's brother, Karim, landed at JFK and called to say he was on his way to Vegas to bring her home." He swallowed as icy shiver broke over him. "I'd never seen such naked fear. She went completely insane. I suspected she'd scored some drugs but I refused to believe she'd relapsed again. I tired to talk to her but she was completely irrational about the whole thing. I'm not sure whose idea it was but all of sudden the idea of getting married was on the table."

Bethany's mouth quivered and he knew he needed to finish this quickly. Hearing him describe his relationship with another woman couldn't be easy for her. Hell, he was in hell reliving it.

"We were in the right place. I had enough people on speed dial to make things happen. Plus, I was getting a chance to win against her asshole of a brother. We got married an hour before we went on the first IL flight."

"And then what happened?"

Regret and sorrow bit deep into his gut, threatened to claw him inside out. He buried his face in her hair and shut his eyes. "Then Armageddon took a left turn into hell."

Twenty-Two

BETHANY STARED UP into Zach's face and watched the ragged anguish eating him alive. His eyes were still tightly shut but his hand was pressing deeper between her thighs as if he was grounding himself.

Reaching up, she touched his cheek and he blindly turned his face into her hand. His eyes remained closed but a film of tears sparkled on his lashes. His jaw was rigid with the pain he was holding in and her heart tore wide open for him.

She was beginning to have an idea of what had gone on with Zach and Farrah but even the insane jealousy ripping through her couldn't stem the sympathy she felt for what he'd gone through…was continuing to go through.

The shimmer of tears grew and his nostrils flared as he tried to control himself. "Oh God, Zach."

A huge shudder raked his frame. "I can't tell you anymore, baby. I'm sorry," he rasped, his voice thick with pent-up emotion.

"I know." Sitting up, she kissed his hard cheek, then nuzzled his shadowed jaw. I know." She scrambled to think of something else to talk about. Anything to take his mind off the past and the turmoil churning in the air. But every other subject she could think of was trivial and inane.

She kissed the corner of his mouth and started to scramble off him. He held on tight.

"Let me up, Zach."

"No."

"If you don't let me up, I can't pack a bag to come home with you."

Intense, shimmering eyes met hers. He slowly inhaled. "Are you serious?"

She nodded. "If you want me to."

He snorted. "I should spank you for that statement."

"You're always looking for an excuse to spank me and yet you never have."

The shadows receded and that heat she was so familiar with slowly replaced them. "Is that a challenge, Peaches?"

She leaned closer and nipped his lower lip. "It's an indirect suggestion that I wouldn't mind experiencing the palm of your hand against my peaches."

His big body jerked. Beneath her, his cock grew into a rigid imprint against her butt cheek. That she'd successfully diverted his mind was blatantly obvious.

The hand between her legs slowly slid up and down. "You're getting wet, Bethany."

She gave a jerky nod. "It's a state of being that only needs you to be close."

His eyes darkened. "Shit, I wish we had time for a Christ-you-undo-me fuck before you pack."

Her insides sizzled with anticipation. "What's the hurry?"

"My attorney is calling me back in an hour. I want to be in a position to fuck you straight after so we need to move quickly. I can take the call here but I think a visit to your toy room is in order."

The sizzling escalated to a full-blown electrical current running through her.

He stood up with her in his arms. Taking her lips with his, he strolled to her bedroom and let her slide down his body.

Remembering what had happened the last time they were in here, Bethany glanced warily at him.

A hard smile lifted one corner of his mouth. "I'm still devising ways to pay you back for your birthday treat, Peaches. But nothing is going happen here right now. You're safe so get packing."

Shivering, she moved away and grabbed her weekender.

Zach lounged against the door and watched her with an unwavering focus that sent tingles up and down her spine.

When she had everything she needed for another workday and the weekend, he held out his hand for her bag. "Ready?"

She nodded. "I just need to grab my laptop and papers then I'm good to go."

In the living room, he shrugged into his leather jacket and waited till she gathered her stuff.

The elevator ride down barely registered because Zach refused to take his eyes off her and she was drowning in him.

Vlad's gaze flicked between them as they passed, the mild concern in his eyes telling her he'd probably seen the photo too.

"Do I need to be worried about him?" Zach arched his brow at her as he walked her outside and held the back door to his car open for her.

"He likes to keep a brotherly eye on me, is all."

"As long as that's all it is," he replied.

The partition to the front was open and she smiled at Philip. He nodded and the car moved into traffic.

"You can't growl at every man who looks at me, Zach."

"You underestimate my motivation to keep you mine," he snapped as he pressed the button to send up the partition.

She rolled her eyes. "And I thought we were getting on so well," she sighed.

He laughed, his teeth flashing in the semi-darkness. "We are, Peaches. As long as you get where I'm coming from where you're concerned, we're completely okay."

She shrugged. "I guess I need to practice my growl where you're concerned too."

"Your helpless purring when I'm deep inside you is all I need."

Her deep blush brought another laugh and her heart lifted to see the anguish greatly diminished. He would never get over the circumstances leading to Farrah's death, and she now understood the bleakness she saw in his eyes sometimes. But seeing him smile again made her heart lift with joy. Which was why she didn't mind that he teased her with hot words and heated glances all the way to his place. She didn't even mind when she stumbled on the way to his private elevator when he described in precise detail how he intended to fuck her.

He installed her bag in his bedroom and mixed her a drink after he came downstairs. After delivering another sizzling kiss, he reluctantly pulled away.

"You have free run of the place. If you need anything, use the buzzer on the wall and Philip will help you. I'll come and find you when I'm done."

She nodded and watched him walk way.

Tall, impossibly gorgeous and totally devastating to her senses, she continued to be stunned by how much more depth there was to Zach. And she admitted she was terrified by what lay ahead of them.

With a past plagued with drugs and a highly turbulent relationship, she couldn't help but dream up scenarios that would be equally devastating of how Farrah had died.

She wondered through the condo, trying not to let her imagination run away with her. She let herself remember the guy who'd had tears in his eyes as he talked about ruining a young girl's life. Whatever came after that, Zach had proved once and for all that he was human, and compassionate; that he felt guilt and regret.

That had to be enough, surely? She shivered and realized she'd wandered into the swimming pool room.

Water shimmered under strategically placed lights, casting moving shadows along the walls.

The water was deep. Much deeper than anything she'd ventured near for the past decade. She risked getting closer to the edge of the water, slowly. Then breathed out when her freak-o-meter didn't start screeching out of control. She walked round the pool and back to where shallow steps led into deeper water.

Gathering the skirt of her dress in one hand, she slowly lowered herself onto the first step and sat on the edge of the pool.

Swimming and water were part of Zach's private life. She was shameless enough to wish to be a part of that life. Flexing her toes in the cool water, she sipped the tequila-based cocktail Zach had fixed for her.

She was finishing her drink twenty minutes later when he walked in.

Sharp eyes darted from her immersed feet to her face and a smile broke out on his face.

She returned the smile, a spurt of pride welling up in her chest.

"Hey Peaches," he said as he came to crouch behind her. His hand slid round her nape and up into her hair.

"Hey," she responded, tilting her head up to watch his face. His incredibly handsome profile knocked the breath from her lungs.

"Think I'll be able to convince you into the water anytime soon?"

She swallowed before she could speak. "I'm willing to give it my very best shot."

His smile widened. "That's my girl."

He rose, went to the shelves holding the towels and brought one back with him. After drying her feet, he picked up her shoes and tugged her after him.

"You told me your high school crush was swimming. So you were a swim jockey?"

He looked back at her and nodded. She noted his smile was a little strained. "Swimming was my whole life back then. I competed all the way to nationals."

"Why was it your whole life?" she asked, half holding her breath in case he shut her down.

But he merely tugged her to his side and hurried along the hallway toward his bedroom. "Because it was my means of escape from home and from my mother."

Her breath caught. He kissed her mouth and pushed her into the bedroom.

"Don't look so surprised, Bethany. I'm a fast learner. And I'm learning very quickly that opening up a little with you gains me serious brownie points. You can ask me another question later and I'll answer. But right now I need to pay you back for my ten days of suffering. After that I'll see about building up more brownie points."

"But...we've made up since then!"

He laughed, a pure predatory sound that jerked her heart to her belly and flipped it back up.

He hooked his fingers under her dress straps and started lowering them. Her strapless bra quickly joined the heap at her feet.

The moment he spotted her indigo thong, the ruthless anticipatory gleam in his eyes that had been sparked since they left her place grew. Every time he turned those grey eyes on her, a fresh tingle of hot anticipation slammed her sideways.

"You think that was making up? You tying me up and having your way with me?" He kicked his shoes away and reefed his shirt over his head. His chiseled chest rippled as he moved and her mouth watered shamelessly.

"My poor, poor Peaches. I haven't even been anywhere near your ass throughout this so-called making up period. So tell me, you think I'm anywhere near appeased?"

She swallowed. "No. I'm thinking this is where you fuck me until I break in half?"

He laughed again. "Oh baby, I love the way you blush when you say that. But yeah, I'm fresh out of mercy tonight."

He picked her up and threw her over his shoulder. His rough stubble grazed one ass cheek as he strode purposefully for the toy room.

Even hanging upside down she guessed which gadget Zach was heading for. When he stopped beside the rocking horse, she whimpered.

"Is that a moan of anticipation I hear?" he mocked.

"No, it's a put me down before I pass out groan."

The hard slap of his hand against her ass was unexpected and stung hard enough to make her eyes water.

"Zach!"

The next thing she felt was his fingers digging beneath her thong before the sound of ripping satin tore through the air. Before she could protest, her twin globe received an equally sharp smack.

Three more smacks per cheek followed that left her gasping and extremely turned on.

"Are you ready to behave, Peaches?"

She bit her lip and nearly answered in the negative. But the need to have him inside her trumped any other desire ripping through her. "Yes," she answered hoarsely.

"Then you think you can dig out your nails from my ass so I can put you down?"

Twenty-Three

SHE STARED DOWN and realized her fingers were gripping his hard ass cheeks through his jeans. Face flaming, she released him slowly, letting her fingers linger over his tight glutes.

He set her down, and smoothed back her hair, his eyes filled with humor and hunger. Her vision swam with the headiness of being close to Zach and knowing she could soon have him again.

Eyes on her face, he slowly cupped her breasts and played with her nipples. Then he lowered his head and sucked one tight bud into his mouth.

Head falling back, she grabbed his arms to keep from buckling. He suckled and teased until she groaned from the pleasure rocketing through her. When he was satisfied he had her on the knife-edge of delirium, he pulled back.

"You ready for me to show you how the horse works?"

She gave a jerky nod. He turned her to face the smooth, faceless gadget.

It was chest high and made of expensive, highly polished wood set on an inch-thick black granite platform. The horse's neck was wider than normal, she guessed because it could offer the rider a chance to ride backward while lying against its neck.

The saddle was equally as wide with twin curved seats. With one hand bracing her stomach, Zach leaned forward and slid his hand underneath the front saddle.

A smooth whine followed a click and a small crack opened in the saddle. The finger-like gadget that rose brought another blush to her cheek.

"Touch it," Zach crooned in her ear.

Lifting her hand, she brushed her finger against the pale finger and felt its vibration. He pressed another button and two more openings three inches long appeared on either side of the finger. Soft rubber tubes rotated outwards in a slow rhythm.

"Those two are called pussy-spreaders," he whispered in her ear. "They hold you nice and open while the finger goes to work on your clit. Normally, I'd object to anything touching you, but I have a feeling I'll have my hands full behind you."

Without giving her warning, he picked her up and placed her on the back saddle. He waited until she had a leg on either side and was grasping the saddle before he let go.

Eyes fixed firmly on her, he unbuttoned his jeans and kicked them off.

Naked and rampantly aroused, he was so breath-taking, she felt dizzy just looking at him. He caught her staring and smiled. One hand grasped his thick cock and he lazily stroked himself. With the other, he smoothed her hair over her shoulders so the long chocolate-colored strands drifted down her back.

"You look so fucking gorgeous up there, Peaches," he muttered gruffly. He stroked himself again and a drop of pre-cum glistened at his wide head.

She didn't realize she was licking her lips until he gave a hard groan. "As much as I want that mouth on me, I want inside you more. Slip your feet into the stirrups and slide into the front saddle. Then slowly lower yourself down for me," he instructed.

Bracing her hands on the wide saddle, she did as he asked. Wild sensation shot through her body as the gadgets went to work. The spreaders parted her wet folds and kept her parted as the fat finger vibrated against her sensitive clit. "Oh…oh, God!"

Zach's face darkened as need and rough envy tightened his features. "Having fun without me, baby?"

She shook her head quickly. "It just feels…different." Nothing would ever beat the touch of Zach's hands and mouth on her but the gadget had been created for a reason and that reason was making her core scream with even more hunger for Zach. "I want you."

His nostrils flared wide. "You'll have me. Cross your hands behind you, baby."

Breath fracturing out of her lungs, she complied. Releasing his cock, he circled her waist with his hands, pressed her down harder onto the gadget as he flicked the tip of his tongue against her nipples.

The twin sensation at her breast and between her legs ripped sharp cries from her lips. Wet heat oozed between her legs and her whole body trembled as pleasure slammed into her.

After a full minute of the studied assault, he trailed his mouth up to her neck and gently nipped on her earlobe. "Did you like that?"

"Yes," she gasped shamelessly.

"Good." He placed one foot into his stirrup and swung himself into his saddle.

His strong thighs bracketed hers and heat from his body immediately engulfed her. One hand slid around her waist and his thick cock brushed against the crease in her ass.

"Perfect," he crooned, anticipation thickening his voice even further. Somewhere behind her, she heard another electric whine and the horse tilted forward slightly, exposing her more from behind. Zach caressed her ass, squeezing her smarting rump before parting her from behind. She turned and watched his face as he stared down at her ass.

His tongue rested against his bottom lip and his eyes, when they reconnected with her, raged with lust. "Are you holding on, Peaches? This *will* get rough."

She gripped the saddle in front of her and tried to breathe.

Hard hands gripped her waist and tilted her even further forward. Her clit pressed harder into the vibrating finger and she felt the head of his cock nudge her entrance

"God, baby, you have no idea how fucking incredible you look right now."

"Fuck me, Zach. Please." She felt as if she'd been waiting for an eternity for this. As if the other times these past two days had meant nothing because she'd been in charge and not him.

She'd never believed herself submissive, but feeling his total power over her body, obeying his every instruction, sent her excitement shooting up another few hundred notches.

His fingers slid along her crack, fingered her hole before plunging a finger inside her. She squeezed around him and his breath hitched.

"Christ, you're so ready for me, aren't you?"

"Please…" She angled her ass closer, desperate for him to take her.

After several long seconds of lazily finger-fucking her, he withdrew. She bit her lip and waited.

The first thrust lifted her off her seat. Zach buried himself deep, not taking the time to let her accommodate him. She screamed as ecstasy ripped through her core. He filled her so completely her vision blurred.

"Do you feel me, baby? Do you feel how hard I am for you? This is what you've done to me. Are you pleased with yourself?"

"Y…yes," she gasped.

"Good. Because I fucking adore you for it. I live for this, Bethany. To be with you like this." He lifted her and plunged her back down on his rigid length. Another grunt ripped from his throat. "Every day. Every night. This!"

Stupid tears rose in her eyes, crashing against the pleasure, the pain and the fear of what the future held for them. "Oh, Zach," her voice broke as emotions shook her body.

She wanted to blurt out the words slamming through her brain but she bit her tongue. She would only tell him when she knew it meant something to him, not because he demanded it. They both knew it was there. For now, she would hold it in her heart and express it another way that didn't need the words.

His grip tightened and he fucked her hard, relentlessly. As ever, sharply in tune with her body, he lifted her off the saddle every time she hovered on the brink of orgasm. Without the clitoral stimulus, her headlong rush into bliss was curbed. He slowed down long enough for her excitement to abate before he set the raw, blistering pace again.

He fucked her without mercy, until her hair grew damp and sweat poured down their bodies. At one point, he banded an arm around her waist and twined her hair in a tight hold, using it to control his thrusts.

When he started to lift her again, she shook her head, her need wild and uncontrollable. "Please, Zach, I want…God, I need to come."

"And I need to make you understand how I felt this past week, baby," he said hoarsely. "You keeping us apart may have seemed like the right thing to do for you, but it shredded me. So I'm taking this. *Because I fucking need it!*"

The pain in his voice sent a shaft of echoing anguish through her heart. Weirdly, and as much as she wanted the release that clawed through her, she understood his need to conquer her.

They dealt with their issues differently, she realized that. She was the retreat-and-lick-her wounds type and he was the stick-together-no-matter-what type. By withholding herself from him, she'd wounded him.

"Zach?" her voice was barely above an audible croak.

"Yes, baby?" he rasped back.

"I understand."

His breath punched out. He leaned into her and his stubbled jaw brushed hers. Banding both arms around her body, he brought her down hard onto his cock with a rough growl. "Thank you."

From then on, all she could do was hold on tight as he ravaged her. He eventually allowed her an orgasm; followed by several more in quick succession once he was satisfied her surrender was complete.

When she became too boneless to move somewhere in the early hours, he arranged himself on a leather recliner and settled her on top of him, her body on the opposite side to his. Spreading her thighs wide, he lazily licked her throbbing pussy.

The soothing movement made her melt even more. But beneath her cheek, his cock was beginning to grow again.

"No obligation at all, Peaches, but you can suck me off if you want," he said in between licks.

His superhuman recuperation skills had long ceased to amaze her. Feeling drowsy and languid, she grasped his cock and stroked him. Holding him was a treat she didn't think twice about foregoing.

"How about a hand job?"

She felt a smile against her inner thigh. "That works for me too."

She stroked him until the need to taste him grew too strong to deny. Then she ended up giving him exactly what he'd asked for. As he drew closer to losing control, his antics between her legs altered, grew more urgent. He sucked, licked, bit and ravaged her as if he hadn't already spent hours feasting on her.

Renewed hunger tore through her, sending a shuddering climax pounding through her seconds before he filled her mouth with his hot, gushing seed.

After they caught their breaths, he picked her up and headed for the bedroom. As they passed the horse, heat stormed into her cheeks.

"You know I'll never be able to ride a horse with a straight face ever again, don't you?"

His laughter was deep and supremely satisfied. "I hope you won't. From now on I want everything meaningful in your life to remind you of me."

The dark possessiveness in his voice sent a pulse of pleasure through her body. Zach may be irrational in his demands, but it turned her on that he made them anyway.

Walking her to the bathroom, he washed her from head to toe, then washed himself as she dried her body. They fell into bed and he pulled her close. Just as she was about to fall asleep, a thought brought her wide awake.

"What happened with your attorneys?"

Zach's jaw tightened and a hard light entered his eyes. "Karim didn't turn up for the conference call."

Her heart lurched. "You think it's because of the photo?"

His jaw clenched and released. "Yes."

"What are you going to do?"

"Find a different route to make him play ball." He tilted her face and looked into her eyes. "I promise you, Bethany, one way or the other, this will be resolved."

Twenty-Four

"Morning, Peaches. Time to wake up." Warm lips kissed along her shoulders and down her spine.

She groaned and buried her head deeper into the pillow. "Why? It's Saturday. And it's stupidly early," she protested.

"I want to hit the pool." He trailed his lips from one dimple above her ass to the other.

"And you want me to leave my warm bed and come and watch you swim. What's in it for me?"

He worked his way back up and nuzzled her earlobe. "A newly energized lover who may give you a poolside fuck if you come keep him company."

She groaned again. "You just spent half the night fucking me, Zach."

He paused at her neck. "Is that a complaint?"

She knew better by now, so she shook her head. "Throw in a coffee and I'll consider your offer." Even as she said it, the smell of freshly ground coffee hit her nostrils.

He pulled away. She turned over to see him smiling and holding out a steamy mug. "I know how grouchy you get without your caffeine fix."

Accepting the cup, she took a grateful sip. He got out of bed, naked and unashamedly magnificent. At the door, he paused and stared back at her. "You coming?"

She stared down at her naked state. "I need to throw on some clothes first."

His mouth compressed. "You don't need to but if you insist, you can grab a T-shirt from in there." He pointed to the dressing room and walked out.

She took another sip and set her cup down. Zach might have no compunction walking around butt naked, but she'd never felt comfortable walking around in the buff. She didn't think she ever would.

Walking into his dressing room was like walking into a shadow of Zach's lingering aura. His smell and potency permeated the room and she had to force herself to focus on finding a T-shirt instead of sniffing in the air like an eager puppy.

By the time she got to the pool, his huge body was cleaving rapidly through the water. Watching him swim, much like watching him do anything, was a heady experience. The man was a fucking god amongst other men, with a stamina that defied reason.

He'd set a timer by the poolside and it read fifteen laps done already.

She made her way slowly to the side of the pool where he'd found her last night, took two steps into the water and perched on the edge. The water lapped her legs as she finished her coffee.

Setting the cup aside, she leaned back on her hands and continued to watch Zach.

God, he really was magnificent. The timer hit sixty laps and he continued to swim, his energy not showing signs of depleting.

Recalling him expending that energy on her last night, her belly grew hot. Heat arrowed between her legs and she bit her lip on a soft moan. By the time he hit eighty-five, she was struggling to breathe.

Jesus, she was so pathetic. And helplessly addicted to everything about Zachary Savage - his inhuman strength, his determination, his body.

Her legs slowly slid open and water lapped against her heating sex. She rocked her hips and sensation built. Her eyes started to drift shut and her breath grew shallower as memories of last night rushed into her mind.

He'd feasted on her like a man starved for a century. And she'd loved every single minute of it.

Dimly, she heard the timer beep. She opened her eyes to see him stroking toward her, his wet hair slicked back and his magnificent eyes taking in her shameless stance.

"I see you started without me." His eyes lingered on her peaked nipples, visible through his T-shirt before drifting down.

"Watching you swim made me hot," she confessed breathlessly.

His eyes dropped to her open sex and his nostrils flared. "And wet."

His hands surged out of the water and traced her inner thighs. One thumb brushed her clit and a cry ripped from her lips.

"I can't get enough of you, Zach."

Grey eyes grew molten hot and ravenous. "I never want you to. I want you to remain as insatiable for me as I am for you."

Rising like an ancient sea god out of the water, he bore her back, parted her thighs wider and delivered the poolside fuck he'd promised.

*

The rest of the day passed at a steady pace of final preparations for the IL trip. Since she needed to do nothing on the actual flights, she concentrated on double and triple checking the arrangements for the ground events.

At about midday, Zach received another phone call from his attorneys. Her heart tripped over as his face hardened and he walked away from where he'd been sitting next to her in the living room.

She forced herself to concentrate on her work but when he remained locked in his study for two straight hours her anxiety started to escalate.

What if he never found a way round the non-disclosure agreement? Zach had shown her in Paris that his integrity meant a great deal to him. She had no doubt that there was far more than his integrity at stake here. But it was still a major issue. Knowing he would hate himself if he ever had to compromise that too in order to find a solution round his promise he'd made her heart ache.

When he emerged just mid-afternoon, his hair was in disarray from raking his hands through it and his jaw was set in a tight knot. Not that he looked anything less than jaw-dropping in his designer khaki shorts and white T-shirt.

She rose and went to him. He caught her in his arms and kissed her like she was his lifeline and he was near death.

When he reluctantly set her free, she looked into turbulent eyes. "On a scale of one to zombie apocalypse, how bad is it?"

One corner of his mouth twitched upward. "The fires have started and the bodies are stirring."

The rock of despair that had lodged beneath her breastbone that last night in Marrakech and never really gone away, dropped into her belly. She witnessed that same despair in his eyes and smoothed back his hair. "Do you want to get out of here for a while?"

"Unless we're using the chopper, it may not be wise. Philip tells me there are reporters downstairs."

Her despair grew. "Taking the chopper to go get an ice cream cone wasn't quite what I had in mind."

He smoothed a strand of her hair behind her ears. "Sorry, baby. I can arrange for the ice cream to come to you?"

She frowned and shook her head. "Not quite the same thing. But does that mean I won't be able to go home to pack for the IL trip?"

"I have a service that you can use. Or we can get you new things. Is there anything in particular you need from your place?"

She nodded. "My passport."

He grimaced.

"I suppose I can get Keely to go get it for me."

He thought for a moment and nodded. "It'll give you girls a chance to catch up too. I'll even make myself scarce if you want me to."

Her mood lightened. She gave him a quick kiss. "Thank you. I'll call her now."

He caught her hand as she started to walk away. "Does that win me brownie points?"

She smiled, feeling lighter than she had five minutes ago. "It does indeed, Savage. And you'll gain even more when you answer my question of the day later."

To his credit, he didn't flinch or look uneasy. The only sign of his distress was the slight darkening of his eyes and the shallow rise and fall of his chest as he nodded. He kissed her fingers and released her.

Her smile widened as she walked away to call Keely. Her man was doing better. He was willing to attempt change in order to keep her. There were a great many things out of her control. Maintaining an open channel of communication was one she would fight tooth and nail to hang on to.

Keely was in a much calmer mood when Bethany called.

"Dinner at your rich boyfriend's Upper East Side penthouse in exchange for a quick trip to your place? Why not?" There was mild snark in her tone but Bethany chose to overlook it. Keely was still smarting and Bethany didn't really blame her. She would forgive her in her own time.

She gave her the list of things she needed and hung up.

By the time she returned to the living room, Zach was once more shut off in his office.

Trying not to let it affect her mood, she returned to the living room and continued working.

⁂

Zach walked into the kitchen as she was uncorking the bottle of red Keely had chosen from Zach's extensive wine collection. He'd changed out of his shorts and T-shirt into a pair of slim black chinos and another indigo shirt.

He crossed over to her side, took the bottle from her and carried on with the task.

"Everything okay, Miss Benson?" His glance held a touch of wariness which Bethany found cute.

Keely rolled her eyes. "It's fine, Savage, you can call me Keely,

I won't bite. As to my state of being, it's nothing a hot new *interesting* boyfriend won't cure. The men I've been attracting lately bore me rigid."

Zach nodded seriously. "I know a few guys. I'll make some calls."

Keely's eyes widened. "Whoa, hold your horses there, Savage. I can find my own dates, thanks."

"And I can put you in the position where you can assess and select your next...conquest."

Keely's head whipped to where Bethany stood at the kitchen counter. "Is he seriously trying to set me up?" Without waiting for an answer, she turned back to Zach. "I bet you can't find me one hard core nerd among all your high flying friends."

"Is that a challenge?"

Bethany groaned. "Oh God."

Zach lifted a brow at her and Keely glanced between them. "What did I say?"

"He devours challenges for breakfast. And more often than not, he sees one where there is none."

"Oh. Right. Well." Keely smiled and Bethany watched Zach's reaction to her friend's traffic stopping smile. To his credit, he didn't react. She released a breath she hadn't realized was trapped. "If your heart is set on winning some sort of challenge, then by all means, have at it."

"What are you doing next weekend?"

"Why?"

"We'll be in Amalfi. I'll fly you over and you can join us for a dinner party. I'll invite a few friends."

Keely's mouth dropped open. Bethany tried to keep hers from following suit. "Umm, I'll check my calendar and let you know." Her eyes met Bethany's with a *WTF just happened* expression clear in her eyes. Bethany fought not to laugh.

Zach poured the first glass and offered it to her. Then he slid one to Keely and set the bottle on the counter. Going to the fridge, he took out a bottle of water and walked over to Bethany.

His kiss was short and sweet but no less mind-altering.

"Thai food will be here in forty-five minutes. Is that okay?"

She nodded. "Great. Thanks."

He nodded to Keely and walked his fine ass out of the kitchen.

Bethany eyed her best friend. "Are we good?"

Keely rolled her eyes. "Of course. My diva fit needed to be thrown but I'd never stand in the way of you going after what you want. You know that, right?"

"Bethany nodded. "Thank you."

Keely glanced back at her. "So," she drawled, thoughtfully passing a forefinger over the rim of her wineglass. "He doesn't really strike me as a ruthless killer of first wives."

"He isn't," Bethany replied, the knowledge a rock-solid certainty in her gut.

Keely nodded. "Are we one hundred per cent certain of this?"

"I'm in a relationship with a rich, powerful guy who wears his secrets like a second skin, Keel. Nothing is ever one hundred per cent guaranteed. Do I think he'll take a butter knife to my throat while I sleep? I'm certain he won't. Am I terrified that I still don't know him nearly as well as I want to and that I'm falling harder for him regardless? Fuck. Yes." Her breath shuddered out.

Her best friend studied her for several minutes, then leaned forward and covered her hand with hers. "I hear you. But Aunt Keely wants to know, what now?"

Bethany clutched her glass tighter and tried to smile through the anxiety storming through her body. "Now, I stay the distance and see where this takes me."

Twenty-Five

THE INDIGO LOUNGE plane took off mid-afternoon on Monday. Her first time on the trip, she'd been so overwhelmed by Zach that she hadn't really found time to experience the unique concept he'd created.

Of course, he was no less overwhelming now and she would probably never get used to the force of his magnetism but at least she was learning to absorb the mind-altering shock that he was hers without it affecting her thought processes too much.

The seat-belt sign winked out at thirty-thousand feet and she stood up from where they'd been watching the clouds from Zach's suite.

"You wanna buy me a drink at the bar, big guy?"

He remained seated and eyed her attire and a frown started to form. "You sure you want to go out like that?"

She looked down at her leather dress, the same one she'd worn when she accepted his indecent proposal three weeks ago in this same suite. "There's nothing wrong with my dress, Zach. The only change is I don't have any pantyhose on."

His frown deepened. "But you're wearing panties, right?" he bit out.

She sighed and linked her fingers through his, choosing not to remind him that there'd been a time when he'd forbidden her from wearing any. "Yes. As ordered to." She pulled him up. Or tried to. He looked intensely irritated.

"God, what now?"

"I'm wishing I hadn't burned that chastity belt."

She laughed. "Sorry. Can't help you there."

His mouth twitched and he finally rose. Tightening his fingers around hers, he brought them to his lips. "I'll just have to be your human chastity belt, then."

The image his words evoked made her cheeks burn. He quirked a brow at her.

"I see that turns you on, Peaches. I can give you a demonstration right now if you want?"

"You get that the more you try and keep me here the more I want to go out, right?"

His jaw tightened. "Unfortunately, I do. Come on."

They left his suite on the third deck of the plane via the private lift. Zach bypassed the second floor in favor of the first and she tried not to let her smirk show. They had seven hours on board before they landed in Rome. She was dying to see how he intended to keep her from the second floor.

The lift opened onto the main lounge. The venture capitalist CEO she'd met at the pre-flight drinks, Mike Henson, was at the bar with his Russian girlfriend when Zach steered her in and pulled out a seat for her. His narrowed gaze fell to her bare thighs as she perched on the stool and his mouth pursed.

"Behave," she whispered.

He gave a low growl, turned to the bartender and ordered a *caipirinha* for her and a beer for himself.

Mike straightened from where he'd been leaning against the bar and came toward them.

"Hey Savage, I was just saying to Olga that I think this plane is your best one so far," he said.

The bartender placed their drinks in front of them and Zach handed over hers. "Glad it's living up to your standards," he replied.

"Shit, it's a dream! If you ever want a partner in any future venture, you know where to find me."

"Thanks, I'll bear it in mind."

Another two couples drifted in. Gabriel Antonelli introduced his stunning black girlfriend, Angela, and Damon Sinclair introduced his wife, Birdie.

As the introductions were reciprocated, Bethany noticed how Zach kept his body between hers and the men and curbed a smile. Her guy was unashamedly territorial. She had no problem with that.

Although she was beginning to get irritated with Olga subtly eye-fucking Zach.

The conversation inevitably drifted to business but she noticed there wasn't that aloofness when Zach interacted with the guests on her first Indigo Lounge flight. When the other couples drifted away, she looked at to Zach.

"They're your friends?"

"We move in the same circles and get together every now and then."

"So they're your friends."

He shrugged. "More like business acquaintances I'm familiar with."

She frowned. "Do you have any real friends?"

His eyes shadowed as he stared down at her. "Yes. You."

She should be used to the way he frequently kicked her feet from under her with his words alone, but Bethany had a feeling she would never get used to Zach's power with words. "I seriously like you, you know that?"

His smile was a little forced, and the hand drifting down her cheek trembled slightly. "You more than like me, but I'll take this for now. You want another drink?" he asked.

She drained the last of her cocktail and shook her head. "I want to keep a clear head. Technically, I'm supposed to be working."

"Not while we're flying."

Stepping down from the stool, she tugged down her dress. "I know, but getting to know the guests now will help me service them better later."

He froze. "Fucking wrong choice of words there, Peaches."

"God, are you going to be like this throughout the trip?"

His nostrils flared. "Things are still unsettled between us. I can't help think something's around the corner waiting to fuck us up even more."

She reached for his hand and slid her other hand around his nape. "Shit is going to happen no matter how much you may try to prevent it. What you can control is how you live in the moment, right now."

He swallowed and the fierce light from his eyes burned right through to her soul. "You're mine. Nothing and no one is going to alter that. I won't let it happen."

She smiled and his breathing altered. Her hand slid from his nape to his chest and as she kissed him, his heartbeat escalated. "I like that sound of that. Know what else I like the sound of?"

"Will I regret asking?"

"I like the sound of you taking me to the second deck. I wanna see who's getting frisky with whom."

His breath hissed out. "God. You're a closet Peeping Tom. How did I not know this about you?" he grumbled.

She laughed and tugged him to the glass staircase.

They entered the bar area and she felt Zach's fingers tighten on hers. Glancing at him, she saw his face set in hard, unreadable lines. She noted why a second later.

One of the guests, a young German heir to a sport car giant was busy fondling his companion who was naked from the waist up. She had both hands tied behind her back, giving him free access to her heavy breasts.

As Bethany watched, he slapped one breast and made a sound of pleasure when her nipple immediately peaked. Cupping her, his other hand reached between her thighs. At the first touch, her head rolled back and her mouth dropped open.

The man's eyes flicked to them, his eyes glazed. He started to smile at Bethany, then noticed Zach and immediately looked away. To his credit, he became completely engrossed by the sight before him again. Leaning down, he rolled his tongue over his woman's nipple, sucked hard on it and groaned.

"Seen enough?" Zach rasped. She glanced at him, wanting to

see his reaction but he'd retreated behind an inscrutable wall as he stared down at her, one eyebrow raised.

"Umm...maybe." Bethany wasn't sure how she felt about witnessing another couple's blatant enjoyment of each other. She felt hot and guilty at the same time.

"You don't have to be ashamed about how external stimulus makes you feel," he whispered in her ears. "As long as you bring all your wants and needs to me, we'll be fine. Deal?"

Biting her lips, she nodded. Zach's hand slid around her waist and he guided her forward, past the couple who were now completely lost in each other. The passed another couple getting heavy in the next spot and walked through to the games room.

Bethany's stomach twisted as they walked into the chill out room to see Mike and Olga and Damon and Birdie lounging in the seats. Two of the screens had descended and as they moved into the room, Bethany heard hoarse Italian swearing followed by a very feminine cry of pleasure. Gabriel and Angela.

"Join us," Olga invited, her eyes latching on to Zach.

Bethany had never really tested their relationship against the rigors of close proximity. Sure, she knew how Zach felt about Chris, her ex and she'd made her feelings clear about the belly dancer who'd got a little too close in Marrakech. But this was different. Olga was blatantly eyeing up her man. She needed to set boundaries. Fast.

"We'd love to," she responded.

Zach's hand tightened around her waist. When she glanced at him, his face was still expressionless. "You sure about this, Peaches?" he murmured.

She sent him a thousand-watt smile. "Absolutely." She took a seat on the last remaining lounger and slid her hand onto Zach's thigh when he sat down next to her. Hard muscles bunched in gratifying reaction to her touch.

Olga, dressed in a silver sequined micro-dress that left very little to the imagination cleavage-and-leg-wise, stood. Mike's smile looked a little strained as he watched his girlfriend sashay over to Zach, card in hand.

Zach's face remained the same as he took the card from her. Again he glanced at Bethany. She felt her smile slipping but held her nerve.

Zach shrugged and opened the card. "How many billionaires does it take to screw in a light bulb?" A tiny smirk twitched his mouth.

Olga let out a tinkling laugh that grated on Bethany's nerves. "Silly question." She stared straight at Zach. "I say he should forget the light bulb. And screw me."

Whoa.

Zach barely blinked. "Your turn," he said to her.

She pretended to tilt her head in thought. "Well, how important is the light is to him? Because if he has me, he won't need to worry about the darkness."

Lame. So fucking lame. And yet, the change that came over Zach's face made her want to scream with happiness.

He flung the card away and pressed the screen button on his seat. "Sorry, Olga. She wins."

Mike had a full-blown smirk in place as the screens descended. Olga looked like she was chewing nails.

Twenty-Six

ZACH CAUGHT HER as Bethany flung herself at him before the screen had fully descended.

"Baby, what the hell are you trying to do to me?" he grated out.

"I saw your face. You liked what I said," she murmured as she settled herself in his lap, her thighs bracketing him and her hands sliding into his hair.

He clamped his hands on her hips and pressed her flesh.

"Like it? You fucking turned me inside out."

She made a soft sound and rubbed herself against him. He hardened instantly. "I like turning you inside out."

"I know. Any reason why you want to prove that right now?" he asked, although he could guess the answer. Dark satisfaction shot through him.

"I wanted to put that Siberian bitch in her place. She's been eyeing you like you're Beluga caviar on her cracker."

He laughed and cupped her firm rump. "I hate caviar."

She jerked back and looked into his eyes. "Really?"

"Really."

"Good." She undulated her hips and his mind reeled. Her dress rode up a little higher and the scent of her arousal hit him like a blow to the heart.

"Bethany?"

"Hmm?"

"If you want me inside you, we have to return to our suite. I'm not fucking you with people listening in, baby. Your pleasure sounds belongs to my ears alone. But it looks like you have something to prove so have at it. But I say when to stop."

Her beautiful eyes were stormy with need when she stared down at him. "I thought you didn't fuck where you work."

"I'm making an exception for you. Besides, when I'm with you, it's not work."

"So, heavy petting is allowed right here?" Her hands drifted down his chest and over his stomach.

"Hmm.'

She put her hand on his hard crotch and squeezed him. Intrigued by how far she would go, he watched her slowly slide down his zipper and take out his rigid cock. His eyelashes fluttered but his eyes remained on hers, eager to see her face, watch her pleasure as she pleasured him.

She pumped him a couple of times and Zach gritted his teeth and swallowed a groan. He was unraveling, already spinning out of control from her touch alone.

Her miniscule smile told him she knew her effect on him and was pleased about it. She gripped him harder, worked him faster, her fingers warm rings of exquisite torture. Her lips parted and her pink tongue darted out to wet her lower lip. Another groan ballooned in his chest.

Christ.

"Baby…" His gaze dropped to his cock in her hand and he lost his train of thought. He was agonizingly hard and growing desperate by the second.

"Zach," her voice was thick with need. He speared a hand through her loose hair and dragged his fingers over her scalp the way he knew she loved.

"Peaches, do you crave me inside you?"

"Always," she breathed.

"Time to return to our suite?"

She nodded eagerly. "Yes."

He grinned at the reluctance with which she released him. Gingerly, he zipped himself up and dropped his shirt tails over his crotch.

She stood and sent him a saucy grin. "That's not going to keep them from guessing what we've been doing," she said.

He let out a frustrated growl. "Next time you decide to mark your territory, pick a quick getaway that doesn't involve a dozen guests and two flights of stairs between us and a bed."

She mock frowned. "Should I be worried that you think I'll need to mark you often and consistently?"

He smiled. "I love being marked by you. Even though blue balls could become an issue if we don't time it properly." He grimaced at the agony tearing through his groin and pressed the button to lift the screen.

She caressed soft fingers down his cheek. "Oh, you poor baby. I promise I'll make it better very soon."

Her sheer enjoyment of his discomfort made his teeth grit but he couldn't stop the pure vein of happiness from growing in his chest as he watched her beautiful face and breathtaking smile.

This woman knocked his numb heart into kicking life. And he intended to do whatever it took to keep that life force beating. A return to his previous existence, to that soulless numbness, was unbearable.

※

Rome was hot and gloriously culture-filled. And the spot Karim chose to launch his first salvo.

Zach saw the first email from his lawyers half an hour after landing. He barely managed to contain his rage as he read the clear threat in the email.

Beside him in the limo Bethany arranged to ferry the IL guests to his hotel, she turned sharply, her senses tuned perfectly to his mood.

"Something wrong?"

"Yes." He stopped for a moment, marveled at how easy it was to talk to her now. To share his joy and his pain. "The zombies are sabre-rattling."

Worry clouded her eyes. She put a hand on his thigh and he covered it with his own. "Explain."

He looked out the window at the passing view. Early evening

sunlight glinted over the Coliseum's ruins. Shorts and T-shirt clad tourists aimed their phone cameras at the ruins and for a moment he yearned to be one of them, with no worries or bitter past or threats of losing the one precious thing in his life.

He refocused on Bethany. "He wants me to leave the non-disclosure alone."

"Or?" she pressed.

"Or he'll unearth a few skeletons."

"Your skeletons?"

"Yes." He sighed and passed a hand over his face. He needed a shave. Badly. But Bethany had protested when he'd threatened to shave this morning. Her reason for wanting him to leave it unshaved brought a fleeting smile to his face and a hard kick to his groin. His Peaches loved a good and rough Princess Treatment. And he had no intention of denying her. He refocused when her hand tightened on his. "I never told you why I cut my mother out of my life."

Her breath caught. "No, you didn't."

A wave of shame slammed into his gut and spread outward. "I have a vague recollection of my father. Nothing concrete. But even before he walked when I was four, I knew something wasn't right with our *family unit*." He stopped and sucked in a breath. "There were too many *uncles* drifting in and out, you know?"

She made a distressed sound and the wave of shame crept higher, threatened to engulf him.

"At first, I would just stay in my room. No one bothered me and I didn't go hungry or anything like that. I just recognized very quickly that staying in my room was the best thing all round."

"Then I got older. Things began to make more sense." She winced and he realized his fingers had tightened. He loosened his grip immediately. "I couldn't avoid the truth. And she didn't really bother to hide it from me once I hit puberty."

"Are you...are you saying that your mother was—"

"A glorified prostitute? Yes. And the thing was, she wasn't doing it for the money. She just did it because…" he shrugged and noticed his whole body was coil-tense, "she enjoyed it. My mother enjoyed giving herself freely to men just for the hell of it. I asked her once why she did it." His jaw locked for an instant, so tight he was stunned when something didn't break. "She told me she enjoyed the attention. Of course, she couldn't be like every other mother and join the fucking PTA or book club. She let other men use her. Because she enjoyed it. When I was old enough to stay away without supervision, I did. I spent hours at the pool and only came home when it was strictly necessary."

"And your father?"

The long-buried scab ripped raw. "He wasn't interested enough to stick around when I was a kid. I have no interest in getting to know him now. Kudos to the man, though. He paid enough child support to allow my mother to support her exemplary lifestyle." He couldn't stop the bitterness from spilling out. "You know, sometimes I hated him for that? For supporting us from wherever the hell he was? I thought that maybe if he didn't, my mother would've been forced to get a real job."

"Zach…I'm so sorry…God, I don't know what to say." This time her fingers gripped him hard enough to hurt..

He risked a glance at her and saw sympathy, concern and a sheen of tears in her eyes. But no judgment.

No judgment.

His breath fractured out of him and he swallowed hard to keep from losing it.

She was so giving. So damned generous, with her body and her soul. She was currently guarding her heart due to his intense stupidity but he intended to do everything in his power to win it back.

"You're still here. That's all that matters."

Silence followed, soothing the jagged edges of his confession.

"So, Karim is threatening you with your mother's past?"

Bitterness soured his mouth. "Yes, he'll leak a story unless I let the Farrah issue go. I've refused. As for my mother, I wish the past tense applied where she's concerned."

Her eyes widened. "You mean she's still…"

"She never stopped. Not when I threatened to leave and never come back. And not when I made good on the threat."

She leaned closer and slid her arm around his waist. Her nose nuzzled his throat and he closed his eyes and reveled in the softness and goodness of her.

After several minutes, he opened his eyes and looked down at her. "Do you have a question for me today?" Again, he noted that this - letting her in, was getting easier.

Her smile lit her up from the inside and his brain fried. God, how was it possible she had no idea how gorgeous she was? His thumb traced her lower lip and he watched her eyelids flutter with pleasure.

"I *had* a question for you. You just answered it."

Surprise jerked through him. "You wanted to know about my mother?"

"I wanted to know about your childhood."

He nodded, then breathed in deep. "And are you okay knowing there won't be any fond family Thanksgiving dinners?"

Her mouth brushed his throat again. "I'm okay knowing we'll have Thanksgiving dinner together some day."

He splayed not too steady fingers through her hair and angled her face to his. "I intend for us to have many. Get used to the idea."

"Yes, sir."

"Are you sassing me, Peaches?"

"I wouldn't dream of it." Her smile indicated otherwise. He started to lower his head, to taste those sweet lips that had the power to wreck his world and put it back together again. Her question stopped him.

"So what's going to happen now with Karim?"

Renewed anger churned through his gut. "I won't let him threaten me. I won't let him threaten us."

"Zach…"

"Let me worry about it, baby."

"I don't want you to go through this alone. The alpha thing is sexy and all but there are some things I will insist on sharing."

"Understood. Now enlighten me as to what else you think is sexy…"

The atmosphere had lightened considerably by the time they arrived at The Indigo Palazzo Roma in the heart of the Italian city just off Piazza Navona.

His uncompromising business ethic coupled with his drive for perfection in all things usually worked well to charm and impress his IL guests.

But for the rest of the afternoon as he watched Bethany swing into work mode and seek to deliver the very best experience to each guest, he surmised that perhaps on this occasion, his guests were enthralled for a different reason.

She put each guest at ease while maintaining a distance that made the Neanderthal in him stop wanting to rip things apart. Their dinner at La Pergola, the three-Michelin star restaurant came with a wine list that made even the Wall Street CEO and self-confessed seasoned connoisseur's eyes bulge.

Zach sat back and watched her effortlessly charm his guests. When a few of them drifted off after coffee to admire the rooftop view of Rome at night, he stayed at his table and allowed himself an unashamed view of his woman. Her dark gold silk-clad body had been teasing him all evening. The material had especially clung to her ass in a way that made his groin burn every time she walked away from him, which had been often, much to his irritation.

He finally managed to corner her an hour after they arrived at Gilda, the exclusive club, where she'd arranged after-dinner chill-out drinks.

She smiled when he turned her into his arms on the dance floor. "Having fun?"

"Yes. What can I say? I enjoy my work. Did you see Jerry Daniels' face when the *sommelier* brought out the wine list? I thought he was going to have a heart attack." Her eyes sparkled and Zach thought she'd never looked more beautiful.

"You knew he was a wine collector?"

She raised a perfect eyebrow. "You doubt that I did my homework?"

"I never doubt you, Peaches."

Her breath shortened and her eyes dropped to his mouth. Flames fanned into roaring life and his cock followed suit. "How much longer until we can ditch this circus?"

She laughed. "It's *your* circus."

"Exactly. So I'm calling it a success and you're clocking off for the night." He stood and held out his hand. "I can tell you're horribly jet-lagged. You need a bed *asap*."

She rolled her eyes but slid her hand into his when he stepped off the dance floor. Her knee-length dress caressed her body as he strode over to the group and ensured everyone's need had been catered to for the evening. Then he watched her expertly hand over the reins to the Italian assistant and hostesses she'd been working with all afternoon.

By the time they reached his limo, he could barely keep his hands off her. He had her on her back and panty-less within seconds.

He was inside her a minute later. He held himself deep inside her and watched pleasure darken her eyes.

"To what do I owe this keen attention, Savage?" She licked the pad of the thumb he traced over her mouth.

He pulled out and slowly slid back into her snug heat, burying himself so deep, he earned himself a sweet, lusty groan. "What can I say, Peaches? Watching you work made me hot for you."

Her mouth closed over his tongue and sucked it deep. Then she reached down to where they were joined and boldly cupped his balls. "Hmm."

His vision blurred. "Fuck!"

He muttered, groaned, then finally shouted that word before they got to his hotel.

Bethany wasn't sure what woke her. But the sense of déjà vu hit with frightening force. Only this time, Zach was in a deep sleep, his head on the pillow just above her with both arms tangled around her in a back to front unbreakable hold. She listened for several minutes before she forced herself to breathe slowly, regulate her heartbeat.

Putting it down to strange sounds in a strange city, she was just starting to drift back into sleep when she heard it.

Her tablet. Sending out an alert meant for her. Sheena had sent her several during the evening and probably hadn't stopped to work out the time difference.

The temptation to leave it till morning was strong.

But as she found herself reaching toward the bedside table for her iPad Mini, that lingering sense of impending danger grew stronger.

The headline in the email from the unknown sender hollowed out her stomach. But it was the paragraph that followed that made her blood ran cold.

Twenty-Seven

*S*AVAGE *S*ETS *H*IS *Sight On Another Innocent.*
Shall we pity Bethany Green or be bug-eyed with envy? New York events organiser Bethany Green has landed herself the big fish in the form of Zach Savage. But before women the world over start rending their garments, we advise caution.

Savage has a history of turbulent relationships, one of which ended in tragedy, intrigue and a cover up. Sources previously close to a deceased ex have further revealed a major cover up including missing hospital records after said ex's death.

So before you lament the loss of this billionaire bachelor, perhaps you should count yourself lucky to have escaped his dangerous snare…

Bethany swallowed and read the email again, trying to keep the icy churning in her stomach at bay.

Missing hospital records…a cover up…

She noticed the attachment to the email and activated it. The photo that opened up made her heart stop.

At least now she had a face to go with the woman who has made such an impact on Zach.

Farrah Nisa was gorgeous. The kind of hurt-your-eyes stunning that men like Zach Savage attracted with minimum effort. Zach hadn't been exaggerating there.

God, no wonder he'd built a shrine for her.

Pain, jealousy and a healthy amount of self-loathing for her very uncharitable thoughts congealed in a ball of misery in her gut.

She stared harder at the sultry Farrah's photo, searching for answers she knew she wouldn't find. Then she scrolled back up and read the message again.

A full body shiver raked over her.

"What the fuck are you doing?" Zach rasped in her ear.

She jumped and slammed the tablet shut. Or she tried to.

Besides the insane talents he'd been blessed with, Zach also possessed super quick reflexes. He snatched the iPad from her and flipped back the cover.

Heart in her throat, she watched his face as he scanned the page.

"Who sent this to you?" he demanded, his face as mask of pure, icy fury.

"I don't know. There was no identifiable email address. Just a bunch of numbers and figures."

He threw back the sheets and lunged out of bed. Tension gripped his body and stiffened his shoulders as he stalked naked to the dressing room, her tablet still in his hand.

"Zach?"

He came out seconds later, dressed in dark blue lounger pants. "I'll deal with this."

"How...who sent it?"

"I don't know. But I'll find out." He strode purposefully to the door of their suite and yanked it open.

Bethany scrambled out of bed, threw on a robe and raced after him.

Philip appeared in the doorway as she reached the living room and she saw Zach hand him her tablet. "...source of the email. It may have been hacked. Have it checked out."

The thickset man merely nodded, unruffled by the fact that he'd been woken in the middle of the night.

"And the LA situation needs to be escalated," Zach added. The cold menace in his voice made the hairs on her nape quiver.

Another nod and Philip calmly shut the door behind him.

"What's the LA situation?" Bethany blurted, unable to stop the shivers that raked her body.

He slowly turned and faced her. His face was a mask of fury

and deadly control. "Karim."

"What are you going to do?"

"He came after you. All bets are off."

Her hand tightened over her belt. "What does that mean? In plain English, please."

"It means he will be given one last opportunity to deal with my lawyers. Or he'll have to deal with me. Only a handful of people have the information in that email. It's designed to look like a newspaper article but I'm certain it won't be published anywhere. He's an attorney, he knows the law."

"So this was supposed to scare *me*?"

His jaw tightened. "Yes."

Fear clambered up her gut and lodged in her chest. "What are you going to do?"

Her emotions must have communicated themselves to him because he paused in his pacing and came over to her.

He grabbed her waist in a tight grip and pulled her into his body. "Nothing that will jeopardise us, I promise. But he needs to know that he can't mess with you."

"Zach, I can take care of myself."

"Then why are you shaking? Why do I see pain in your eyes?" His voice was husky with worry and fury and barely leashed control.

"Because…my imagination fell far short of grasping just how beautiful Farrah was. Now I know…and I…"

A rough sound jerked from his throat. "*That's* what you're worried about?"

"I'm worried about other things. But I know you'll tell me what you can when you can." She held her breath. "The hospital records going missing. Is it true?"

His mouth compressed. "Yes," he answered tersely.

She shut her eyes and breathed out shakily. "Did you have something to do with it?"

"No. Not directly." His tone pleaded for her to stop her line of questioning.

She placed her hand on his naked chest and felt his heartbeat jolt at her touch. "It's okay, I won't ask anymore. I can go back to trying to deal with how gorgeous Farrah was and how awful I feel for hating her because she had you first."

He speared his fingers in her hair and angled her face up to his. "Don't do this to yourself. I belong to you, Bethany. Do you need a reminder fuck? Because I can oblige if it helps you stay grounded in the fact that I'm yours and you're mine."

"God, Zach…" she sighed out his name and he groaned and pressed her back against the doorway.

His lips brushed the corner of her mouth. "Keep saying my name like that and I'll throw in a Christ-you-undo-me fuck too."

She laughed. "How many categories are there?"

"We can work our way through it and find out." He cursed as a knock came at the door.

Reluctantly, he dropped his hands and walked over to open it. Philip silently handed him her iPad, nodded and retreated.

"Does he have anything?"

Zach's mouth tightened and he set her tablet on a console table. "He will by morning. Go back to bed, Peaches. I'll join you shortly."

"I don't…"

"It's okay, I'll behave. For now. I just need to make a couple of calls." He caught her to him and kissed her long and deep, then pushed her toward the hallway leading to the bedroom.

She turned and watched him walk away, her heart in her throat.

Every time she fooled herself into thinking they were making strides forward, something happened to set them back.

Frustration and fear had her altering her course, choosing another small hallway in the suite that led to the balcony outside.

Rome was spread out before her and in the distance the large, imposing dome of The Vatican loomed. She gripped the railing and tried to infuse hope into her heart.

She fell short.

Would they make it? Would they survive? Someone out there

knew what Zach had done. The possibility of losing him rose like the dome before her, threatening to shatter her.

She wasn't sure how long she stood there, trying to fight back the black hopelessness, but she felt his presence the moment he stepped onto the wide space.

"You're supposed to be in bed."

He came toward her, tucking his cell phone into his pocket before strong arms bracketed her.

"All done with your call?"

He nodded. "We're meeting on Friday."

"*We?*"

"Yes. It's time, Bethany."

She swallowed and calculated quickly. "The IL trip wouldn't be finished."

"We'll be done with Thailand and the guests. We'll take a break and finish the private tour after we meet with the attorney."

She hugged him tight and waited, knowing there was more.

"It could turn ugly, baby. But I'll protect you, no matter what."

Her fear escalated. "What are the options?"

He shrugged. "Breaking the agreement could possibly mean getting sued, maybe jail time. I don't care about that—"

"I do!" She reared back and stared into his face. "I do," she reiterated forcefully.

"Fuck, baby, I didn't mean it like that. I won't accept anything that takes me away from you. But I don't want this thing between us any more. I'm not prepared to take that risk. But we need to do it right. Regardless of anything Karim's trying to pull, his family has suffered enough. Hell, he's lashing out because he's in pain, much as I want to tear him a new one. I'm going to do my best to make things right all round."

That core of integrity that had been the first pull to her falling in love with him tugged harder at her heart. He drove her mad with his secrets and veils but from the first, Zach wore his integrity with unashamed pride.

How could she fault him for that now simply because it stood in the way of her truly knowing the man behind the enigma?

She burrowed into his chest and breathed him in, her heart sighing in contentment at just being this close to him. "You know I would never betray your trust, don't you?"

He tugged her head up and kissed her, long and deep. When he raised his head, they both gulped in much needed oxygen. "I know. And if it were up to me, you'd know everything by now, fucked up bits and all."

"You call it fucked up. I call it the building blocks of who you are today."

"You must really, really like me, Peaches. Because only you will see things that way."

She smiled. "I do really, really like you."

His eyes darkened. "Come inside. I need to fuck you again."

Twenty-Eight

THEY FLEW BY helicopter to the Amalfi Coast and Zach's place right on the water shores of Lake Como.

The red brick palazzo was another stunning masterpiece that left her slack-jawed.

"Can you believe this place?" Angela, who'd accompanied them with Gabriel, asked as they moved from room to breath-taking room. "I hear it once belonged to a famous opera singer."

The statuesque African American beauty shaded her eyes as they gazed back at the palazzo from the jetty where they'd wandered. Behind them, Zach was showing Gabriel the workings of his speedboat.

A big boy with his toy.

As if he caught her thoughts, he raised his head and slanted a heart-stopping smile her way.

"Shit. That smile shouldn't be legal," Angela murmured under her breath. "And you two really need to stop with the *I-wanna-fuck-your-brains-out-right-now* looks. It's a health risk to the rest of us trying to keep up."

Bethany face flamed. Knowing how completely besotted Angela and Gabriel were with each other made it easy to join in when Angela's smirk turned to outright laughter.

"You glad we ditched Olga the Ogre?" She waggled her eyebrows.

Bethany laughed again. "It's certainly nicer without her around."

Angela's eyebrow arched. "Right. You're the diplomatic type. I think Mike's about to ditch her. I say the bitch deserves to be ditched right all right. From like thirty thousand feet above the Atlantic."

Bethany's eyes widened.

Angela shrugged. "Yeah, I'm hating on her. She tried to make a play for Gabe too."

"Well, in that case, when the time comes, I'll bring the wire cutters."

Angela smiled speculatively. "You're a keeper. We should hook up when we get back to New York."

Bethany smiled. "I'd like that."

The men joined them and they headed in for lunch of roast peppers stuffed with shredded lamb and pasta.

As they enjoyed coffee, Zach caught her hand in his and trailed his lips over her skin.

Her phone beeped. She ignored it, caught up in the intense gaze of the man who commanded her emotions so very effortlessly.

"You like the house?" He seemed a little nervous.

"Yes, I do."

He nodded. "Good.

She raised a brow. "Good? Is this some sort of audition?"

A corner of his mouth tilted. "Maybe."

"I hate it when you're cryptic."

"It's okay, Peaches," he murmured for her ears alone. "You can work out your frustrations on me later."

Her phone beeped again. Zach plucked it off the table, glanced at the screen and inserted it in his pocket. He ignored her arched look and stood.

"You work for me. The only person who should be commandeering your time is me." He took her hand and pulled her up.

Gabriel and Angela followed and they headed back to the chopper.

Easy banter accompanied the ride back to Rome but every now and then, she caught a look on Zach's face that made her nape tingle.

In the rush of getting packed to head to the airport, she forgot to ask for her phone back.

Three hours after take off, he lowered his superb body over hers, pinning her to their king-size cabin bed. "You want to try out the sky deck? I still have a promise to keep. Something about fucking you as we race toward the stars?"

She tried to lift her hand to smooth back his hair but her hand flopped uselessly back down as her sweat-slicked body shuddered through the afterglow of yet another orgasm. "Give me a year, Zach. I'm sure I will have caught my breath by then."

He laughed, pure arrogance and male satisfaction throbbing through his voice. "You have an hour."

"Oh…joy." Her eyes drifted shut as he turned sideways and tucked her into his side. His steady heartbeat beneath her cheek lulled her deeper into sleep. With a sigh, she gave in.

※

Zach held his breath until he was sure she was asleep. Then he released the anger locked inside him.

Karim had taken the situation to a whole different level. The second message he'd sent to Bethany's phone had contained more clues as to what happened six years ago. His ex-brother in law was skating dangerously close to breaching the terms of the agreement he was fighting Zach to protect.

He meant to threaten Zach. And damn if it wasn't working.

A trace of panic flared alongside his anger. Because he knew Karim couldn't have chosen a better bull's-eye to aim for by choosing to set his sights on Bethany. But what he didn't realise was that Zach would protect the most important thing in his life - Bethany - at all costs.

The fact that his ex-brother-in-law may not also know the whole truth had crossed his mind. It was the reason Zach had gone against his own rigid principles and placed the call to Farrah's parents earlier this evening.

His message had been simple. And succinct.

Now he needed to wait and see what shook out. If they could half the juggernaut that their son was dangerously close to overturning.

And he had to keep Bethany occupied and away from any communication devices.

He sighed. There would be hell to pay when she found out. He had no intention of keeping them from her long-term. Only until he knew he could come clean without jeopardising her safety.

She sighed in his arms and his heart turned over.

He fucking adored her. She was the blood in his veins. The light in the darkness that he'd never thought he'd escape.

She was his life.

She stirred and he realised he held her too tightly. Forcing himself to loosen his hold, he listened to her sleep.

Nothing could be allowed to touch her.

Nothing.

୪

"We've organised your chefs to prepare your meals at eight. Please let your hostesses know if you'd prefer to change the time."

"I hope the chefs make more than just Thai noodles. I'm off carbs for the foreseeable future," Olga pouted, more than a trace of malice in her eyes as she watched Bethany.

As far as she was concerned, she'd made her point with Olga. So Bethany smiled. "I'll personally let the chef know to keep the carbs off your menu, Olga."

"Then we head out for cocktails at the Vertigo Bar before midnight."

They'd been in Bangkok for half a day. Everyone had had a chance to relax at the exclusive hotel spa and napped for a couple of hours to offset jet-lag.

Four hours ago, a designer arrived to take the female guests' measurements for evening gowns which were due back at six.

When they were returned at six, Bethany personally delivered each gown and got a kick out of seeing the women's delight. She was trying on her own after dinner and a quick shower when Zach walked in.

The red and gold gown was made of heavy silk with a thigh split that showed a whole lot of leg when she moved. The high neck and collar were demure enough, but the severe cut at the shoulders left her arms and most of her back bare.

"You're looking pretty pleased with yourself, Peaches."

Her gaze connected with his in the mirror and her heart did another crazy whirling. "I haven't fucked up your trip so far. So yes, I'm pleased."

He stopped behind her, pulled up her zipper and slid his hands over her hips.

"Have a little faith in yourself. I do."

Her heart skipped several beats as his hands gripped her hips in a possessive hold. "You on a brownie point hunt, Savage?"

His eyes remained serious and intense. "Always. I never want to run out." His drifted down her body. "That dress looks incredible on you," he breathed in her ear.

She shivered. "Thank you. You don't look so bad yourself." His evening jacket sat perfectly on his broad-shouldered frame and the open collar of his grey silk shirt gave him an air or urbane sophistication that would most definitely draw female eyes. She tried not to think about that. "I thought you'd gone up to the Krug and cigar bar with the guys?"

"No," he answered simply. They remained like for another minute, devouring each other and letting their eyes say the words neither was ready to spill yet. Zach's hand drifted down to the bracelet he'd given her for her birthday. He raised her wrist and placed a soft kiss on her skin just below the bracelet.

Again, she sensed that air of restless watchfulness about him that she'd caught occasional glimpses since they left Amalfi.

"Is something wrong, Zach?" She shook her head and corrected herself. "Something else I should know about?"

One corner of his mouth twisted up as he trailed his fingers up her arms. "Would you be satisfied with a-same-bullshit-different-day answer?" Despite his offhand remark, a dark emotion throbbed in his voice that made her anxiety escalate.

"General bullshit or specific?" She didn't think that outside of what was happening with Farrah's brother and the non-disclosure situation, Zach was the sort of man to worry about the outcome of any problem.

He loved challenges. He thrived on the adrenaline rush of tackling the impossible and besting it. It was what had made him the powerful, charismatic man he was today.

The only thing he didn't relish was tackling the subject of jeopardising the fragile connection they were building.

That thought made her heart swell and ache for him at the same time. He was fighting for them. She couldn't deny that. And her love for him grew each time he showed her that.

"Specific," he admitted with a harsh exhale.

"What can I do?"

He watched her silently in the mirror, then his lids slid down, veiling his expression. "You're already doing it. You're here with me." He linked his fingers through her and kissed her exposed neck.

She got the strong impression that hadn't been his intended answer but she let it go. She was learning fast which battles to pick and which to concede.

"Have you seen my phone?"

He tapped his breast pocket. "I have it, but you won't be needing it tonight."

She raised an eyebrow at him. "You plan to keep me busy all night?"

His mouth twitched sexily. "Now there's an idea. Any chance of convincing you to ditch the others and play hooky with me?"

"Nope. And you say that but I know you want this trip to be a success as much as I do. Failure is not an option for you."

"No, but I also can't help but wish this trip were over. I feel like we're suspended over a goddamn cliff," he grated out.

She faced him and he pulled her closer, as desperate for contact with her as she was for him.

"Three days, Zach. I'm sure we can find a way to forget about the future and make the next seventy-two hours memorable," she supplied.

His mouth slowly curved in a wicked smile. Her heart kicked into gear and began to race.

"Ah, baby. You want memorable? I can give you memorable. I just hope you can take it."

Twenty-Nine

DECADENCE BECAME THE buzzword from the moment she stepped out of the suite and headed upstairs with Zach.

They mingled with the great and glorious on the sky deck of Zach's hotel before they headed out to a private martial arts tournament at a converted Buddhist Temple.

Watching the sleek-muscled men who'd honed their bodies through years of perfecting their craft made her secretly thrilled at how dedicated Zach was to his own fitness regime.

"Did you bring us here so you could ogle other men, Peaches?" he murmured in her ears.

She turned and locked eyes with his hot, intense eyes. "No. But I do appreciate a fine specimen when I see one," she replied impishly.

"You keep your eyes on me when you say that or there will be hell to pay," he warned.

She held his gaze for several seconds, then she deliberately glanced over to the spot-lit platform where the artists circled one another.

His hand curved over her nape in a firm, domineering grip. "You want test the edge, baby?"

She shivered and glanced back at him. Their private booth meant other guests in the small group couldn't hear them but he kept his voice low anyway. She liked that he reserved his hot words for her ears alone. Words she greedily craved and could never get enough of.

Her hand slid to his thigh and she gloried in the tension that rippled through his muscles. "I want to test *your* edge."

His eyes gleamed and his gaze dropped to her mouth in blatant hunger. "My edges can be rough. You sure you're ready?"

"I'm sure. I want it. I want you."

Hard fingers slid up her nape into her hair and bunched in a sharp, painful hold. "You'll have me. In more ways that you can possibly imagine." The dark anticipation in his voice heated her blood.

Her nipples peaked and liquid fire flared between her legs. His fingers tightened another notch and he watched her, absorbing her tiny wince and her shallow breathing with a dark satisfaction that only made her hotter.

His tongue rested against his lower lip as he stared at her mouth. "I won't be gentle tonight, baby," he warned.

Her nails bit into his hard thigh muscle, and he jerked beneath her touch. "Yes," she said simply.

His nostrils flared and he stared, unblinking, at her for so long, color flared into her cheeks. "I adore your blushes, Peaches. They make me want to dirty you up nice and good. Scandalize you completely."

Her hand moved up and she slowly cupped his crotch. Thick and heavy, she could barely fathom where he began and ended. Her mouth watered just thinking about all that power inside her. "I adore *this*. Your beautiful cock. I adore the way you take me. I adore the way you make me come for you." Her eyes met his boldly. "I adore you."

His eyelids fluttered as he took in a long, shaky breath. "Bethany." His eyes had darkened to almost black and the fingers in her hair trembled. "You make me…" he paused.

She leaned closer, her heart thumping wildly. "Tell me."

A swallow bobbed his Adam's apple. "All my life, I've felt alone. The money, the lifestyle, it doesn't insulate you from loneliness. Hell, sometimes it emphasizes it even more. With you…you make me see my way through the darkness. You make me feel as if…you make me *feel*, Bethany. Period. I'm so fucking grateful to have you in my life." A shudder moved through him.

"Whatever happens when we get back; whatever you find out about me, please know that I'll never hurt you. That I'll never wreck what we have?"

That solemn vow moved her more than anything else Zach had ever said before. Tears prickled her eyes and clogged her throat. "Zach, I—"

Applause broke out and the outside world broke through their charged, intimate bubble. Zach's jaw clenched at the intrusion and she glance around to see the martial artists taking their bows.

Sweat glistened off their bodies and their solemn faces and their audience wore huge smiles.

The evening had been a success. But she, like Zach, wanted it over. "I'm probably going to lose my job for not sticking around until the night ends properly, but I want to return to the hotel with you. Right now."

His cock twitched beneath her hand and a smouldering smile curved his sensual lips. "I'll make sure your client puts in a good word for you." He leaned close and brushed his mouth against her throat. "As long as you let him put his cock inside you in the next five minutes."

A delicious shiver coursed through her body. "We won't make it back in five minutes, Zach. Not even you can move that fast."

One hand dropped to where she held him and he pressed her hand harder against him. Her fingers curled around his solid length and his breath hissed out. "You think I can't get us back in five when I have your tight cunt and the pounding I intend to give it to look forward to?"

She groaned and tried to pull away when the guests began to rise. "I'm learning not to test your motivation, but I think we may have missed our chance for a quick sneak out."

He cursed under his breath when the Indigo Lounge guests headed their way. He pressed his hand over hers one more time before he released her. She watched his face slowly lose the erotic promise it'd held a moment ago and settle once more into the suave, enigmatic billionaire the world saw when they looked at

Zachary Savage.

A thrill went through Bethany at the thought that his special, private look belonged to her alone.

She turned to the guests and smiled in response to their praise for her organisation of the evening and the show. A tiny bubble of pride fizzed through her. She may not lose her job after all.

They drifted out into the warm night air and Philip pulled up to a smooth halt on the kerb.

"Enjoy the rest of your evening," Zach said to his guests, his smile back to friendly-but-not-engaging.

"You won't be joining us at the club?" Olga asked sullenly, her lips pouting as her eyes devoured Zach.

Bethany had arranged it so everyone could use their Indigo Lounge hostess for the rest of the night, and she knew the couple and a few others had opted to go to *Q-Bash*, the exclusive nightclub a few blocks away.

"Bethany's work is done for the day."

She didn't mind that Zach answered for her. Or that he slid his hand around her waist and held her possessively against his side. She belonged to him and she had no problem letting the world know.

He held the limo door open and waited for her to slide in. She expected him to pounce on her the moment they were alone. Instead, he lounged on his side of the long seat, his eyes on her.

He watched her almost clinically, one hand fisted on his thigh, like a predator assessing which part of her to attack first. Her mouth received its fair share of intense focus, followed by her breasts, her thighs and legs.

By the time they rolled beneath the columned portico of The Indigo Bangkok Hotel, her heated core had commenced a desperate, hungry clenching that would drive her insane until Zach assuaged her hunger.

The trip up to their Penthouse suite passed in a haze of heated anticipation and harsh breathing.

The door had barely shut behind them before he hoisted her

up against him. She immediately slid her hands into his hair, luxuriated in the slide of the thick strands through her fingers.

Hungry eyes fixated on her lips. "Give me your tongue," he rasped.

Excitement shot through her. She opened her mouth and slowly traced the outline of his soft, firm lips.

"More," he ordered.

She pushed between his lips, seeking the merciless stab of his tongue. He kept it from her, making her work her way in. She found it and tasted him. Slow and hot and erotic. His arms tightened where they were banded under her ass and he moaned long and deep.

The sound sizzled like lightning through her bloodstream, stinging her nipples and raking deliciously through her belly to flash against her clit. Gripping his hair tighter, she gave him everything she had.

And he took it.

She had a vague sensation of being carried deeper into the suite. Seconds later, she found herself on the wide, waist-high marble center isle in their dressing room.

Rough hands lowered her zipper and cool air washed over her shoulders as her dress was lowered to her waist. Then large hands gripped her and the kiss took a turn for bruising. He ate her mouth like it was his favorite treat and he was intent on gorging himself sick.

Just when she thought she would burst into flames from the scorching assault, Zach stepped back. The look in his eyes was unapologetically carnal and voracious. He shrugged out of his dinner jacket and kicked his shoes away. The smooth, bronzed column of his throat and chest bared as he unbuttoned his shirt. Her mouth watered just watching him undress.

"You look hungry, Peaches."

Her eyes dropped to his flat nipples and she licked her lips. "Ravenous."

His smile was pure male satisfaction as he made short work of getting naked.

Taking a step forward, he reached for her dress. "Up."

She lifted her hips. He pulled down her dress and panties and dislodged her shoes, all in one go. She lowered her ass to the smooth surface and waited, breath locked in her throat as he strolled to a dresser drawer and pulled it open.

He turned, and her belly clenched hard.

"What's that?" she gasped.

His smile turned a lot wicked and her heart leapt into her throat. "A little something I had specially designed for you."

He dropped the leather gadget and the tube of lube next to her. Then he cupped her breasts and slanted his mouth over hers again. His merciless fingers teased her nipples, tugged and grazed until wet heat bloomed between her legs.

Planting himself between her legs, he pulled her closer. Her sex grazed the top of his pelvis. She flushed as he looked down and noted her shameless state.

"Do you know how fucking thrilling it is to see you so wet for me?" he growled. Long fingers drifted down her midriff and slid through the tiny triangle of hair on her pubic bone before his thick knuckle grazed her clit. "Open wider for me."

Her legs parted further. Her man wasn't satisfied. Hooking his hands behind her knees, he raised her legs and planted her feet on the marble top.

Bethany bit her lip. She'd been exposed many times to Zach's avid gaze but tonight there was something in his eyes that set her pulse racing a little faster.

And she still didn't know what the gadget was he'd placed next to her—

"Oh!" Her thoughts fractured as he plunged two rough fingers inside her. She was scrambling to deal with the decadent invasion when he bent his head and sucked her clit into his mouth. "God!"

Just like he'd devoured her mouth minutes ago, he ate her without mercy. Tongue, teeth and fingers electrified her core, sending pleasure shooting into every nerve ending. He stripped her of every other thought except the terrifying beauty of what he was doing to her.

He finger-fucked her hard and fast and merciless, his growls of pleasure against her swelling tissues pushing her close to the edge of her endurance in seconds.

She came hard, screaming her pleasure until her throat stung raw. He lapped her climax with deep strokes of his tongue, an insatiable animal, greedy in his need for her every shiver and shudder.

Before she'd fully come down from her high, he gripped her waist and lowered her from the marble top.

"Turn around," he ordered brusquely. The gleam in his eyes was brighter, heat scouring his sculpted cheekbones in a way that told her he was skating at the edge of his control.

She turned her head, glanced at the gadget and shivered.

"You'll get your present soon enough, baby. First, turn around and grip the counter," his voice dripped power, sex and hunger.

He took his thick cock in his hand and stroked himself as he waited for her to comply. The moment she did, he stepped closer, bracing his powerful body over hers.

One hand splayed into her hair to grip a handful and the other slid down between her legs. He spread her juices all over her sex, then higher, caressing over her butt hole.

She jerked but he held her still. Slowly, he turned her head towards the leather, belt-like gadget. Laying his cheek against hers, he whispered, "You want to know what that is?" His fingers skated over her hole once more.

Dark excitement screamed through her. "Yes."

"It's a diamond-studded vibrating butt plug made for a priceless ass."

Thirty

JESUS.

Her legs weakened at another invasion and her temperature shot up when his teeth grazed her throat.

Her eyelids fluttered at the raw sensation. "You had it made especially for me?"

Why the thought blew her mind, she had no idea.

"Your ass has been a source of singular indecent fascination to me from the moment you went up those stairs before me, Peaches. I get hard and excited just thinking about it." He continued to spread her wetness over her pussy and butt hole. His cock rested thick and heavy against her crack and another memory triggered even more excitement.

"Pick it up, baby," he whispered hotly in her ear.

Her shaky fingers reached for it. The leather belt was solid and expensive. The *tail* hung halfway between the loop, at the end of which hung the curved diamond-studded plug. The diamonds were smooth but cold to the touch.

She didn't insult him by asking if they were real. Zach Savage was too much of a *connoisseur* to settle for imitation.

"Do you like it?" His fingers continued to send her mindless down below but their eyes were fixed on the glinting diamonds in her trembling hands.

"I like it," she replied.

His forefinger caressed her. "Then say, *thank you,* Peaches."

An impish streak shot through her excitement. "*Thank you, Peaches.*"

The smack on her ass was sharp and unexpected. Three more

followed, bringing stinging tears to her eyes. Whimpering, she tried to raise her head.

The fingers in her hair tightened. "Stay," he rasped. "Take your punishment."

He smacked her some more. Unbelievably, she grew wetter. He pushed her forward. The tips of her breasts grazed the cold marble and excited goosebumps rose over her skin.

He smacked her again, harder, then groaned as he caressed her stinging flesh. "Fuck, Peaches. Watching your ass turn pink is fast becoming one of my favorite things to do."

The slap of his hand on her ass was fast turning into another favorite of hers too but she withheld that information and contented herself in rocking back against his rock hard erection. He jerked against her ass and a drop of pre-cum dripped into her crack.

With another groan he stepped back. "It's time, baby."

"Yes."

He grabbed the belt, secured it around her waist and tested the snug fit. The tail had dropped between her butt cheeks, the diamonds cold against her ass.

She turned and watched as he parted her and brought the head of the lubed plug against her sensitive hole.

His face was taut with withheld control and a deep, dark hunger she'd never seen before.

When his eyes met hers, the grey depths were almost black with need. Harsh breaths rippled from his lips as his other hand reached down and circled her pussy in slow caresses. "Relax, Peaches," he crooned.

She forced even breaths into her lungs. He watched her face with keen eyes, gauging her breaths. As she breathed out, he pressed down on the plug and shoved two fingers inside her.

"Zach!" Sensation like she'd never known tore up her spine, shoving her onto her toes. "Oh God, I can't—"

"Take it!" He held his thumb down, his thighs parting her legs wider to step closer. "Take me!" He pinned her to the hard surface and surged inside her. His voice, low and feral rolled roughly over her. "Take me and know that I am yours." His thickness bruised the walls of her sex, filling her, pleasuring her fully and unapologetically. The newer sensation of the plug made its presence known with each thrust, sending a different sort of pleasure twining around that of being thoroughly fucked by a consummate expert.

"Christ, you're so tight, so amazing."

"Only for you."

His breath rushed out, bathing her neck in warmth as both hands circled her waist. "Tell me you adore me, Bethany." His voice was still razor rough with need, whatever edge he was riding taking complete hold of him. He fucked himself deep, deeper, and she felt his body tremble against her. The knowledge that he was as caught up in the sensations riding her made her heart swell and turn over.

"I adore you, Zach. So much."

He made a sound between a moan and a choked cry. "Tell me you're mine."

"I'm yours. Inside and out."

Knowing the next question that was coming, knowing how incredibly close she was to giving in, she planted her feet and deliberately slammed hard into his thrust.

"Fuck!" A full body shudder rippled from his body to his. "I'm going to come, Bethany."

She was already there. "Do it with me, please."

Another shudder. "Yes!"

She slammed back again and felt the world tilt beneath her feet. Ecstasy roared, vicious and unstoppable through her. Through the mind-blowing ride, she heard him roar his own release.

Hot gusts of semen filled her, scalded her tight passage until she could take no more.

Against her neck, Zach panted, sweat dripping from his body onto hers. His hands banded her as if he'd never let her go. And she was beginning to think he never would.

Their breathing slowly returned to the realms of normal. When he pulled out of her, she moaned. He turned her around and slid her arms around his neck. He hugged her close again and buried his face in her shoulder.

"You make me happy, Bethany. You make me feel like I'm not alone."

Tears welled her eyes and spilled down her cheeks.

Words of love filled her heart again, threatening to spill. While she guessed Zach wouldn't reject them this time, the swiftness with which she'd fallen for him, continued to fall deeper for him despite all the threats that loomed in the horizon, frightened her.

"You're not alone. I'm here, baby. I'm here."

His breath rushed out. Bending, he picked her up and carried her next door into the large tiled shower. He set her down and steadied her when her legs wobbled.

A cheeky grin curved his mouth. "I love that I've fucked you so hard you can barely stand."

She noted the tremble in the hand that held her and raised an eyebrow. "Don't go beating your chest just yet, Savage. You don't look too steady either."

"Touché," he conceded, although his strength seemed to be returning by the minute. Certainly, his semi-hard cock was hardening again as his gaze moved over her body to settle on the belt still encompassing her waist.

God, the man was insatiable.

He turned on the shower and turned to her. "You're surprised that I'm getting hard again for you?" he mused.

"Do you ever get tired?"

"Stop looking this fucking beautiful and I'll answer you."

She rolled her eyes and stood still as he untied the belt and gently eased it out of her. Residual sensation made her bite her lip. He dropped the belt on the bench and drizzled soap over her body. He washed her thoroughly and she returned the favour before they headed to the bedroom.

Her stomach growled loudly and he looked over at her. "Midnight snack?"

She nodded eagerly. "Please." She followed him into the dressing room and watched him tug a silk lounger over his delectable ass.

She'd thought him insatiable minutes ago. And yet, here she was ogling him, ready to jump him again. He straightened, raked a hand through his damp hair and her insides turned over with desire.

God…

She looked up and caught his grin. "When you've talked yourself out giving in to your dirty, dirty thoughts, come and find me in the kitchen."

His deep laugh as she punched his arm resonated within her and she found herself grinning as she hunted through his side of the dressing room for a T-shirt.

She tugged it on, breathing the mingled scent of Zach's masculinity, aftershave and cleanliness. With a smile tugging her lips at her stupid, swooning emotions, she was about to leave the room when the beep stopped her.

Turning in the doorway, she tried to locate the source of the familiar text alert. She recalled that Zach had hung on to her phone earlier when she'd asked him for it.

She picked up his discarded jacket and hunted into the pockets until she found her phone.

The text was from Keely but it was only to alert her that she had mail. She closed the text box and activated her email. Sure enough, Keely had sent her a message. Bethany touched on the little envelope next to her friend's name and the box expanded.

The message was short and succinct.

≈

Zach walked into the bedroom ten minutes later, his frown deepening when he didn't immediately see Bethany. He was about to head back out when he saw movement from the corner of his eye.

He altered course toward the dressing room and sucked in a stunned breath when he saw her crumpled on the floor, her features ashen as she stared at her phone screen.

Rushing the last few steps, he dropped to his knees in front of her. "Bethany, what's wrong?"

She looked up and the pain in her eyes sliced through his soul. "Keely sent me this."

Tilting the phone, she showed him the message.

A beautiful life cut short. Are you not afraid you'll be next?

Thirty-One

BETHANY WALKED INTO Zach's San Francisco Palisades home just after midday the next day, expecting another architectural masterpiece that bore very little signs of who Zach Savage was. She was proved wrong immediately.

Well used surf boards lined the wide grey hallway that led to a vast open plan living room that gave floor to ceiling views of Bay Bridge from the exclusive corner of the world Zach truly called home.

The furnishings were big and comfortable and lived-in. A signed baseball glove sat on the large cedarwood coffee tale hewn from a whole tree trunk and swim trophies covered the large fireplace that dominated one side of the room.

The surprising insight into his life however didn't distract her from the man himself. His face was set in harsh lines of fury, much the same as they had been when he'd picked her up off the floor in their Bangkok suite and carried her to the living room.

He'd poured a brandy and stood over her as she'd sipped the strong liquor.

Then, just like he'd done with her iPad, he'd taken her phone and handed it to a summoned Philip. It was returned less than ten minutes later.

"Keely didn't send you that text. Your phone was hacked." Zach's voice, blade thin and lethal had frozen her relief that her best friend hadn't been responsible for the pain clawing through her.

"Who did?"

"The same person who sent you the message to your iPad."

Frowning, she'd stared at him. "But why send it from Keely?"

His look of guilt sent alarm bells clanging wildly. "Because I blocked all non-essential calls on your phone the day we left Italy."

"*What*? What gave you right? And who were the essential people you chose?"

"Your parents and Keely."

"We need to have a serious conversation about the things you feel you need to protect me from, Zach. But first, please tell me what the hell is going on?" she'd demanded.

Fury had pulsed from him as his jaw clenched. "Time to bring this thing to an end."

Now, Bethany watched him pace his living room, his cell phone glued to his ear, and her insides churned.

The whole flight home, he'd kept her in his sights as if she would disappear the moment he looked away. The terror in his eyes when he'd read the message would live with her forever.

It hadn't been terror born of guilt. It had been terror that the simple text message would drive her away once and for all.

His eyes had tracked her as he called his lawyer; his demands uncompromising. After he finished, they'd dressed, packed and headed to the airport.

It was a testament to Zach's power and influence that he'd had a private plane fuelled and waiting by the time Philip drove them onto the tarmac.

For a tiny moment, she feared what he would do to the person who'd sent her texts messages.

"The meeting's in half an hour. Would you like something to eat? Or to take a shower?" he asked, that probing look fixed on her.

She didn't feel much like eating. And she didn't think her stomach could hold any food, seeing as it performed a triple somersault each time she thought of what lay ahead. "I could use a bathroom."

He nodded, came over and took her hand, the apprehensive

look still lurking in his eyes. "I'll show you where it is."

The bedroom he led her to was suspended over a shallow cliff, the view so breath-taking she froze for a second. "Do you like it?"

Just like in Italy, his gaze searched her as he questioned her. She nodded. "The view is amazing. And this place…it feels like a home."

He nodded thoughtfully and pointed to the glass door to the side of the room.

Bethany washed quickly, dug her toothbrush from her purse and ran it over her teeth. Then she re-knotted her hair and adjusted the sleeve of the light blue jacket she'd worn over her white, summer dress.

Zach was waiting outside when she emerged, feeling a little less travel-worn.

"We need to leave now."

She nodded, her heart jumping into her throat. She would know Zach's deepest, darkest secret before nightfall. Zach Savage wasn't prone to making irrational judgments and as Philip drove them towards the offices of Reed, Reed & Clintons, she reiterated to herself that whatever that secret was they would work through it together.

Stanley Reed personally met them in the vast, artistically designed foyer and led them to a plush conference room. Introductions were made.

The portly man's gaze was speculative but his inbred discretion won over his curiosity.

"Are they here?"

Stanley nodded. "They arrived ten minutes ago."

Zach's face grew taut and unreadable and renewed tension bristled through him.

"Let's get this over with."

"I've drawn up all the necessary papers. All we have to do is convince them to go ahead with what we proposed."

"They have no choice. They won't like the alternative." The

dark threat was unmistakable.

Stanley's gaze darted back to her before he stood. Zach remained seated, his breathing choppy. "Give us a minute, Stanley."

His attorney nodded and left.

Zach raised bleak, anguished eyes to her and her fear for them, tripled. "Bethany…"

She surged forward and took his hand. "I'm here, Zach. No matter what, we'll deal with it together." She knew, unequivocally that the man she loved, the man who treated her like she was the most precious thing in his life wasn't a killer. Whatever else was out there, she was sure she could deal with.

His fingers grasped her, meshing painfully around hers. "I'm holding you to that, baby. I can't…I *won't* live without you," he whispered raggedly.

She rose and launched herself at him. He pulled her into his lap and buried his face against her chest, his breath heaving as his body shook. They remained like that for a full minute before he slowly lifted his head.

The anguish hadn't abated but it had eased a little.

"Are you ready?" she asked.

He nodded.

She took and held onto his hand as they left the room.

Stanley waited outside and led them two doors down to another conference room.

Three people were seated inside. The older couple were clearly Farrah's parents. The older woman's resemblance to her dead daughter was acute.

Stanley made the introductions. Fawad and Nabila Nisa didn't offer to shake hands, and neither did their son, Karim. Pure hatred bristled from the younger man the moment he turned his black eyes toward Zach and it ramped up a few thousand degrees when he saw their joined hands.

Zach pulled out a chair for her opposite the trio on the other side of the conference table and sat without letting go of her hand. She knew he craved the support but it helped her just as much.

Stanley Reed took his place at the head of the table and cleared his throat. "Shall we get started?"

Nabila made a tiny rough sound beneath her breath. Raising her head, she glanced at Zach.

Bethany's breath caught as she witnessed the emotion in the woman's eyes. Pain, raw and hellish and all-consuming. But as she watched her another emotion flared up. It took a few seconds for Bethany to recognize it.

Her eyes were pleading with Zach - a desperate plea for salvation. For mercy.

Zach returned her stare, his face twisting with regret for a moment before he glanced at Stanley.

"Bethany, Zach has asked me draw up non-disclosure papers for you to look over. As you probably know they involve Farrah Nisa, his wife," he paused as Karim snorted, "and the circumstances of her death. Are you prepared to consider the papers?"

Her eyes darted to Zach. Grey eyes locked with hers. "It's totally your call. But it's…easier this way."

"Easier for you to lock her in a world of secrets and lies, you mean?" Karim blasted from across the table.

Zach froze. His eyes turned bullet-lethal as they rested on Karim. "Do not push me, Karim. You already stepped way out of line when you decided to come after Bethany."

Fawad Nisa frowned. "What did you do, Karim?"

Karim's jaw clenched. "She needs to know the kind of man he is," he shot back.

"I know everything I need to know about the kind of man he is," Bethany inserted.

Five pairs of eyes turned to her. Zach's eyes held desolation, gratitude and fear. Her lips pursed. It was time to end this, to work on making her man whole again.

She glanced at Stanley. "What do I need to do?"

He opened the black folder in front of him and slid papers across the desk.

"You sign the agreement, then Zach is free to tell you everything you want to know."

"No," Zach bit out, his eyes still on her. "I tell her *before* she signs."

"No chance in hell is that happening." Karim's eyes narrowed on Bethany. "And before you consider signing the document that'll lock you into a sordid world of secrets and lies, let me tell who exactly it is that you're sleeping with."

"Karim," Zach's voice throbbed with warning.

"He took a beautiful young girl and turned her into a junkie."

Zach jerked to his feet. His chair crashed into the wall behind. Karim jumped back but his eyes continued to taunt Zach.

"How old are you, Miss Green?"

"I'm twenty-five."

"My sister would've been twenty-eight two weeks ago. But *he* ended her life."

"Karim," this time the warning came from Nabila. Her eyes darted to Zach and immediately shifted away.

"I meant what I said in that message. You need to be careful he doesn't do that to you, too."

"Karim. Enough!" His father stared him down but anger rolled across the younger man's face. "Mr Savage, I urge you to remember the terms of our previous agreement and reconsider."

Zach calmly resumed his seat. "No. I'm telling Bethany before she signs. That is non-negotiable."

"You trust her to keep our secret?" Nabila asked, her voice husky with the raw emotion displayed in her eyes.

Zach's nostrils flared and he swallowed hard. Bethany looked deep into his eyes and caught a glimpse of the desperately lonely boy yearning for a connection. She vowed there and then to be whatever Zachary Savage needed.

"I trust her to do whatever she feels is right for her. I've trusted her since the moment I met her but I was too damned blind to see it."

His words knocked the air out of her lungs. "Zach…"

"Give us the room please."

"This is…don't think we won't sue your arrogant billionaire ass if this goes sideways, Savage! You'll be looking at serious jail time by the time I'm done with you if you don't rethink this right now."

Zach barely glanced at Karim. "No, you won't. If you want to know why you won't be coming after me, ask your mother."

Nabila's horror-filled gasp echoed in the room. Her husband turned sharply toward her, his eyes widening as her pale, pain-ravaged face crumpled and she began to sob quietly.

Stanley jumped to his feet and ushered the couple out. Karim followed at a slower pace, suspicion and confusion momentarily blanking out his anger.

The moment they were alone, Zach reached for her and pulled her into his lap. He meshed one hand in her hair and then clasped her hand against his chest. "I'm sorry, Bethany. I should've done this a long time ago. I should've told you that night in Marrakech."

"You needed time to sort things out in your head. You've held onto this for six years. Even though I feel like I can't remember a time before having you in my life, it's really been just three weeks since we met, Zach. I wanted too much too soon."

He looked a little shocked at the reminder but he shook his head. "I wanted *everything* from you the moment I laid eyes on you. You had the right to demand the same from me." He sucked in a jagged breath and let it out. "No more secrets, Bethany."

She swallowed. "No more secrets."

Thirty-Two

HE KISSED THE back of her hand and nodded, resolute. "The IL plane took off about an hour before Karim was due to land at McCarran." He eyes clouded with regret at the memory. "I was so damned pleased with myself that I'd won. Farrah was ecstatic and we started partying hard on the plane. We stopped over in LA to pick up a few more people. I suspect they were the ones who brought the drugs on board - I was too off my head with booze to enforce the no-drugs policy. I went to sleep and woke up somewhere over the Pacific. Farrah wasn't in bed so I went to look for her." He stopped and swallowed, his eyes had turned dark with ravaging anguish.

"I found her on the sky deck. She had heroin next to her body. At first I thought she was dead. But I found a pulse. I held her until we landed back in LA. But the damage was too much. She went in to a coma and the doctors declared her brain dead."

"Oh God, Zach."

He shut his eyes and leaned heavily on her. "I was twenty-five. With a wife who was technically dead, in-laws who blamed me for everything, and a police force who thought I was a privileged asshole who deserved jail-time for putting a young girl on life support. Luckily, the cops didn't find enough drugs on the plane for them to charge me. So I dodged that bullet," his voice reeked with bitter mockery.

"Then the doctors started talking about shutting off her life support. I hated that responsibility but as her husband, it was down to me. I tried to talk to her parents about it. Fawad and Karim point blank refused. Nabila…she just wanted Farrah to be at peace. We agreed to hire experts to get as much information as possible. I made it happen. Every single one of them confirmed she was…gone."

Bethany's hand speared into his hair and his arms banded tight around her. She felt a touch of moisture on her chest and realised Zach was crying. Her big, powerfully magnificent man was breaking down in her arms.

"It's okay, baby. I'm here. It's okay."

He shuddered and slowly raised his head. Tears spiked his lashes and smeared over pale, taut cheeks. She wiped them away and kissed his trembling lips.

Gritting his jaw, he continued. "Her family argued back and forth about the decision, and they resented the fact that her life, such as it was, was in my hands. And I…I wanted it to be over."

She jerked and his arms tightened.

"No. I don't mean her life. I meant fighting with her family, watching their suffering and knowing I was responsible."

"You weren't responsible. She chose her own path and you went out of your way to help her over and over when many people would've walked away at the first sign of trouble."

"Knowing that didn't make it any easier. I should've made sure the drugs never got on board the plane or anywhere near her."

She didn't argue. In his own way, Zach was working his way through his guilt. She needed to let him. "How long was she on life support?"

"Six weeks. And every day was hell. I was torn between letting her go and sparing her family the final goodbye. But I woke up one morning and realised I couldn't do it anymore." He released a shaky breath. "I called Nabila and she agreed they would meet me at the hospital. But she got there before me." He gave a fractured laugh wracked with torment. "I think she suspected I would chicken out and I had by the time I reached the hospital. When I got to Farrah's room, she was there on her own without Fawad or Karim. She told me her daughter was now really dead and I needed to do the right thing and let her go. I had no idea what she meant. Until she showed me the empty morphine syringe in her purse."

Ice slithered down her spine. "My God! Did you…what did you do?"

His jaw clenched tight for so long, Bethany thought he wouldn't answer. When his gaze met hers, her heart shredded for him. "I called the doctor and arranged to switch off her life support."

"And you let Nabila go?"

"The way I saw it, the events leading to Farrah ending up on that bed, hooked up to machines, was all on me. What good would it have done to destroy her family as well? Deep down, I knew she would never wake up, but guilt held me back from doing what needed to be done."

"So the doctors didn't suspect anything?"

"No one knew. The only way to find out whether Nabila really injected her with morphine would've been to request an autopsy. I couldn't do it. I turned off the machine and…killed her." More tears welled in his beautiful eyes. He blinked them back and swallowed. "Then I arranged for the records to be destroyed. Now you know everything."

Her insides shook as she grappled with the enormity of what Zach had divulged. She threw her arms around his neck and hugged him tight.

"Thank you."

"Baby, what—" He stiffened as a knock came on the door.

Stanley poked his head through the door. "They're threatening to walk, Zach."

Zach cursed and looked at her.

Taking a deep breath, Bethany stood and returned to her seat. "We're ready."

Stanley's gaze swung from her to Zach then he nodded and retreated.

"Bethany—"

"Go easy on Karim. He loved his sister. He's reacting from a place of pain."

Zach's jaw flexed. "He came after you. I can't excuse that."

"I know. But do it for me."

His eyes gleamed as he watched her. "You know how to knock my fucking legs out from underneath me, don't you?"

Her smile made his breath catch. "I've had a great teacher."

She was aware of Zach's intense gaze on her face as the others walked back in but she wanted to get this done as quickly as possible so she could be alone with him. To tell him what he'd been yearning to hear. What he *needed* to hear.

Farrah's father looked shell-shocked and her brother was much more subdued than he'd been twenty minutes ago. Nabila's eyes met hers and skittered away. Despite what she'd just learned about her, Bethany's heart ached for her.

She turned to Stanley Reed. "I'm ready to sign the agreement," she said.

⁂

"You're very quiet, Peaches."

Zach watched her raise her head from where she'd rested it on his chest. Clear blue eyes met his and some of his panic abated a little. She'd been silent since they left his attorney's office and the coward in him hadn't wanted to push his luck. But not knowing what she was thinking had finally become unbearable.

"It's a lot to process."

He held his breath. "But?"

"But I'm glad I know. We can deal with it, Zach. We *will* deal with it. I'm not going anywhere."

His breath fractured out of him and he pulled her soft body closer. "You don't think I'm a monster?"

"You're not a monster, Zach. You were caught up in a series of circumstances that you couldn't control. You hated that loss of control and have been punishing yourself for it ever since. It's time to let it go. To let Farrah go. I'm insecure enough to admit that I don't want any woman, dead or alive, coming between us. I can't handle it."

"You won't have to. Nothing and no one will come between us. Believe that."

Her eyes clouded and her mouth trembled. "Karim said she would've turned twenty-eight two weeks ago. That night you were dreaming about her. It was her birthday, wasn't it?"

Tension gripped his neck as the ground shook beneath his feet. They'd come so far. But still he couldn't let go of the fear that he could lose her. "Yes."

"God, Zach, I'm barely managing to process the fact that you bought the Marrakech house for her. After she was dead. Please don't tell me you took me there as some form of guilty substitute?"

Shock jerked through him and he grabbed her arms so she could face him properly. "Are you fucking insane? How the hell did you come up with that?"

"Because you built a shrine to her!"

His jaw worked. "No, I didn't."

Her mouth dropped open. "What?"

"I didn't build that memorial. Her family did. She told me how much she loved the place. When I saw it, I knew why. I didn't think it was a big deal to buy the house and let them put up the memorial. And frankly, I wasn't in a position to deny them."

"You didn't build it?"

He shook his head. "No. And I took you there because I had no choice. I didn't want to be without you after I met you, and I knew deep down that would be the last time I went there. Before I came up to bed that night, I went to say goodbye."

The shadows slowly receded from her eyes. "God."

"Is that a good 'God' or should I be even more terrified than I am right now?"

Her eyes widened. "You're terrified? Why?"

"I don't deserve you, Bethany. Every time I hold you in my arms, I'm scared it'll be the last time."

She yanked herself from his arms and released her seatbelt.

His breath slammed out of his lungs when she launched herself onto his lap and took his face between her hands. "You really, really need to get over the fact that I'm going to walk any minute. Or I'll have to teach you a lesson."

Excitement washed away a little of his panic. He forced himself to relax in the seat as she spread her fingers in his hair and dragged her nails against his scalp.

"Hmm, I should warn you I was never a very good student."

"You're asking to be punished, Savage?"

"What can I say, I'm having very dirty thoughts about teacher."

The swiftness with which the atmosphere turned from pain and misery to happiness blew him away. But that was what Bethany brought to his life.

Happiness.

Something tugged hard in his chest as he watched her stunning face turn even more exquisite with her saucy smile. "Well, it's a good thing you happen to be teacher's pet."

Her hands went to his shirt button and started undoing him. His hands slid from her waist to grip her ass as she undulated her hips over his hardening cock.

Her mouth bypassed his hungry lips straight for his jugular. She tongued his escalating pulse and laughed under her breath when he cursed.

"Bite me," he urged roughly.

"Hmm," she complied. He jerked at the not-so-gentle graze of her teeth. "You taste so good," she murmured.

"Bethany?"

"Do I need to tell Philip to keep driving or do you want to go home?"

She slowly raised her head and stared down at him. Her face was grew serious as she took his face I her hands. "Let's go home."

Thirty-Three

Zach slid a finger into her tight, wet heat and felt her jerk against his hold. They'd fucked for hours since returning home, but they were as insatiable for each other as they had been the first time they made love.

Her eager response to his touch blew his mind, made him crave more of her with each orgasm he pulled from her body. But more than that, he'd felt a different, almost spiritual closeness to her after coming clean about his past that made his chest hurt every time the emotion surged through him.

If he had a choice, he would stay here with her forever.

"You having fun down there, Peaches?" He added another finger and gloried in her moan.

"Hmm." She pumped his straining cock a few times before her mouth closed over him. The sensation of her hot, expert suction made his breath shudder out.

Her beautiful body was spread out over him, her pink pussy wide open to his hungry exploration. He adored her body, would happily dedicate hours to worshipping her. That he was getting a blowjob out of it while he did so was a pleasurable bonus.

She sucked him harder, determined to unravel him. Raising his head, he tongued her clit before sucking it into his mouth.

Her cry was pure bliss to his ears. "You like that, baby?"

"God yes, I love that. Love your mouth," she panted.

His heart jolted and a dart of anxiety surged. The words he craved every time they fucked remained unsaid. He knew he would have to work hard to earn it but he was greedy enough to want it here, now.

He worked harder on her clit, watched her body jerk and shudder beneath his hands. When she came into his mouth, her release was so powerful she burst into tears. Fuck, she was so beautiful. Moisture dampened his own eyes as her tears drip onto his thighs.

Getting up, he walked them into this outdoor, enclosed shower. The sun was still high enough to warm their skin as he turned on the cool water. He stood with her for long minutes, just happy to be with her and embrace the heady feelings coursing through him.

He would earn her love.

Because he loved her.

More than he could bear. More than he'd ever dreamed it was possible to love another person.

"You're thinking awfully hard there, Savage. Or is the problem somewhere else?"

Her hand grasped his still raging cock. He rested the subject of earning her love for a moment and just stared at her stunning face.

"I'm beginning to think you've upped the sass lately because you love getting spanked." He delivered a sharp smack and watched her eyes grow dark with desire. "If that's what you need, all you have to do is ask." He spanked her again then soothed her stinging flesh with a firm caress. He continued to lazily explore her as they kissed. She nipped at his mouth then sighed with pleasure when his middle fingers slipped between her crack. He teased her puckered hole and slowly pushed in.

She froze. "Zach, no."

He frowned. "What's wrong?"

She flushed. "Nothing." He raised an eyebrow and she bit her lip. "I just…Chris—"

He jerked back. "Are you telling me that every time I touch you there, you think of that fucking bastard? That every time I come anywhere near that sweet spot, you think of another man?"

Bethany's heart jumped into her throat, stopping her denial for a second. But it was a second too late. Fury washed over Zach's face.

Rough hands turned her around. "Put your hands on the wall."

"Zach, wait! It's just...I've never understood the big deal—"

"Did you enjoy your little present back in Bangkok?"

Unable to lie, she nodded.

"The wall, Bethany. Now."

"What...what are you going to do?"

"I'm going to erase that bastard's memory from your mind once and for all."

Slowly she turned around. Looking over her shoulder, she saw him grip his thick cock and pump it once. Twice.

He stared down at her ass, his breaths coming out in harsh, aggressive pants.

Apprehension, real and hot and fuelled with enough adrenaline to knock out an elephant coursed through her. His cock was a whole different animal to the butt plug.

And the mood he was in, the fury stamped on his face, didn't give her comfort.

"Zach," she tried again.

Grey eyes slid up her back to clash with hers. "Your ass belongs to me. Your body belongs to me. I can't have you thinking of another man when we're apart. And I sure as fuck am not going to allow you to think of another guy when we're this close."

"I...wasn't. Not really..."

Another wave of fury surged. She bit her lip and jumped at his ferocious growl. "Put your hands on the fucking wall, Bethany."

Knowing she only making things worse, she clamped her mouth and placed her hands on the wall. Slowly excitement filled her.

She'd never done this before. Chris, before he'd confessed to his love of male assholes had suggested it a few times but she'd refused, too uncomfortable with the idea.

Now...her breath hitched with a completely different emotion.

God—

"What are you thinking about, Peaches?" His voice was a low, growled warning. A warning of punishment should she give the wrong answer.

She quickly shook her head and forced her eyes shut. No thinking about Chris. Not now, not ever. "I'm thinking of you. Of this."

"Then look at me. Are you thinking of how your beautiful ass is going to take my cock?"

She slowly opened her eyes and turned her head to look over her shoulder the way she knew he loved. "Yes."

He breathed out in satisfaction.

"Good. Now watch what I'm going to do you. I want you in no doubt as who's fucking your ass, Bethany. Who's owning your body, mind and soul. Understand?"

She nodded quickly and looked down.

Jesus. He was so big. There was no way he would fit. No way—

She cried out as his fingers slid over her clit, and pushed inside her, testing her wetness. And she was plenty wet. He spread her juices over pussy and up against her hole. Then he reached up on the wooden shelf and grabbed a tube of lube. He smeared a blob against his finger and rubbed it against her hole. Pressure scrambled up her spine as he spread another blob on his cock and slowly rubbed himself before positioning himself between her spread legs.

Her hands shook. "Jesus, this is happening."

A raw, masculine smile curved his mouth. "Yes, Peaches, it's happening. And from now on, every time I touch your ass, you'll remember me and only me. You'll take my cock inside you and you'll remember how fucking beautiful it feels. Understood?"

"Yes."

"Now, keep your eyes on me. I want to see your pleasure. You can watch mine." He gripped her waist with one hand and his wide head pushed against her. "Relax and breathe for me, baby."

A shocked laugh ripped from her. "You expect me to relax? You're fucking huge."

"I know," he replied without a hint of arrogance. "Try anyway."

At the first touch of his smooth head, she tensed. Then forced herself to relax. He pushed again and smooth became hard. She bit her lip to stop a groan. She felt herself opening up, unfurling at his searing demand. Excitement tore through her. She arched her back and he groaned.

"Yes. Work me in. God, Bethany. Yes, that's it. Oh, fuck!" he muttered hoarsely.

His cock head popped in and electric pleasure sizzled up her spine. Her channel burned at the forceful invasion but the exquisite delight was beyond anything she'd ever experienced. She took another inch of him, cried out as he took over, filling her with sure, powerful thrusts.

"Christ you look so fucking amazing." His voice was barely recognisable with the depth of his rough pleasure. "The way you're taking me..." He slowly established a rhythm, holding her steady with an iron grip on her waist as he fucked her ass.

"Look at me."

She raised her eyes to his. Pleasure scoured his cheeks, throbbed the body possessing hers.

Eyes connected, he surged deeper and fuelled the flames of ecstasy roaring through her. "You're mine. Every single inch of you."

His dark ownership of her triggered her climax but he controlled it, refused to let her soar until he was good and ready. Then he slid a hand between her legs and plunged two fingers inside her.

"Come for me, Bethany. Now."

She came with a scream that ripped through the air. She bucked, cried, and trembled in his arms as the most sublime orgasm she'd known tore her apart.

He pulled her back and banded his arms around her. Against her ear, his breath was harsh but his voice was full of awe, adoring her as she trembled in her arms. "You're a dream come true. *My* dream come true."

He held her like that, skin to skin as he groaned his release, long and hard inside her. Several minutes later he still trembled.

His hands shook as he pulled out of her and washed her. Turning off the shower, he dried her body then swung her in his arms and took her back to bed. He pulled the covers over them and cupped her face to deliver a sweet, adoring kiss. His mouth quivered against hers and emotion welled inside her.

God, she loved him, especially when he was caught in the grip of his own overwhelming emotions.

"Zach…"

Something in her voice must have given away her feelings. His breath hissed out and those intense eyes devoured her.

"Tell me you love me," he demanded hoarsely. "Please baby, I need to hear it."

Bethany opened her mouth to tell him. But found herself shaking her head. "No. *You* tell me you love me. You never have. Because you don't love me. Why should I be the one to bare my heart and soul to you?"

He looked shocked. Genuinely shell-shocked as if he'd been shot.

"What the fuck are you talking about? Of course I love you! Why else would I be ripping myself inside and out for you if not because I'm insane about you?"

In that moment, Bethany was sure she knew what it felt like to be completely insane with both fury and love.

She went to pull out of his arms but he caught her back.

"Wait!"

"Let me go, Zach. You've just ruined what should've been a beautiful moment. I am not fucking psychic! How would I know you love me? There are a hundred different emotions besides that love that could be motivating you."

His eyes widened. "Like what?"

"Obsession. Possessiveness. *Insane sexual chemistry.*"

A haze of red flared across his taut cheekbones. "You think that's all this is? That my heart turns over every time you look at me because I'm crazy about the *sex*?"

"Those are powerful emotions, Zach."

"God...Bethany, I love you," he repeated. "I love you. So much. So very much that sometimes I wonder if I'll ever be able to take a breath without craving you."

She trembled at the strong, powerful words. "Do you want to?"

"Hell no. But I want your love, too. I foolishly threw it away when you offered it. I'm not ashamed to beg you for it. But only if you feel it." A shadow of anguish clouded his eyes. "Do you feel it, Bethany?"

"Tell me you love me again."

"I. Fucking. Love. You."

Her heart soared, joy and love and screaming happiness fizzing inside her. Her smile felt as wide as the sky and his breath hitched as he gazed down at her.

"Bethany?"

"I feel it, Zach. With every breath in my body, I feel it."

Epilogue

"Get up, I have a present for you."

She groaned and burrowed deeper into the pillow and tucked another one over her head for good measure. "Give it to me later."

"No, it's nearly ten. You have to get up anyway. Your parents will be here in half an hour."

"God, I can't believe you invited them to brunch without telling me."

"It was a spur of the moment thing," he answered before yanking the pillow away.

She turned over and watched him stride naked into the dressing room. "Sure, which was why you arranged it two days ago, then dragged me onto yet another plane and flew us back to New York last night?"

His shrug was unrepentant. "They love you. I love you. I thought it was time we bonded over our mutual interest."

She rolled her eyes. "When you put it like that, it's so *sexy*!"

He laughed as he tugged on blue jeans and paired it with a fitted stripped grey shirt that did amazing things to his physique and eyes. Strolling back to bed, he gazed down at her. The adoration in his eyes fractured her breath.

"I know they were concerned about that photo of us this week."

"I explained things to them. They know who you are now and they're okay with it."

"I still think they deserve to have their concerns put to rest properly, don't you agree?"

Her heart melted. "I love you."

His smile widened. "You still have to get up, Peaches."

With a groan she rolled over. The smack that landed on her ass made her yelp. She rose and lunged for him and he caught her up in his arms and strode into the bathroom before setting her on her feet.

"Shower. Now. I'd join you but I'd prefer your parents not to receive audible evidence of me defiling their daughter." His eyes raked heatedly down her naked body, then he swallowed and jerked around to walk out of the bathroom.

"What about my present?" she asked.

One wicked eyebrow arched her way. "You'd definitely have to shower and dress for that one. It's in Bora Bora."

∽

Sugar white sand crunched between her toes as Bethany lifted yet another shell and looked underneath it. So far she'd searched from trunks of palm trees to the fruit sculpture their chef had created this morning for her. She'd even considered diving into the natural water feature outside their bedroom at Zach's villa, but she hadn't quite reached that stage yet.

But she *was* fast reaching the end of her tether.

"Do you give up, Peaches?" Zach strolled a few feet behind her, his bare chest making her insides heat up all over again.

"No."

"Do you really want to tie me up that badly?" The dark anticipation in his voice made her pulse race.

"Yes, I do want to win that badly."

Half a day of Zach as a slave to her every whim was too tempting a chance to pass up. Trouble was, she had to find the tiny flat white box he'd hidden somewhere on the premises.

His Bora Bora villa wasn't huge, which was an advantage. But it was breath taking in an utterly distracting way. The water was impossibly blue; the sand impossibly white, and the man she loved impossibly gorgeous and utterly bent on impeding her search.

"Just say the word and I'll end this. We can go back to bed and

I can have my way with you until the sun goes down."

She blew out an exasperated breath and faced him. His blue shorts were snug enough that she would've noticed if he had anything in his pocket. And his chest was bare, so no hidden treasure there aside from the obvious hard torso she loved to explore.

And she hated that his baseball cap and sunglasses hid his expression so she couldn't get further clues…

His baseball cap.

She walked slowly toward him, swaying her hips in a seductive way that made his arms slowly drop from their folded stance. Her tiny white bikini had already caused major concentration issues for him and when his lips parted and his tongue traced the inside of his lower lip, she knew she had him.

"Zach?" She reached him and tugged off his glasses.

Molten grey eyes stared at her, their focus unwavering and adoring. "Yes?"

"I need to kiss you."

"You don't need to ask, baby. Just take what you need."

"Take your cap off."

He tensed. "Ah…"

"Do you want to win so badly? It'll be equally pleasurable for you if I win."

His nostrils flared. His eyes dropped to her hips and he swallowed before glancing back at her. "Take what you need."

She closed the gap between them and slowly slid the cap off. His tension increased. She looked from his face to the cap. Taped inside was a flat box from a jeweller whose name made her jaw drop.

She looked from the box to Zach's face.

Guarded expectation blazed from his eyes and he swallowed again. "No matter what your decision, I love you. I'm thankful that you love me in return. Know that. Believe that."

"I do."

He nodded. She opened the box. The diamond ring was huge

and gorgeous and a perfect fit when he placed it on her finger.

Her heart leapt into her throat. She tried to speak but no words were adequate for the feelings rampaging through her.

"Speechless, Peaches? I believe that wins me a year's brownie points."

"You win all the fucking points, Savage. A lifetime of them."

"And I intend to collect. Often and thoroughly."

Tears swam into her eyes. "God, I love you."

His smile slowly disappeared and his eyes grew solemn with a deep, unwavering promise. "Not as much as I love and cherish you, Bethany. Always."

Zachary Savage would probably never be the guy to wear his heart on his sleeve, but she knew him inside and out. And she loved every single inch of him.

That he felt the same about her was pure icing on the cake.

COMING SOON

SPIRAL
BY
ZARA COX

THE INDIGO LOUNGE SERIES #3

JUNE 2014

INTRODUCING

NOAH KING AND LEIA MICHAELS

Another sizzling story set in the luxurious and sinfully sexy world of The Indigo Lounge.

Are you ready to SPIRAL out of control?

Dear Reader

Thank you so much for reading HIGHER, the concluding sequel to HIGH.

I really hope you enjoyed it.

THE INDIGO LOUNGE SERIES is by no means finished.

I will be introducing two hot new characters, Noah and Leia, in June 2014 and I hope you will take them to your hearts as much as you've taken to Zach and Bethany.

If you'd like to find out more about these new characters, please stay in touch, via Twitter – @zcoxbooks or on Facebook – Zara Cox Writer

Alternatively, you can email me – zaracoxwriter@yahoo.com

I'd love to hear from you.

Happy reading!

xxx

ACKNOWLEDGEMENTS

As always, my thanks go to my Minxy Buddies, especially to Kitty French, for her continued support. You've all become more than writing buddies. You're my rock and my lighthouse and I don't know what I'd do without you all!

Also to Kate, for your continued unwavering support and general cheerleading skills when things get a little rough. I'm humbled and honoured to have you in my corner. Thank you, my friend!

To JoJo, yes, it's almost time to say goodbye to wheelie chair conversations and "kitchen meets"! I leave you with Zach to cheer you up.

And last, but not least, to my husband, Tony, for being my most supportive, incredibly patient rock, and for bringing me coffee and chocolate when I pulled all-nighters for this and all my writing projects. I love you.

ABOUT AUTHOR

Zara Cox has been writing for almost twenty-five years but it wasn't until seven years ago that she decided to share her love of writing sexy, gritty stories with anyone besides her close family (the over 18s anyway!).

The Indigo Lounge Series is Zara's next step in her erotic romance-writing journey and she hopes you'll take the journey with her.

Printed in Great Britain
by Amazon.co.uk, Ltd.,
Marston Gate.